"Circle the wagons!"

They were moving before Travis even finished barking his order, taking up defensive positions along the top of the gully.

Travis snapped, "I want that personnel carrier in one piece! Draw the bad guys out into the open!"

The machine gunner on top of the APC fired several wild, ineffectual bursts above their heads, missing them by a mile.

Powczuk smirked. "What a bunch of amateurs!"

"Stan, Jack!" Travis said. "Give them some encouragement. Send some misfires their way. Make 'em think we're a bunch of frightened idiots!"

The two team members complied, firing sparse shots toward the tank without actually hitting it. Their shots whined through the trees and plowed up ground.

Shouted orders could be heard inside the personnel carrier, then the troops came rushing out of the vehicle via two doors in the rear hull. They formed a ragged skirmish line and ran yelling toward TALON Force's position.

"All right, playtime's over!" Travis ordered, "Shoot to kill!"

The team let loose a hail of fire. . . .

P9-AQD-201

TALON FORCE

SKY FIRE

Cliff Garnett

A SIGNET BOOK

SIGNET
Published by New American Library, a division of
Penguin Putnam Inc., 375 Hudson Street,
New York, New York 10014, U.S.A.
Penguin Books Ltd, 27 Wrights Lane,
London W8 5TZ, England
Penguin Books Australia Ltd, Ringwood,
Victoria, Australia
Penguin Books Canada Ltd, 10 Alcorn Avenue,
Toronto, Ontario, Canada M4V 3B2
Penguin Books (N.Z.) Ltd, 182–190 Wairau Road,
Auckland 10, New Zealand

Penguin Books Ltd, Registered Offices:
Harmondsworth, Middlesex, England

First published by Signet, an imprint of New American Library,
a division of Penguin Putnam Inc.

First Printing, May 2000
10 9 8 7 6 5 4 3 2 1

Dedicated to a couple of Barchian *baroudeurs,*
Pete Dawson and Ivan Miskoski

Special acknowledgment to Patrick Andrews

People sleep peacefully in their beds at night
only because rough men stand ready
to do violence on their behalf.

—George Orwell

Cosmodrome Chyitiryeh
Kazakhstan in Central Asia
2212 hours

It was midnight black and a perishing cold wind whipped relentlessly and without mercy off the Central Asian Desert. The gusts hummed intermittently through the electric fence around the cosmodrome that was one of the Russian Federation's busiest rocket-launching centers. Inside the facility's Satellite Processing Building was a state-of-the-art U.S. communications satellite that had been designed and manufactured to bring international sporting events to the American public. Several television networks had invested heavily in the project, which was hailed as the dawn of a new era in sports broadcasting.

The spacecraft was scheduled to be launched the next morning under contract with a newly organized Russian launch services agency. The mighty Kosnik Rocket would drive the satellite to an altitude of 98 miles, where it would coast before the final upper stage took it into geosynchronous orbit to do the job for which it had been designed.

Now, as the encapsulated and fueled satellite awaited transport to the launch complex to be attached to the Kosnik Rocket, its American crew slept away the night in the stark quarters furnished them by their Russian hosts. A tank regiment made up of hearty Tartars had been billeted in the building back in the days of the U.S.S.R. The former occupants thought the accommodations quite comfortable, but the Americans felt as if they were camping out. Nevertheless, they slumbered in contentment, securely confident in the knowledge that the satellite and all its systems had checked out A-OK. It had taken weeks of toil, checking, rechecking, and countless inspections, but now it all added up to a mission success.

While the American engineers and technicians were in bed, a young Russian soldier shivered in the night cold during his stint of guarding their satellite. His name was Senior Private Yuri Koblenko, and he hadn't been paid in almost a year. Yet he was a contented trooper.

There were canned meats, preserved fruits, sausages, and dried vegetables in the small apartment he and his wife shared with two other families in the cosmodrome's complex for married soldiers and their dependents. But it wasn't his government who had issued him that bounty of food they would all enjoy for the next six weeks. The victuals came from an outside organization, and their gifts had made him fiercely loyal to them. This group of benefactors even sweetened the deal with generous amounts of extra cash that would come in handy on the next trip to Moscow. All in U.S. dollars.

Suddenly Yuri heard a truck approaching his post from the desert. The young soldier was expecting its arrival, knowing it belonged to the people who had provided all that money and food. The roar of the distant vehicle's engine grew louder, and its headlights blinked a predetermined signal. Yuri took his flashlight and answered with the correct number of flashes.

Within a few minutes a large KrAZ-214 seven-ton truck appeared in the lights of the compound. Yuri quickly opened the gate to allow the vehicle to enter the area. After relocking the barrier, he followed the truck to the building. Yuri glanced inside the large double doors of the Satellite Processing Facility. Another soldier from the interior opened them up wider and stepped out to signal all was well and ready.

There were a dozen men in the truck. At orders from their boss, spoken through clenched teeth, they quickly jumped out, some going inside while others began pulling the heavy tarp off the cargo compartment. The supervisor urged them to make haste, using rude curses and threats. They worked almost frantically under his bullying supervision.

A forklift rolled out of the building and drove up to the tailgate. A few deft pushes and pulls of levers and the powerful little vehicle backed off carrying a fully prepared satellite. The forklift turned and entered the building.

Yuri stamped his feet to get some circulation back in them as he watched what he could of the activity. The men began opening the space capsule. At that point, the young soldier decided he should get back to his post.

Two hours later, the forklift came out of the processing center. This time it had the American satellite on its lift. This was put on the back of the truck and the tarp cover was replaced. Once again the gang boss urged his men on, this time punctuating his tirade with punches and kicks.

Yuri walked over for another look inside the building. He saw that the replacement satellite was being prepared to be placed into the same capsule that had held the American spacecraft.

The frantic work continued through the night. By the time dawn was a reddish hint on the far flat horizon, the job was done. The new satellite was fully encapsulated and ready for launch.

The boss's bellowing now increased as he ordered his men to withdraw from the area. The workers rushed from the building and got back on the truck. Within moments they were out of the compound and rolling across the desert at high speed. Yuri closed the gate and relocked it.

Two hours later, another truck arrived. This vehicle was from the regular motor pool that served the cosmodrome. Its crew took the encapsulated replacement and loaded it on their vehicle. Then it was driven away. The driver turned north toward the Kosnik Launch Complex. The satellite capsule would be locked into place on top of the Kosnik Rocket prior to erection. Then, as per prescribed procedures, the launch sequence would begin.

Senior Private Yuri Koblenko smiled to himself as he thought of the ham and canned peaches he and his wife would enjoy at supper that night.

0009 hours

It was just after midnight, and the cosmodrome complex was well into the launch countdown. At T-minus 1.6 seconds, the six Stage-One RD-0253 engines were ignited. The thrust was increased to 100 percent at T-minus 0. At T-plus 0.5 seconds the liftoff confirmation was announced.

The roar of the powerful engines shook the air as the rocket began its unstoppable climb. The viewers were unable to look at the brilliance of the multiple burns that seemed as bright as the sun to unprotected eyes. Even the veterans of many launches were in awe of the majestic performance of what was considered to be one of the best rockets in the entire world.

At T-plus 10 seconds the Kosnik executed a roll maneuver to align the flight azimuth in the desired direction. Stage two's RD-0210 engines kicked into their ignition sequence after a bit more than two minutes and were taken to full thrust when stage one was jettisoned at a speed of nearly 3,700 miles per hour. Five and a half minutes into flight marked stage three's ignition and this was followed by stage two's shutdown and separation.

The process continued through its cycle until the rocket was 98 miles above the earth's surface. At that point the final upper stage with the satellite was separated from the Kosnik. Then the capsule opened and the satellite was kicked into its proper orbit of a flight azimuth of 37.5 degrees with an inclination of 63.4 degrees.

In the Launch Control Center, the Russian and American aerospace engineering crews cheered and congratulated each other as the tracking computers indicated the satellite was heading into a correct parking orbit at an altitude that guaranteed a working life of some fourteen years.

Then bitter disappointment set in.

For some unfathomable reason, their equipment was unable to acquire the satellite. After a futile hour of failure trying to establish contact and control, a frustrated American engineer ripped the earphones off his head and flung them across the room.

"Son of a bitch!" he bellowed. "The goddamned thing is acting like it's not even ours."

Off the East Coast of Scotland
1640 hours

The North Sea behaved itself for a change as the crew due for relief gathered bag and baggage at the leeward side of the helipad. One of the workers, a pneumatics technician named Ian MacGregor, glanced over the dancing whitecaps on the waves at the gray sky.

Ian and his mates had just finished a month-long tour of duty on Barkley Oil Company's Number Three Offshore Rig. They were a tired, wind-burned crew with all the muscle strains and physical bruises from the thirty-plus days they had spent battling the elements and merciless work environment required to keep the drilling program in full operation.

Now they waited for their relief team to show up. Ian continued to gaze out at the watery horizon for a sight of the helicopter that would be coming to take them back to Dundee. That was where he wanted to be more than any place else on the Planet Earth. Good Scotch whiskey and a willing Scot wife who got as horny as he did during his absences awaited his pleasure.

As he scanned the far distance, something caught his eye. He looked up just in time to see a small but blinding point of light.

In the next millisecond, Ian MacGregor, his working companions, and the Number Three Offshore Rig were vaporized in a flash of roaring flame.

Chapter One

Travis Barrett stepped out of the elevator and walked down the hall of the Pentagon's third floor, second corridor. He was in familiar environs and did not have to follow the signs or colored lines on the floor to get to his destination.

Travis was dressed in a business suit he had bought off the rack at a cut-rate men's clothing store in Fayetteville, North Carolina. He didn't wear the attire too often, and consequently, it had the look of having been on a hanger for a long time. The only tailoring done to it had been the measuring and sewing of the hems.

Because of the suit and the scuffed, nondescript briefcase he carried, casual observers assumed he was a low-paid Department of Defense civilian employee with some sort of mundane administrative job. Travis's impressive physique belied his bargain clothing. The man stood six feet two inches tall with a lean, muscular body. He seemed the sort of desk jockey who followed a very rigorous exercise regimen during his free time.

Major Travis Barrett's real profession was that of an Army Special Forces officer. And he was a hardcore West Pointer and professional soldier right down to the pith of his military soul. At present he was on detached duty to a very unique operational group called TALON Force.

Travis continued down the hall and turned into a side corridor until he reached a little-used area. There were numerous empty offices and the floor did not appear to receive regular attention from the building maintenance staff. Several of the fluorescent tubes in the ceiling lights were burned out and had not been replaced. Nor had the floor been touched by a broom or mop for a considerable length of time. Obviously, no high-ranking or important personnel occupied that part of the Pentagon.

The Green Beret reached a door that identified it as the Base Commissary Inventory Section. A poster was mounted on the wall to one side that had an illustration showing a young sailor, his wife, and two children. The service family was happy and smiling as they wheeled a shopping cart down a grocery aisle. The words printed across the picture read: *Shop at Your Base Commissary for the Best in Quality, Quantity, and Price.*

Someone protesting the low pay for enlisted personnel had expressed himself by taking a black marker pen and neatly writing *We Accept Food Stamps* along the bottom of the advertisement.

Travis, although recognizing the truth in the words, did not approve of graffiti. As far as he was concerned, it was a case of vandalism, pure and simple. Humor was not part of the officer's persona at the moment.

He rapped on the door, then stepped inside. A young, very sexy, bosomy woman at a desk looked up. She wore an extremely low-cut blouse that showed off her mammary accomplishments to advantage. The receptionist also had the look of a bored, undereducated young lady working at a monotonous job that didn't require much skill. There were photos of Tom Cruise, Leonardo DiCaprio, and Brad Pitt under the glass on her desktop.

"Yeah?" she asked, giving Travis a bold, approving look. "Who d'ya want to see then?"

"Mr. Barrett to see Mr. Wong."

"Really?"

"Really."

"Do you have an appointment to see Mr. Wong?"

"I suppose," Travis said. "He called *me.*"

"In that case, go right in, Mr. Barrett," she said. "I'm sure Mr. Wong is expecting you."

As Travis walked past her desk he bent down and quickly whispered, "You make a good cheap-tart receptionist, Olsen."

She smirked back. "I love driving you big hunky macho types into fits of sexual frustration." Lieutenant Jennifer Olsen, United States Navy, was the undercover ace of the

TALON Force's Eagle Team. This buxom bombshell had uncanny skills in disguise, seduction, and other sleight-of-hand activities.

Travis went through a door and continued down a corridor to the end office. He stepped into a good-sized meeting room to see Sam Wong seated at the long conference table in the center of the room.

Sam, a very thin, delicate-appearing Chinese man in his mid-twenties, was reading a computer magazine. He held a temporary commission in the rank of captain in the Army Reserves. Sam looked at Travis through a pair of oval glasses.

"Hello, Sam," Travis said. "Am I the first here?"

"Yeah," Sam said. "I've been waiting for everybody with Jennifer."

"Yeah," Travis said. "I like her cover. Or should I say *un*cover."

Sam grinned. "You know how Jennifer likes to stay in practice."

"Maybe she should have stayed in show business," Travis growled. "When are the others due in?"

"We're staggering everybody's arrival and bringing them in from different directions," Sam said, taking a loud, slurping sip from a can of Mountain Dew. "I regret having insisted that you dress civilian. Those were my orders."

"I'm sure there're good reasons for it," Travis said. He set his briefcase down on the table and walked over to a coffeepot. "How come we're going through this drill?"

"Because this is probably the most dangerous mission we've had to undertake," Sam said. He paused. "Let me qualify that. The most dangerous to the entire world. I suppose we'll be risking our asses like we always do."

"You've been briefed already?"

Sam nodded. "Not fully. Just enough to scare the shit out of me."

"Is there some nut flying around the globe with a hydrogen bomb?" Travis asked as he poured a cup of coffee. "Are we going to make a *banzai* charge against ten thousand deeply entrenched, armed-to-the-teeth, do-or-die suicidal fanatics?"

"You don't know the half of it."

The door opened and a muscular black man stepped into

the room. He, too, was in civvies but, unlike Travis, he was very much at ease in the well-cut business suit he wore. Captain Jacques DuBois, U.S.M.C., stood nearly six and a half feet tall and was built like an NFL linebacker. He was a Force Recon Marine, and he smirked at Travis. "I see why you prefer wearing uniforms, boss. Who's your tailor? Omar the Tentmaker?"

"Clothes don't make the man," Travis retorted.

Jack chuckled. "Good thing they don't."

Sam groaned.

Travis and Jack went over to the table and took seats on opposite sides. They had just settled down when Lieutenant Commander Stan Powczuk, a Navy SEAL, walked in followed by Air Force pilot Captain Hunter Blake. Greetings were exchanged and five minutes later microbiologist Sarah Greene joined them. This U.S. Army captain was a triple scientific threat as a medical doctor, board-certified surgeon, and microbiologist. She strutted in on killer legs developed through years of snowboarding, both recreationally and in competition.

"Well, well," she said, getting a cup of coffee. "It looks like the gang's all here."

Jennifer Olsen, who had stepped out of her receptionist role, came in and took a seat.

"It's getting hot in here," Hunter said with a smile.

"Aren't you glad there aren't more of us?" Sam remarked. He got his cell phone and punched out a beeper call. He turned to the others at the table. "Our briefing will begin in a few minutes."

The people gathered in that briefing room made up an elite, ultra high-tech team designated as the Eagle Team of TALON—Technologically Augmented Low-Observable Networked—Force. They were the *crème-de-la-crème*, all drawn from the best the United States Armed Forces and security services had to offer. Superbly conditioned and trained, they were issued a Battle Ensemble of combat gear linked by proximity wave transmission to biochip sensors and transmitters embedded beneath the skin of each TALON Force trooper.

Now, sipping coffee and soft drinks, they waited for the introduction to their latest operational assignment. A quarter of an hour passed before Eagle Team was joined by someone they all knew very well. Brigadier General Jack Krauss, in Army uniform, was the TALON Force commander. He had lost his right hand in combat, but this no-nonsense veteran didn't consider such a minor inconvenience a reason to bow out of active duty on a medical retirement.

The general nodded a silent greeting as he walked in, halting at the head of the table. He set his briefcase and cap in front of him. He pulled out some documents and slapped them down. Jack Krauss was an intense individual and not a man to waste a lot of time.

"ALAS," he said.

Stan asked, "You have some problems, sir?"

"Yeah," Krauss said. "ALAS. A-L-A-S. Aimed Laser Attack Satellite. It's a nasty son of a bitch that's orbiting Earth at this very moment."

"Who does it belong to?" Jack DuBois asked.

"Some very unpleasant, devious individuals who are not dedicated to creating a better world," Krauss said. "Unless it's better for them."

Travis shrugged. "Sounds like all the little playmates we play such lovely games with."

"Fill us in," Sarah urged Krauss.

"This goes back a few years," Krauss said. "So bear with me." He took a deep breath and began, "Prior to the Soviet Union's breaking up, some of their leading aerospace technocrats saw the handwriting on the wall. These guys were a Warsaw pact team. Russians, Poles, East Germans, etcetera. They had brought some hardware into existence that we hadn't even taken off our own drawing boards at the time. They had designed and constructed a laser-firing satellite with the capability of being fed exact coordinates of any spot on earth, then blasting it into a vacuum."

"Fully operational?" Hunter Blake asked.

"I'm afraid so, my friends," Krauss said.

Jennifer sat up straighter. "And it's up in orbit?"

"That's the bad news," Krauss said. "The good news is that they've only got one. Their manufacturing techniques are slowed by the primitive environment they must work in."

Stan Powczuk nodded. "Okay. So how did all this shit get rolling?"

Krauss explained, "When the Soviet Empire crumbled, these guys took off in a carefully orchestrated clandestine operation. They relocated to the hinterlands of Kazakhstan in Central Asia. And they took along plenty of mostly American cash. There were some hidden bunker complexes the Reds had built for their government brass to hide in if we Running Dogs of Capitalism decided to launch a nuclear attack against their Workers' Paradise. The exact location of these places isn't even on the map."

"Understood," Travis said. "What're their plans? To bring Communism back?"

Krauss shook his head. "It was originally, of course, but the current situation has changed all that. They've formed into an organization called the Frateco. That's the Esperanto word for brotherhood."

"Why would they choose *that?*" Sarah asked.

"They chose the term because the artificial Esperanto language was invented by a Dr. Ludwik Zamenov in the late 1800s. He was a Russian-Polish physician who created the lingo as a way to promote understanding and rapport along the German-Polish and Polish-Russian borders. The members of the Frateco thought the name most apropos in their own activities as Russians, Poles, East Germans, and others who were members of their group."

Hunter asked, "If they're not dedicated to Commie imperialism, what the hell are their aims?"

"The CIA tells us that from all indications they've realized they could never have their former glory of the old days," Krauss said. "So they've turned to extortion in a big way."

"Details," Sam Wong said. "Please! Details!"

"All right, Sam," Krauss said. "They managed to switch their ALAS with a normal communications satellite that was to be launched from a cosmodrome in Kazakhstan a month ago."

"Jesus!" Jack exclaimed. "That sounds nearly impossible. What about local security?"

Krauss snorted a sardonic laugh. "The Russian troops garrisoned there haven't been paid for a year. They're living on substandard rations issued them by their government. The soldiers' wives and children are hungry."

Travis nodded knowingly. "We're talking heavy-duty bribery here."

"Exactly, Major," Krauss said. "The Frateco now enjoys a fierce loyalty from a good number of the garrison personnel after giving them decent food and plenty of it. Generous cash payments have also sweetened the deal."

Sam pensively scratched his chin. "Then the switch of satellites was made by Russian soldiers?"

"Yes," Krauss said. "So when the latest Kosnik Rocket was launched a few weeks ago, it did not carry the intended satellite. The launch crew unknowingly put a super weapon into a very precise and neat geosynchronous orbit."

"Understood," Sam said. "So how do they control the spacecraft?"

"What they've done is designed a Mobile Control Center—or MCC—with all the computer gadgetry inside to operate ALAS," Krauss said. "The MCC is moved from place to place out there on that vast goddamned desert to keep it from being located. Meanwhile, they contacted the West through NATO and gave a complete description of all the harm they can do. After demanding a billion dollars, they performed a very convincing demonstration. They used ALAS to blast an oil rig in the North Sea into nothingness."

"Wait a minute," Jack said. "Is that the one that was reported on TV news? It was supposed to have capsized and sunk with all hands during a storm, right?"

"The same," Krauss said. "But it wasn't a storm. Hell, after that laser strike, there were dead fish floating in a twenty-mile radius around the site. The incident proved that ALAS could hit even that small a target with deadly accuracy and at the precise moment they said it would happen."

Jennifer scowled. "It's a worldwide hostage situation!"

"An accurate assessment, Olsen," Krauss said. "Now their demand is *two* billion dollars or the next target is Detroit, Michigan. No jokes, please."

Sam gulped. "They can do that?"

"Listen, Sam," Krauss said. "That satellite was a hundred miles overhead when it beamed down on the speck of an oil rig in the North Sea. One instant the rig was there, the next instant the spot was nothing but boiling water and poached fish."

Sarah Greene spoke up. "Then if they can hit anything on earth, they can hit anything in the sky too. Or in space."

"Exactly," Krauss said. "Dr. Greene, do you realize what effect the loss of all the world's communication satellites would be? A catastrophe, not to mention the Frateco would also amuse themselves by annihilating a few million human beings."

"They could knock out our Shuttle Program," Hunter said.

Travis was getting impatient. "Our mission?"

"Your mission," Krauss responded, "is to find the Mobile Command Center for ALAS." He looked at Sam Wong, the electronics and communications expert. "You must use the instrumentation inside the vehicles to cause ALAS to self-destruct." Then he turned to Travis. "And then you folks are to destroy their laboratory and factory complex in those hidden bunkers. It won't rid the world of the organization, but it'll keep them from manufacturing any more ALAS weapons."

Sam, ever the techno-nerd, asked, "What about the plans, blueprints, scientific data, and all that stuff?"

Krauss replied, "We know they're not at the location. That, boys and girls, will be another mission when we have better intelligence."

"We'll worry about that at a later time," Travis said. "Meanwhile, can you tell us how to locate all these places we're supposed to do away with? They're not on any maps and it's obvious that no one can locate that Mobile Command Center."

"We do have an asset," Krauss said. He went to the door and opened it. A Slavic-looking man stepped inside. He was a bit short but muscular and had a tough countenance. Krauss indicated him with a nod of his head. "This is Sergei Mongochev. Former captain of the Russian military. And a defector from the Frateco."

Stan sized up the newcomer. *"Vi gavaritya pa angliski?"*

The Russian smiled. "Yes. I speak English. A little rough, but I speak it and understand everything."

Travis Barrett was a naturally suspicious man. "Why did you defect?"

"I join Frateco through desperation as did many members of garrison at cosmodrome," Mongochev explained. "My loyalty to Russian government go down when Frateco help me to feed my family."

Travis was persistent. "*Why* did you defect?"

"I have faith in my people," Mongochev said. "I grow ashamed of doing wrong. Mother Russia must take her rightful place in world. Gangsters, criminals, renegades, all bad elements must be destroyed before we win back our glory."

"I see," Travis said. "So how did you go about with this defection?"

"I make deal at American Embassy in Moscow while on furlough. I tell all. They help me and my family go to America. Give us new identity. Protection while I help my beloved country. When I am able, I will return to Russia to continue my work as a patriot."

Travis's suspicions were unabated. "How much money did you get?"

Mongochev shrugged. "Only money to pay expenses."

"He's cleared by the CIA, Travis," Krauss said. "Mr. Mongochev knows the location of the Frateco's laboratory and factory complex. He also has the times and locations of the Mobile Command Center as it moves around. There're two weeks left on that schedule. So we can't dick around."

Jack DuBois leaned forward. "Then let's get it on!"

"Right," Krauss said. He pointed to Travis. "You'll have to draw up your own operations plan." He turned to Sam. "We'll need *all* your electronics skills when we get to the MCC. It'll be up to you to figure out how to activate the self-destruct mechanism. You'll have Mongochev, Travis, and Stan to translate the Russian instruments and documents you'll find."

"I speak crappy Russian," Stan said, "and I'm especially not real sharp on aerospace terminology."

"Give what help you can, Commander," Krauss said. "Mongochev can fill in the blanks. Where you'll really serve best is in demolitions. Our esteemed Russian asset also knows all the architectural, construction, and material details of the complex. So get with him and work out how much explosives it will take to destroy the place." He indicated Jack, Sarah, and Jennifer. "The rest of you will pro-

vide additional firepower as well as any of your individual
skills and expertise that may become necessary."

Hunter Blake, the Air Force pilot, frowned. "Is there
anything for me to do? Carry extra canteens maybe?"

"You've got one hell of a job, Captain Blake," Krauss
said. "And you'd better stay sitting down for this next bit.
We'll be taking a most unique advantage of your skills as
a pilot." He walked over and took a chair beside the Air
Force officer, leaning close to him. "The Central Asian desert is an immense emptiness. For that reason a powered
aircraft can be heard for literally hundreds of miles. We
know the Frateco facilities out there are radar poor. What
they have must be totally devoted to ALAS. But people
on the ground are aware of airborne intruders while they
are still far away."

"Christ!" Hunter exclaimed. "That means that we won't
be able to get close enough for a parachute infiltration, not
even with the X-37 rocketplane. What are we going to do,
walk in? And if we are, what the hell does my ability as a
pilot have to do with it?"

"We've reached a solution with some very special people
you'll meet later," Krauss said. "You'll be going in by
glider."

"Oh, shit, not again! We had one hell of a trip on our
last mission in Cuba," groused Stan.

"Well," Krauss said, "they might hear your tow aircraft,
but when you cut off tow and glide toward the objective,
the airplane's engine noise will fade when it turns away.
You can come in silently and at night."

Hunter smirked. "Should we pray for a full moon?"

"The latest weather forecast shows no clouds during the
operational phase," Krauss said. "And there will be a full
moon at this time of the month. With good visibility, you'll
be able to land relatively close to your first target. That
would be the Mobile Command Center." He gestured at
Travis. "Take out the MCC personnel without destroying
the vehicles. You'll need them for the ride to the factory
complex. That'll also make it easier for you to enter the
area."

"Makes sense," Travis interjected. "After we've accomplished the mission, I take it we'll head to the cosmodrome
for exfiltration."

"Sorry," Krauss said. "There are elements of the garrison there we can't trust. Rather than *exfiltrate,* you'll be *extracted.* You'll be taking along a retrieval mechanism in which an aircraft will dive down low and grab your glider. You'll be towed back to a safe area for landing."

"We have a personnel extraction system that's been used for years in Special Forces," Travis said.

"The one you'll employ out there in ol' Kazakhstan is based on a World War II design," Krauss said. "Don't worry that it's an old concept. It works."

"Interesting," Jack said. "We go in by glider and we come out by glider." He thought a moment. "Y'know, it's kind of like Sun Tzu said, 'The wise general's blows fall like thunderbolts from the nine-layered heavens.' "

"Oh, yeah?" Stan remarked. "What did he say about exfiltration?"

Jack smirked. "The Great Master said that a general could withdraw, but he must do so swiftly to avoid being overtaken."

"And Sun Tzu was so right," Krauss said. He had grown weary of all the talking. "Now hear this! You'll be using a clandestine air base in the former East German territory for take-off to the operational area." He stood up and went back to the head of the room. "You'll be preparing for the mission at the China Lake Naval Weapons Center in California. That's a high desert area that is similar to Kazakhstan in both terrain and weather. We can only give you a week. That includes all planning, working up skills with the glider, tactics, grand strategy, and all other aspects." He gazed at the team. "Questions? No?" He pointed to Travis. "Take over, Major."

Krauss turned abruptly and left the room.

"Well, folks, here we go again," Travis said. "All on our lonesome."

"Please not to be forgetting me," Sergei Mongochev reminded him.

Chapter Two

The clandestine facility out in the far reaches of the China Lake Naval Weapons Center in California was nicknamed Desertville by those who used it. However, its official designation was Area Seven, and it appeared on all maps as no more than an untitled cluster of buildings.

Any casual observer from the air—such as a civilian pilot who had inadvertently strayed into restricted airspace—would assume it was a small settlement in the arid hinterlands of the vast Mojave Desert. To that unintentional intruder, it seemed just a place where rustic desert rats went to buy supplies, get drunk, and bed some cheap piece of tail. After their brief debauchery those ol' boys no doubt returned to their isolated shacks in the harsh environs far from populated areas.

The sham community consisted of a cluster of nondescript buildings alongside a paved road. A full mile of that bucolic "highway" was actually a runway capable of supporting maximum loaded C-5A transport aircraft. There was also what appeared to be a hangar typical of a small town's airport, although it was uncommonly large. Several of the smaller edifices scattered around the area were Quonset huts used for command, storage, living quarters, and communications.

The team had shown up onsite the night before and moved into the phase of the operation known as *Isolation*. And the term was literal. Upon their arrival, the seven team members and their Russian asset had come under the full control of a crusty individual named Ozzie Nettles. This mysterious and eccentric man's job was to keep them locked securely away from the rest of the world—and vice versa. Nettles, officially entitled the station chief, was also known among the well-indoctrinated as the Mayor of Desertville. Some even addressed him as "Your Honor."

In spite of its appearance, there was none of the usual small-town pleasantness about Area Seven. In fact, the locale had an ominous air about it. The activities there were not the sort that would appeal to the faint-hearted. The people passing through were preparing themselves for some of the worst cases of applied violence known to civilization.

The team, dressed in black fatigue uniforms, had just finished breakfast and had left the mess hall for some pre-training coffee in the dayroom of their Quonset hut. Duffel bags were stacked in an orderly pile in one corner of the room.

The group had just settled down with their first steaming cups when the door opened and Ozzie Nettles stepped into the room letting in a blast of cold air.

"Hello, folks," he greeted as he headed directly for the coffeepot. He poured himself a generous cupful of the strong brew and took a swallow. "Busy day ahead of you, hey?"

"Busy *seven* days, Your Honor," Travis Barrett corrected him. "And what brings the august presence of the Mayor of Desertville into our humble midst?"

"Hot coffee for one thing," Ozzie said raising his cup. "It's colder'n a witch's tit in an iron brassiere out there."

Sarah shuddered. "Reminds me of when I went snowboarding topless at Killington one January. On a dare, of course."

"I wish I'd seen that," Ozzie said. "But I'm really here to fetch Blake."

"You mean our dickhead *extraordinaire*?" Stan Powczuk asked.

"That's Captain Dickhead to you," said Hunter.

"We're about to run a pre-operational inventory and inspection of our Battle Ensemble," Travis pointed out.

"Sorry," Ozzie said. "The folks that are going to train Blake are on a tight schedule. One was even brought out of retirement. And I understand he's a crotchety old geezer."

Hunter frowned and said sardonically, "Now there's a harbinger of state-of-the-art methodology and equipment."

"Don't knock experience, Cap'n," Ozzie said. "And they're waiting for you. Let's get over there."

Travis spoke to Hunter. "Go ahead. We'll take care of your gear for you."

Hunter looked up from the worn sofa where he sat with Jennifer and Sam. "I take it I'll be doing some flying today."

"Yep," Ozzie said. "They're all set up for you. It's a bit blustery outside, but if you learn to handle that glider in these conditions, you'll be more than ready for Kazakhstan."

Hunter finished his coffee and stood up. "I'm going to need every minute of flying I can get, good weather or no."

"Then let's not waste any of those minutes," Ozzie said, draining his cup. "C'mon!"

The two stepped from the Quonset hut, leaving the team basking in the warmth of the metal building's gas heater. Hunter hunkered down in his flight jacket, cramming his hands deep into the pockets as he and Ozzie walked through the frigid gusts of wind that played around them.

Ozzie pointed ahead. "There's your mentor waiting for you."

Hunter glanced toward the hangar and could see an elderly gentleman standing by a small door.

"That old fart?"

"Yeah. But don't underestimate him," Ozzie advised. "If he wasn't an expert in his field, he wouldn't be here. They'd have left him in his rocking chair."

"I suppose," Hunter conceded. He picked up the step, making Ozzie hurry to keep up with him. When they reached the old man, the station chief made a quick and simple introduction.

"Hunter Blake. Dan Farley." They shook hands, and Ozzie said, "I've taken care of my part of your activities. I'll leave you alone. Have a fun day." He gave Hunter a hopeful look. "Good luck."

As he walked away, Farley turned and, without speaking, led the way inside the hangar. A large glider sat in the middle of the edifice's expanse. It was a fiberglass job and looked formidable to Hunter.

"Aluminum tubing," Farley said, anticipating the question. "She's roughly modeled after the World War II CG-15A glider."

"Uh-huh," Hunter said. "Vital statistics?"

"Sixty-five foot wing span," Farley said. "The fuselage is a tapered fifty feet in length. The troop compartment is fourteen feet long, six feet wide with a height of six feet."

"A big guy can't stand up straight in there," Hunter remarked, thinking of Jack DuBois.

"He couldn't go for a long walk either," Farley said. It was obvious from his slow restrained movements that bad health was plaguing him in his senior years. "The final twenty-five feet is nothing but fiberglass. The guy'd fall through."

"Now *that* would ruin his whole day."

Farley snuffed. "Hell, it'd ruin the whole rest of his life."

"Which would last the time it took for him to hit the ground."

"Yep," the old man agreed. "Remember, it's not the fall that kills you. It's that sudden stop." He cackled at his own joke.

They went around to the door in the side of the fuselage. When they stepped inside, Hunter was surprised. "There's only a place for a pilot. No copilot?"

Farley shrugged. "If something happens to the pilot on a mission of this sort, there'd be no time for a backup to do anything."

"Have you had combat experience with these babies?" Hunter asked.

"Yep," Farley said, slowly easing his frail body down into one of the webbed seats along the side. "I paid my dues when I flew gliders into Normandy and on Operation Market Garden."

"Yeah," Hunter said. "They made a great movie about that last one. *A Bridge Too Far.*"

"They made movies about D-Day too," Farley said.

"They sure did," Hunter said. "What did you think of 'em?"

"I never saw one," Farley said. "Anyhow, in those days a lot of the pilots had a partner, but I never did. Just the senior-ranking man of the troops I was transporting."

Hunter felt a new respect for the older man. "Then you really know what you're talking about, huh?"

"You better hope like hell I do, kid," Farley cracked, "or you'll be giving Saint Peter the finger long before I do."

Hunter knew better than to pry further into the man's credentials or even ask which agency he represented. He noticed some poles and cables stored overhead. "What's that Rube Goldberg gizmo for?"

"The retrieval system," Farley said. "That's what you'll use to get pulled back into the air after your mission. We have some written instructions explaining how it works."

"I'm not going to practice with it before we go on the operation?" Hunter asked.

Farley shook his head. "If you tried it out and it didn't work you'd crash and bend the glider. The mission would have to be called off."

"You make my friends and me sound expendable, Mr. Farley."

"All I know about your mission is that it's the most consequential ever to be put into operation," the old man said. "That means any precommitment risks must be minimized."

Hunter shrugged. "Well, at least they're making an attempt to get us back safely. On our last mission we flew into Cuba in a plastic glider that we melted after we landed." He sat down in the pilot's seat and worked the wheel and rudder pedals. They were a bit stiff.

Farley read his mind. "They're new."

Hunter checked the instruments. An altimeter, turn-and-bank indicator, vertical airspeed indicator, airspeed indicator, and compass made up the panel. He grinned. "No fuel gauge, hey?"

"Nope," Farley replied without smiling. He first heard the joke in 1942 as a corporal in the U.S. Army Air Corps Glider Pilot Training Program. He hadn't thought it particularly funny then, and he sure as hell didn't in his old age.

The sound of an approaching plane buzzed in the distance, then grew louder. Hunter listened as it made an obvious approach for landing. "Anybody you know?"

"Tug plane," Farley replied. "Now you'll have a chance to fly this beauty."

"What about performance data?" Hunter asked. "Such as glide ratio."

"Sorry," Farley said. "It's never been flown before."

"That would explain why the controls are so stiff," Hunter said.

"And a few more things too," Farley said.

"Did you folks check out a model in a wind tunnel?"

"We didn't have the time or facilities for crap like that," Farley said.

"What do you *estimate* the glide ratio to be?" Hunter asked insistently.

"You don't want to know," Farley said flatly. "Anyhow, if you're a real pilot you'll want to discover all the *minor* details for yourself."

"That's me all over," Hunter said. "A real pilot."

Now Farley cracked a weak grin. "It helps sometimes to be kind of stupid."

Hunter grinned back. "You're very perceptive, sir."

"You and I are more alike than I thought," Farley said.

They stepped out of the glider in time to see a couple of station crewmen opening the large hangar doors. The arriving aircraft taxied from the runway up to the opening. It was a Fairchild C-123 provider. It moved up, then turned around with its tail facing the glider. Some airmen appeared from a side door of the airplane. They hooked one end of a towline to the tail of the C-123 then stretched it out until it reached the glider.

"What's that wire coiled around the rope?" Hunter asked.

"Telephone line," Farley answered. "That way you can talk with the tug plane without worrying about breaking radio silence."

"What if the telephone line breaks?"

Farley was not apologetic. "Then you won't be able to talk to the pilot." He was showing some impatience now. "Get in. We'll give you a lift."

Hunter went back inside the glider. He settled into the pilot's seat and buckled himself in, watching the crew prepare to hook him up under Farley's supervision.

Farley gestured to Hunter. "Hit the red button overhead to open the towline hook."

Hunter complied and the end of the towline was placed in it and the device clamped shut.

"Now," Farley said. "Let's see how it'll work when you want to cut loose. Hit it again to open it."

Hunter repeated the sequence but the hook remained clamped down without opening even an inch. "Hey!" he shouted. "If this happens upstairs, I won't be able to get loose! I'll be married to that goddamn tug plane."

Farley looked at one of the crewmen. "Spray some WD-40 on the damn thing."

Hunter rolled his eyes.

The man sprayed the hook, and Hunter tried again. This time it worked.

Hunter set the telephone headset on his head. He thought about what sort of obituary would be written for him if this glider thing turned out to be a fiasco.

I can see it now, he told himself, it'll read: Captain Hunter Evans Blake III, Air Force Academy graduate who was checked out in a myriad of aircraft ranging from a 1909 Curtis Pusher to the F-117 Stealth Fighter, died today when he got into an untested, untried, uncertified, unsafe, unflyable excuse for a glider and allowed himself to be towed into the sky to a stupidly fatal aircraft accident that was just waiting to happen. The late Captain Blake was not an intelligent man.

Hunter spoke aloud to himself, adding, "But he sure had a hell of a lot of fun along the way."

The mental picture of his obit faded when a crackling voice came over the headset. "Tug pilot to glider pilot. Ready for takeoff? Over."

Hunter smirked. "Sure. I've got nothing else on my schedule for this morning. Out."

0800 hours

The team, without Hunter Blake, but with Sergei Mongochev, finished their coffee in the Quonset hut dayroom.

"Okay," Travis announced. "Let's get to work. Time to inventory the gear. We don't want anybody showing up a day late and a dollar short."

Stan interjected, "You mean a battle sensor device late or Smart Rifle short."

"Whatever," Travis said, not appreciating the interruption. "Everyone grab your equipment case and form a wide circle around the room."

Sergei went off to one side to watch. As an outsider he would not be as fully equipped as the rest of the team.

"Let's do this by the numbers," Travis said. "As I call out an item, remove it from your case and hold it up."

Jennifer asked, "What about checking them out?"

"Sam will take care of maintenance and repairs later this afternoon," Travis said. "Now! Battle sensor helmets!"

Everyone dug inside their hard-sided equipment cases and retrieved the headgear from its molded foam cradle, holding them high. Travis noted that all Force members had them.

The helmets, made of light but tough micro-filters, were for more than skull protection. They were also portable communications and computer network stations. This allowed communications between members and also with the Joint Task Force Headquarters where Brigadier General Jack Krauss worked. The headgear was also used to pinpoint a TALON trooper's exact location on the globe. All this was accomplished by routing proximity bursts to those communications biochips embedded under the skin by the right ear of each team member.

In addition, the helmets also held the battle sensor devices. These folded down over the left eye like a monocle. Its laser pathway provided images in the eye of the trooper, using the retina to produce holographic images of what the trooper was looking at or visually searching for. It also displayed status reports, maps, and battlefield telemetry from distant locations. The battle sensor devices also designated targets at a maximum range of 3,000 meters and permitted the user to see in the dark or through smoke and haze up to 2,000 meters.

"Helmets all present and accounted for," Travis said. "Now! Wrist Band Radio Frequency Field Generators."

These "nonlethal" weapons directed short, intense RF energy to disable electronic devices. With a range of 200 meters, they were activated by voice command via the micro-biochip transmitter. These handy high-tech gadgets could screw up unarmored vehicles' ignition systems and incapacitate most electronic equipment, including computers.

The audit continued with the hyper-capacitor belts that contained charged cells of micro-conducting material to act as emergency power for the Battle Ensemble.

The automatic trauma medical pack was a micro-engineered medical system that kicked in to provide an injured trooper with life-saving drugs, fluids, stimulants, and sedatives. The proper treatment was determined through embedded biochips that transmitted data to the Battle Ensemble's health sensors. From that point on, wounds would be automatically sealed and the proper medications injected.

The final item was the low-observable camouflage suit. This was the neatest part of the entire Battle Ensemble. It was made of a bulletproof fabric that determined, through micro-sensors, the visual qualities of the wearer's immediate physical environment and copied its exact shades, colors and luminosity. This allowed him or her to blend into the natural surroundings like a chameleon.

The automatic battlefield motion sensor was also part of the low-observable camouflage suit. This item alerted the wearer of danger by detecting millimeter wave changes in movement out to seven hundred meters away. In case of peril, a minor electric tingling sensation warned the trooper of impending danger. In truth, the motion sensor was a sixth sense that could also take over if the battle sensor device's thermal sensor malfunctioned.

Each trooper was also armed with the 4.55-millimeter XM-29 Smart Rifle. These weapons fired bullets directed by a wave sensor with an aiming device located under the barrel. The bullets came in 50-round magazines and were also armor-piercing. A four-shot 20-millimeter grenade launcher could also be attached to the weapon. In addition, the new silenced .45 semi-automatic pistol was issued as a backup and for nasty close-in work.

Sergei Mongochev, without the necessary imbedded biochips, would be dressed in an empty shell of the battle sensor helmet and wear regular fatigues designed for desert operations. He would, however, enjoy toting and using an XM-29 Smart Rifle as well as a .45 pistol.

When the inventory ended, Travis was pleased to find everyone properly equipped. He spoke to Sam. "I'll give you time this afternoon to run diagnostic and technical tests on the gear."

"Yes, sir," Sam replied. "I've got the minilab with me."

"Listen up, people!" Travis barked. The team com-

mander was ready to begin the day's real activities. "Grab
your helmets and rifles! Fall in outside! Move it!"

They wasted no time in storming out of the hut to form
up. Travis marched to the front of the group, holding a
couple of the grenade launchers tucked under one arm.

"Okay, Eagle Team," Travis said. "As you know, we're
standing on the threshold of a new operation. It's just like
an NFL team starting a new season. And like they do in
professional football, we're going back to the basics."

The team members, knowing it was going to be a physically demanding morning, mentally prepared themselves for
a few hours of sweat, strain, and more than a little attitude adjustment.

Travis continued, "First thing we must do is get organized for the big game ahead. I'm dividing you into two
teams. Alpha and Bravo. Jack will lead Alpha Team. His
team members will be Sarah and Sam. The Bravos will be
honchoed by Stan, and will carry Jennifer and Hunter on
their illustrious roster. Hunter will join Bravo when his flying duties are done. Sergei, as our asset, will stay with me."

Travis motioned to Jack and Stan with the grenade
launchers. "You two guys each take one of these. Affix 'em
to your rifles. You'll be our artillery when we need it."

The two team leaders took the launchers. With his hands
free, Travis took a corona-sized cigar from his cargo pocket
and stuck it in his mouth unlit. As Jack and Stan knelt
down to attach the lightweight weapons to their XM-29s,
Sergei, curious about the unfamiliar weaponry, watched
them.

The Russian asked, "They have own trigger?"

"Yeah," Jack answered. "You don't fire these hummers
with the rifle."

"I am not familiar with XM-29," Sergei said.

Travis gestured to Jack. "Give him some familiarization
firing with it the first chance you get."

"Right, boss," Jack said.

As soon as Jack and Stan were ready they stood up. By
then the team had separated into their respective teams.

"All right," Travis said. "We're going to use three basic
formations. The column. The diamond. And skirmish line."
He looked at Jennifer. "When's the best time to be in the
column formation?"

"During times of reduced visibility like night, thick vegetation, or fog," Jennifer replied. "I take it each team will be in line and parallel with the other."

"Correct," Travis said. "Alpha will always take the left side and Bravo the right." He looked at Stan. "What about the diamond formation? When will we use that one?"

"When we need all-around security," Stan snapped. "Like moving across open terrain with no cover."

"Right," Travis said. "Again, the Alphas will be on the left with one individual in the lead. The Bravos will be on the right with one of them acting as Tail-End Charlie. Sergei and I will occupy the center." He took a deep breath. "What about skirmish lines?"

Sergei raised his hand. "I think we use skirmish line in attack. Everybody in line face enemy and charge or shoot. Or charge *and* shoot."

"That's one way of putting it, I suppose," Travis said. He spat a stream of tobacco juice on the ground. "Each squad leader will be behind his people and I'll bring up the rear to maintain control."

"What about echelons?" Sam asked. "You know, echelon right and echelon left."

"There ain't that many of us," Travis said. He shifted his rifle. "Now let's get in some practice."

They spent the next two hours running at top speed, shifting from formation to formation. Everyone made sure they covered their individual fields of fire as the formations changed. Travis was satisfied with the coordination between the team leaders and himself, and the team leaders and their people. He cut them no slack, however, and the constant running had them breathing hard in spite of their excellent physical conditioning.

Travis wrapped up the training with an intense practice session of fire and maneuver as each team simulated laying down cover fire while the other moved toward objectives where a pretend enemy was supposedly dug in.

0830 hours

The air transport was at full throttle as it raced down the runway. Captain Hunter Evans Blake III and his glider, attached to the aircraft by the towrope, were airborne long before the big towplane reached its own take-off speed. Hunter, realizing the glider might fly up and over the tug, put forward pressure on the stick to keep his altitude in line with the C-123. Memories of his sailplane days at the Air Force Academy came back. Once both aircraft were airborne, he had a choice of either high tow or low tow. He chose a high tow to avoid getting slapped by the towline if it suddenly snapped. He had a distinct feeling that Murphy's Law was in full force at that moment. In other words, if something could go wrong, it certainly would.

Hunter spoke into the connecting telephone. "Tug pilot, this is glider pilot. Let's try a slow turn to the left. Over."

"Roger. Out."

The C-123 rolled slightly left. Hunter started his following turn too early and went inside the host's flight path. He overcorrected on the controls because of unfamiliarity with their sensitivity. He swung outside at a fast rate, but edged back into the correct position.

The tug straightened out, then eased into an easy, slow turn to the right. Once more Hunter started too early, but he quickly and smoothly corrected his position with just the right pressure on wheel and rudder.

"Tug pilot, this is glider pilot," Hunter said. "Let's start out with some alternating right and left turns. Make 'em a little quicker the next couple of times, then let's try some real evasive maneuvering. Over."

"Roger, glider pilot," came back the answer. "Start turns—*now*!"

Sergei Mongochev used a shovel and metric tape measure to trace a correctly proportioned and sized outline of the ALAS Mobile Command Center in the desert earth. This crude one-dimensional model measured 6.5 x 4.5 meters.

Next, he created the same design of the MCC's auxiliary vehicle that contained the generator and living quarters for the crew. This was approximately 75 percent the size of the MCC.

"Always they park in L-shape like this," the Russian explained. "Is because of length of power cables. Okay?" He walked out and marked three spots, each some fifteen yards away from the simulated control center. "Always is the guards here. One at each post. Okay?"

"Understood, Sergei," Travis said.

Sergei added, "Also on auxiliary vehicle is DShK machine gun. Big one. 12.7 millimeters. Okay?"

"Got it," Travis said. He addressed them all. "I want to emphasize that this initial movement onto the target is going to require absolute stealth. And do not—I say again—*do not* damage any equipment once you are inside. We'll need every bit of it in working order if Sam is going to be able to get ALAS to self-destruct."

Jack flexed his huge hand menacingly and smiled. "That means no shooting, right?"

"Right," Travis said. "Even a ricochet could knock out a piece of sensitive equipment."

They organized for the assault on the objective. Each team came in from a different side. Stan took out one simulated guard post, Jennifer and Sarah another, and Jack did in the third simulated sentry. Then they eased up to the doors etched in the dirt. At Travis's signal they made entries into the bogus MCC and its auxiliary vehicle.

They worked on the routine for two solid hours, never satisfying Travis. He yelled at them even when they had reached a point where the time to execute kills and entries had been honed down to a lightning fast forty-three seconds.

"You don't have all fucking day!" he bellowed during the sixteenth rehearsal of the operation. "Move it! Move it!"

The two teams, sweating in spite of the cold, grumbled to themselves, but all fully appreciated the fact that the dangerous task they faced demanded perfection and nothing less.

Finally Travis relented. "Well, hell. I guess that's the best you can do. Take a break." As they settled down, he announced. "After you've caught your collective breaths, we're going to do a team at a time. The other team will simulate being the crew inside the vehicles. And you pretend baddies try to damage the equipment." He grinned slightly. "A bit of enthusiastic physical contact will add to the realism of the practice."

Sam, smaller and lighter than even Jennifer and Sarah,

groaned aloud. He knew his larger teammates would deal him a few bruises before the day's training was over.

0915 hours

Hunter grew more confident as the towing continued. The turns were now tighter, and he held the glider dead-on in the tug plane's flight path, maneuvering exactly and precisely in the big aircraft's prop blast.

"Glider pilot to tug pilot," he said into the telephone headset. "Let's simulate a long-distance tow. Over."

"Roger," came the reply. "We have to stay in this air space because of security parameters, but I can make some diagonal runs that'll last long enough to give you some practice. Out."

As they made straight runs, Hunter tried different positions behind the C-123. After another hour of flying, he was convinced that the low tug caused less strain on both him and the glider.

"Glider pilot to tug pilot," Hunter said. "Let's get back to the airfield. I'll release about five miles out on your command. Over."

"Roger. Out."

They made a wide, sweeping turn. Hunter studied the terrain, and was ready when the tug pilot gave him the word to release. Hunter hit the button and the towline hook opened properly. The glider suddenly slowed as he turned to the right and the tug to the left.

Now Hunter was one with the glider. It was just the motorless ship and himself moving slowly downward through the sky. He pulled back on the wheel and tried a couple of stalls. He found the aircraft would stop flying and nose over at around sixty miles an hour.

Finally he banked and headed downward for the landing spot he had chosen on the runway. Once more he was forced to experiment as he used the spoilers on top of the wings in combination with flaps as he both steepened his descent and flattened it out during the landing.

"I know you, baby! I know you!" he yelled with delight as the craft responded to his manipulations of the controls.

He came in smoothly and easily on the skids, skimming

along the runway and coming to a halt some twenty-five yards from the hangar. He noticed a pickup truck coming out toward him. Hunter unbelted himself and walked to the door to step out into the cold. The vehicle came up and stopped. Old Dan Farley doddered up to him with a quizzical expression on his face.

"Well? How'd it go?" he asked. "At least you got down in one piece."

"It was better than that," Hunter said. He turned and fondly patted the glider's fuselage. "I've made a new friend."

The team had completed three solid days of training and rehearsal. Their activities evolved into a simulated landing and exit from the glider as would be done during the attack on the mobile Control Center. Travis wanted the team to participate in at least one live glider flight, but Ozzie Nettles, as station chief, would not permit it.

"If you're gonna die in that crate, it'll be on the operation," Ozzie said. "Not on a practice flight." He thought a moment. "We do have some sandbags we use to test cargo chutes. You could put those in the glider to give Blake the feel of handling a fully loaded aircraft."

Travis, as a good soldier, did not argue. "Well, if that's the best you can do . . ." He turned his attention back to the ground phase of the operation.

The attack training was expanded to include the raid on the Frateco factory complex. There would be no finesse in that phase of the operation. It was bust in, shoot it up, and blow the damned place to hell. No prisoners were to be taken. At this point they went to a live-firing exercise, using some abandoned buildings to simulate the factory with mannequins as Frateco people. The reports of the rifles and fire-and-maneuvering further loosened the team's collective kinks.

The team was hard, sharp, and ready. Even Travis was satisfied. The only downside was the lack of practice with the glider. They were all perturbed they could not try out the actual glider recovery that was to be used at the completion of the mission.

During the evenings in Desertville, the team relaxed in their dayroom. To keep boredom from setting in, they organized a Ping-Pong tournament. Little Sam Wong, quick as a cat with twice the reflexes, quickly established a lead and held on to it until he won the championship. Jack, all six and a half muscular feet of him, started off in last place and maintained the position right up to the last. He became known as the Cellar Dweller. Stan, who had been elected league commissioner, announced that the only reason he wasn't sending Jack to the minor leagues was because there weren't any.

The championship game was between Sam and Jennifer. Sam swept the series with a record of three and zip, making him champion of champions. The celebration of his victory was short-lived, however, when Ozzie Nettles made an unexpected and somber appearance.

"Folks, we've just got some real bad news. ALAS has struck again."

No one on the team said anything. They gazed somberly at the station chief, waiting for the full scoop on the disaster.

Ozzie spoke through clenched teeth. "The sons of bitches decided to show off again. They wiped out a small Aboriginal town in Australia's outback. And they've announced that if their demand for ransom is not met, they'll hit Detroit within the next five days."

Travis broke the team's collective silence. "My God! There's nothing anyone can do. A city that size couldn't be evacuated in three times as long."

"Yeah," Sarah agreed. "It would be better not to even attempt anything like that."

"It would be a catastrophe," Ozzie said. "The world's population has got to be kept in total ignorance of this situation."

"Will this new development affect us?" Travis asked.

"You will dismantle the glider tonight and have it ready to be loaded aboard a C-5A transport before dawn," Ozzie said. "Operation Sky Fire is now live and in color."

Travis Barrett reached for his field jacket. "Let's go, Eagle Team. We've got some big-time packing to do."

Chapter Three

The Kazakhstan-bound Russian Aeroflot An-24 transport flew away from the sunset through the darkening Eastern European skies toward its Central Asian destination. The weather was clear and the westerly winds gave the aircraft a helpful push along the course it flew.

A large spring-loaded hook was fastened under the aircraft's nose. This was the apparatus that would be used to snatch the team's glider from the ground at the completion of their mission.

The glider was attached to the An-24 by a towline wrapped with telephone wire. The motorless aircraft, held out of the prop wash in a low-tow position by Hunter, rolled slightly with an up-and-down motion. Because of Hunter's instinctive and skillful touch on the controls, the flight was as pleasant and easy as possible for pilot and passengers. After the initial excitement and apprehension of the takeoff and the first hour of the flight, everyone on the team now felt confident. In fact, with the exception of Hunter and Sam, the TALONs peacefully dozed in their seats.

Sam sat to the pilot's right rear. Because Hunter had to give all his attention to flying and communication with the tug plane, Travis had detailed Sam to act as navigator. This was necessary because a radio-silence mode kept the An-24 from using its sensitive navigational equipment.

Sam employed the "straight-up" communications in his battle sensor helmet to maintain a constant fix on their position. When a correction in the course was needed, he would announce a change in the azimuth and Hunter would relay the message to the Russian pilot on the telephone.

A dozen hours earlier, when the team and glider had arrived at the clandestine airstrip in Germany, they had immediately gone into a hectic routine of dragging the glider out of the C-5A's fuselage and carefully, but as quickly as possible, reassembling it. It was at that time they met the An-24 pilot, Major Anotoli Karlinski. The devil-may-care Russian was a former Aeroflot pilot who, like all such pilots, also held a commission in the Russian Air Force. He had moved into a special operations branch of a joint Russian and American group. This quasi-official organization was geared to go around the usual diplomatic procedures during exceptional situations where a bit of clandestine tiptoeing was necessary.

Karlinski was happy as hell to be participating in this particular program. He had been briefed on the mission on a need-to-know basis, but he sensed these Americans with their Russian asset were plunging madly into harm's way. They were his kind of people and he was looking forward to helping extract them after their mission was completed by snagging them and their glider off the ground with the retrieval device.

Now, winging through the dark night, Sam made another routine check of his positioning instruments. "Two degrees left," he said to Hunter.

Hunter relayed the message. "Two degrees left."

"Da. Ya panyimayu," Major Karlinski replied. "Two degrees left."

Sam ran another set of numbers. "One hour fifty-nine minutes to release point." He turned and looked down the fuselage at the other team members, dozing in their seats. Jack and Stan, however, sought more comfortable accommodations and had sprawled on the floor. Stan, in his usual gruff manner, tried to push the large Marine captain away to get himself more room.

Jack looked at him and muttered, "Watch it, shorty!"

Stan, with a bad case of a Napoleon complex, bristled at the insult. But he was too tired to take on Jack at that particular moment. Both settled down, and within minutes they were sleeping like innocent babies. Sergei Mongochev opened his eyes and stretched. He noticed Sam and nodded to him with a smile.

Sam returned the silent greeting, then went back to his navigational duties.

The glider swung and rolled a bit through some turbulence, then settled down once more. After a couple of minutes, Sam tapped Hunter's shoulder. "We're closing in." The brilliant young computer scientist got up from his seat and stepped over both Jack and Stan as he walked down to Travis and shook the mission leader awake. "It won't be long."

Travis nodded. "Right. Get the word to General Krauss."

"Yes, sir."

Sam returned to his seat. He powered up the communications suite of his battle sensor helmet. The commo biochip embedded under the skin near his right ear routed the signal to Brigadier General Jack Krauss at Special Operations Command.

"Sky Fire! Sky Fire!" Sam said quickly, giving the code word that indicated the mission was about to turn serious.

Meanwhile, Travis bent over the low overhead of the fuselage, going to each individual member of the force to make sure they were awake and alert.

Now Hunter had a real job ahead of him. His test flights had shown that the glider would sink at a ratio of 1 foot to 15 forward feet when taken off tow. It was imperative that he didn't waste a single foot of that sink. At a maximum altitude of 10,000 feet, they had to be released 28.41 miles from the target.

Sam tapped Hunter again. "Altitude?"

"Angels ten."

"Off tow in one minute," Sam reported. "Mark!"

Hunter relayed the information to Karlinski.

"Understood," came back the Russian's reply. "*Zhilayu udachyi!* Good luck!"

"*Spasibo.*" Hunter thanked him in one of the few words he knew in Russian. He raised his hand to the release knob above his head and waited.

A couple of beats later Sam gave the fateful command. "Execute!"

Hunter hit the release, giving Karlinski a farewell "*Da svidniya!*"

The An-24 made a steep turn to the left while Hunter

veered sharply right. Karlinski had been instructed to fly to the aerodrome at Leninsk and feign engine trouble until alerted for the retrieval portion of the mission.

Hunter, again following Sam's directions, made a sharp move left to a course of 88 degrees. The glider sailed gracefully through the sky, lowering itself toward the ground. The promised full moon was there, giving Hunter an excellent view of the terrain beneath them.

"There isn't much out there," he remarked, "but at least it's flat and treeless so we shouldn't hit anything." After a pause he added, "I hope."

"Look!" Sam said pointing ahead and downward.

The shadowy view of the Mobile Control Center with its auxiliary vehicle was visible in the near distance. Sam had done his job to perfection. Hunter now maneuvered to get them to a safer distance. He dropped the flaps and kicked up the spoilers as he headed for a convenient landing spot on the desert floor. The glider complained about the sudden slowing with a groan in its aluminum frame. After a slight shudder, its flight trajectory smoothed out again.

"Prepare for landing!" Hunter shouted.

The team, expecting the worst, tensed up for what could well be a controlled crash. The skids hit the sand, throwing back a shower of the pebbly stuff, looking like a powerboat plowing through water. For a brief moment, Hunter had no control over the glider. But he had brought it in at a perfect landing angle with the nose up at 15 degrees, and it went straight and even for fifty yards until slowing to a complete stop.

Now Travis took over. *"Out!"*

The two teams exited the glider and immediately took up a prearranged defensive perimeter. Travis, in the center of the formation near the aircraft with Sergei, watched and listened for a full minute.

"Clear!" he announced in a stage whisper. "Let's go. Diamond formation and mind your fields of fire."

The ground portion of Operation Sky Fire was underway.

Kazakhstan Desert
0300 hours

The man in the small sandbagged position yawned and sat down on the ground. He leaned back against the wall of his crude fortification with his AK-47 in his lap. Several months before he had been a warrant officer in a motorized rifle division stationed between Moscow and St. Petersburg. Most of his duties in the unit had involved road repair rather than soldiering. Without proper pay or rations, his unit was going to hell and morale had dipped low. Every morning at reveille there would be fewer soldiers present for duty as they fled the miserable existence of the current Russian Army.

The warrant officer's own desertion and subsequent induction into the Frateco had come through the machinations of one of his best friends. It was true he was no longer a leader and was required to do the duties of a common soldier such as he was performing now, but at least he was paid regularly and well. He had been pleased to note that his new annual earnings bested that of his former colonel.

The warrant officer yawned again and closed his eyes. No need for alertness way out there in the wilds of Kazakhstan. He took a deep breath and sank into slumber.

Within five minutes he was so deeply asleep that he didn't feel Stan Powczuk's knife slice into his throat. Although his legs drummed the ground, he died as he had been slain: silently and quickly. Another man from his old unit who was posted as a guard nearby left this mortal world the same way.

It was Jack who ran into trouble at the third sentry position. The soldier there was a veteran of the Afghanistan War, and he was prone to flashbacks. He sat in his sandbagged post, his mind taking him back to the Hindu Kush Mountains where the Mujahideen rebels owned the night.

Jack's approach toward the Russian was silent and stealthy enough to overcome any sane man. But a potential victim who lived in the world of schizophrenic paranoia not only heard nonexistent enemies but even more easily perceived real ones.

Just as Jack came over the sandbags, the large Russian

turned and came at him with his own knife. Jack whipped to the side of the man, avoiding a vicious slash. The two stood facing each other in the confined space.

Neither made a sound as every nerve fiber vibrated with gushes of adrenaline. Jack purposely twitched an elbow. This goaded the Russian into an attack that was quickly broken off when he noted the feint.

Now they circled slowly and deliberately to the left, each controlling his breathing, the knife blades moving gently back and forth in the moonlight.

Then Jack sprang into action. His left hand locked like a vice over the other's right wrist. At the exact same instant, the American drove his knife up under the Russian's ribcage with a twist. Jack pumped the blade back and forth as he drove his left hand into the opponent's throat. The Russian staggered back and sat down. Then he died.

Jack eased over the sandbags and headed for the rallying point.

Travis, tensed and ready, was relieved when Jack showed up. The mission commander asked, "Trouble?"

"A bit," Jack answered, "but nothing worth talking about."

Now the entire silent-kill group had returned all present and accounted for to the perimeter. Travis leaned over to Sergei.

"Okay. Ease into the command center and check it out."

Sergei nodded and crawled away to disappear into the darkness. Travis checked his luminous-dial watch and waited. There was still plenty of time before dawn, but he couldn't tolerate any delays. The retrieval of the glider had to be done just after sunup, before the garrison at the cosmodrome began their duty day.

Sergei returned in ten minutes and made his report. "Two technicians only in MCC. Everybody else in auxiliary vehicle. Four men. Asleep."

"Good," Travis said. "We'll pull it off just like we did back at Desertville, you hear? Alphas to the MCC and Bravos to the auxiliary. Move out and make it quick and quiet." He turned to Sam. "Go with the Alphas. Get in there and start the self-destruct sequence as quickly as you can."

"Okay, boss," Sam said under his breath.

Jack, with Sam behind him, moved to Sarah's position and motioned her to follow them. When they reached their target they paused long enough to sling their XM-29s across their backs. No matter what happened, there could be no shooting on their part. Even if the two men inside turned and opened fire on them, they would attack with knives. The situation demanded they be ready to sacrifice their own lives to make sure ALAS's orbit was ended permanently.

Jack pulled his knife as a signal for Sarah and Sam to do the same. When they were ready, he led them to the door.

Meanwhile, Stan, Hunter, and Jennifer headed for the auxiliary vehicle. They, too, had their rifles slung, but each carried one of the .45 autos with silencers.

As the two teams made ready to attack, Travis kept his eyes on them, ready to lend assistance where and when necessary. Everything would hinge around whatever actions Jack and his two teammates took.

Back at the MCC door, Jack rose up and peered inside. One of the technicians inside was asleep, but the other was monitoring the equipment while sipping a mug of tea. Jack turned to his comrades in arms and nodded, then he went through the door.

The working technician paid for his alertness by dying first with Jack's knife blade shoved into his throat. He grabbed desperately at the big African American's wrists in a blind, fearful instinct to remove the sharp instrument from his windpipe. It was all over in moments.

The second, mildly disturbed by the almost noiseless activity, turned sleepily to catch the astonishing sight of an attractive, petite woman in combat gear moving rapidly toward him. He saw her knife too late. Sarah struck with the efficient swiftness of a surgeon. Death was noiseless and instantaneous. Sam stood aside as the corpses were rolled away from the instrument panel.

Over at the auxiliary vehicle, the Bravos found the interior simpler than they had expected. It was no more than a wide compartment with a driver's station and a turret for the machine gun. Everyone inside was in sleeping bags. The team aimed their silenced automatics and popped fusillades of .45 caliber slugs into the sleeping forms. One twitched violently as he died, while two others gasped aloud. The sleeping men now sank into a deeper, more permanent slumber.

The Bravos went to the MCC. Travis assigned Sergei and Stan to assist Sam in activating the self-destruct. The rest of the team was put outside to watch for unexpected intruders. After making sure a 360-degree area around the vicinity was within everyone's field of fire, Travis joined the trio inside to see how things were going.

All the operating manuals in the vehicle's book compartment had been pulled out. Sergei and Stan pored over them, finally finding the one that covered the self-destruct.

"You'd think this would be kept in a safer place," Sam commented.

"Is not possible. Book must be with MC," Sergei explained. "If self-destruct is necessary, is because ALAS is out of control. Impossible to wait. Technicians on duty must begin operation."

"Then it looks like I'm the technician on duty," Sam observed.

They perused the manual and found the proper code. Sam ran the computer through the sequence but nothing happened. They went through the series six times before Sergei made a completely unexpected discovery.

"This is not complete manual," he announced. He showed it to Stan.

"Shit!" Stan yelled after he read the final section of the book. "It says here the other part of the code is at the computer lab at the Frateco main bunker. It is given verbally to the crews just before they go on duty at the MCC. It's changed daily."

"Aha!" Sam exclaimed. "Then *that's* the safety factor."

Sergei looked at the dead technicians. "Men who know code can tell us nothing."

Travis nudged Sam. "You've got a computer that can run through the code sequences, right?"

"These folks use the Cyrillic alphabet," Sam explained. "That's nine more letters than we have in English. And some of theirs represent sounds that take two of our letters to make."

"So?" Travis said. "What's that got to do with binaries and all that shit you computer nerds work with?"

"The numbers are going to be linked to letters in code

words," Sam said. "I could do it eventually, but it would take time. Like a couple of days, maybe."

"In that case, let's head for that damned bunker," Travis said sharply. "But we can't attack it like we planned. We've got to get in and find that code."

"I will help," Sergei said.

"Right. You'll do the talking for us," Travis said. "We'll head over there in the auxiliary vehicle. Stan, you drive. The rest of us will be inside. We may have to make use of those .45s again, folks. Let's boogie!"

After removing the bodies still in the sleeping bags, the team got inside. Stan started the engine while Sergei situated himself in the machine gun turret. He began dispensing directions to Stan.

The ride was smooth across the hard-packed earth, and it took twenty minutes before they turned down the gully that led to the entrance of the complex. When they pulled up, a guard walked up and shined his flashlight into Sergei's face.

"What the hell's going on?" he asked in Russian.

"Power failure," Sergei said. "We have come to fetch a repair team."

The guard studied Sergei's features. "Do I know you?"

"Of course," Sergei said. "I am a brother of the Frateco."

"*Da.* I recognize you," the guard said. Then his eyes opened widely. "Wait! You are the defector!"

He turned and ran toward the guard shack, but Sergei responded by pumping three bullets into his back from the silenced .45. The man's arms flew out as he stumbled forward a couple of steps before hitting the ground. His partner emerged into the open, and Sergei finished him off with some more quick shots. The guard was knocked back against the sentry shack, then fell forward on his face.

Sergei leaned down toward the interior of the vehicle. "Okay, Stan. We go."

"Do you know that guy?" Stan asked.

"Yes," Sergei replied. "Ex-KGB. Real son of bitch."

"It seems there's a lot of sons of bitches in the Frateco," Stan commented.

"True," Sergei said. "Drive slow and go to big building on right."

"You got it," Stan said.

The vehicle rolled slowly across the compound yard as casually as if they were there on official business. When they reached the building, Sergei climbed out of the turret and dropped to the ground. He went to the building and eased open the door, disappearing from sight.

A worrisome five minutes passed before he returned. "Okay. We go," Sergei announced.

The team followed him into the building. An elevator stood open to their direct front. The sight of a dead guard inside explained Sergei's delayed return. They got inside the elevator and went down three floors before stopping. The invaders stepped out, then went down a short hallway to a door.

Sergei reported, "Four men inside. Monitors. But we must be fast, okay?"

"Fine," Travis said. "Bravos go in and do your thing. Sergei, go in behind them with Sam to help him out."

Stan led the way in. The four men inside turned casually to see who had come calling. They leapt from their chairs at the sight of the intruders. Jennifer motioned the technicians away from the control unit toward the wall. The Frateco men raised their hands in an instinctive plea for mercy.

"You asking for break?" Stan asked in choppy Russian. "How about innocent people you killed on oil rig and others in Australia? And not to forget the rest you plan on killing."

"Please!" a nerdy-looking technician begged. "We are prisoners of war, *da*? The Geneva Convention states that—"

He was interrupted as .45s spit death into them, spilling the quartet to the floor. A couple writhed and moaned, then stopped moving. Blood seeped from the corpses.

Sergei knew what he was looking for. As he searched for the correct manual, Sam studied the large screen on the wall to the front.

"Simple but effective," he remarked in unabashed admiration.

A large screen showing a map of the world traced ALAS's orbital path as it swung around the globe. Computer enhanced radar signals pulsed brightly to show the exact position of the Aimed Laser Attack Satellite.

Sam sat down at the main computer terminal. The sequence of codes he had entered at the MCC was on the CRT. He turned to Sergei. "We need the rest of the progression."

Sergei found the manual he needed. He quickly scanned the contents, then turned to the right page. "Okay. Is today's date. Take look."

Sam had a bit of trouble since the last of the order included characters from the Cyrillic alphabet. He had to search the keyboard, hunting and pecking for the correct ones. Finally it was all in. The last thing he did was type in the location code from the big screen. A bright red light suddenly began blinking from ALAS's position.

"Aren't there locks where it'll take a couple of keys to complete the procedure?" he asked Sergei. "Surely it will take more than a keyboard to destroy that satellite."

Sergei shook his head. "This has not the—how you say—sophisticate, er, sophistication. This is all made simple for to bring out here."

"Then all I have to do is hit 'enter,'" Sam said. He looked at the Russian keyboard. "I take it the key is in the same position as on other computers." He pressed down and looked up at the tracking screen. Suddenly it shimmered with a brilliant color, then went dead.

Sam smiled and stood up to face the others with a grand gesture. In his best impersonation of a Shakespearean actor, he said, "Alas, ALAS is no more."

"I hope you're not expecting a curtain call," Travis snapped. He whipped his glare at Stan. "Goddamn it! What the hell are you waiting for? Let's plant those charges!"

"Ex-fucking-scuse me!" Stan said. "I've been loitering around doing nothing for two whole seconds."

"Knock it off," Travis growled. "We've got to destroy this place."

Sergei reminded them, "All charges must be inside bunker. Outside can resist nuclear bomb."

"Right," Travis said. He grabbed Stan's sleeve. "Let's do it."

The Green Beret and the Navy SEAL went to work. Jack took over the force and moved them outside to watch for signs of any wandering Frateco people. The twenty pounds of explosives were time-fused and set in a manner to detonate themselves along with the present charges the

Frateco had placed in the area. With the job done, Travis and Stan joined the others.

"Let's go!" Travis said.

They remounted the auxiliary vehicle and casually drove back out the gate where the two dead guards were still sprawled at their posts. After leaving the compound, Stan went straight back to the MCC. This time only Travis got out. He made a quick job of planting more of the plastic C-4, then rejoined his men.

"Back to the glider!"

They rolled rapidly across the desert until reaching the aircraft. Hunter Blake looked at the glider like he was seeing an old friend after a long separation.

Suddenly the explosives at the compound went off. Not only the TALON Force charges, but the preset Frateco explosives also detonated.

The concussion swept through the air like a semisolid wind and the night lit up for a brilliant millisecond. Less than half a minute later, Travis's accurately timed charges at the MCC followed.

Eagle Team looked at each other, numbly realizing they had accomplished a mission that would save millions of lives if not the whole planet. It was the cleanest job they'd ever done.

Hunter was impatient. "So—what the hell are you waiting for? You aren't going to get any medals, you sneaky bastards. Get that retrieval apparatus up and ready."

Sam turned to his battle sensor helmet to make contact with the tug plane.

Chapter Four

0500 hours

Hunter yelled to Jack as he walked toward the glider. "I need a hand here."

"Sure, fly boy," Jack replied. "You call. I haul. That's all."

"What a poet," Hunter remarked, motioning Jack to follow him into the fuselage. "We've got to get the retrieval gear set up."

They went inside and loosened the straps holding the apparatus to the overhead, then wrestled the equipment outside.

Travis gestured to Sam. "Sammy, call us a cab."

"Already good as done," Sam said. He had activated the "straight-up" communications in his helmet, and as soon as he was linked up, he broadcast the request.

Hunter, dragging the gear to the right position with Jack, spoke to the team's diminutive communications expert. "Bring the aircraft to these coordinates on an azimuth of two hundred seventy degrees." Next he got Travis's attention. "Get me a couple of people off the perimeter to help put this thing up."

"Stan! Sarah!" Travis snapped. "Give Hunter and Jack a hand."

As the two joined the effort, Hunter pulled a packet of papers from his cargo pocket. "Now let's see how this retrieval gizmo goes together."

Jack gave him a look of surprise. "Wait a minute! I know they wouldn't let us use it in training, but didn't you find out how to set it up?"

Hunter shook his head. "Nope. That old guy Farley said it was a piece of cake."

"I don't think that geezer gives a shit if we make it out or not," Stan said.

"He cares," Hunter said. "But in a morbid kind of way."

Stan grunted. "Now isn't that gratitude? You save the world and they still consider you expendable."

Travis threw in his two cents. "You knew that when you volunteered for TALON Force."

"Hey!" Hunter said. "Everybody pipe down while I figure this out." He perused the instructions. After a minute, he said, "Okay. The poles will be set to the left of the glider." He looked at the others. "Well? What the hell are you all waiting for? Turn it to face due west."

From that point on, the detail worked as Hunter read the instructions aloud to them. The poles were set fifteen feet apart. A cable with the retrieval rope was slung between them at the top. Then the other end was attached to the glider's tow hook on the nose.

Travis looked up at the top of the device. "How high up is that cable?"

"Twenty feet," Hunter answered.

"Mmm," Travis mused. "And how fast will the tow aircraft be going when it snaps us up?"

"Two hundred–plus knots," Hunter replied.

"I see," Travis said. "So let's get this straight. We'll be sitting in the glider, and the tug plane will come in going a bit over two hundred knots an hour at an altitude of twenty feet and snap us off the ground?"

"You got it," Hunter assured him.

"Mmm," Travis said again. "In other words, we'll go from zero to two hundred knots in the wink of an eye."

"Yeah," Hunter said. "It's gonna be a real kick in the head."

"Literally," Travis said without a smile.

Sam spoke up. "Tug plane five minutes out."

Travis bellowed, "Into the glider! Now! *Now! NOW!*"

Those on the perimeter joined them as the team made a quick but orderly entrance into the fuselage. Everyone sat down and wasted no time buckling their harnesses as tightly as possible. Stan Powczuk looked at his companions.

"Well, I guess we should congratulate ourselves on a job well done," he remarked.

Jennifer grimaced at him. "Shut up! You want to jinx the operation?"

"Chill out, Olsen," Stan said. "We haven't had any problems so far."

"Well, keep your stupid thoughts to yourself," Jen snapped. "Every time you start crowing like a bantam rooster, things go to hell in a handbasket." She looked at Sarah. "I hate it when he talks like that."

"Don't pay any attention to him," Sarah said, "and he'll shut up. Eventually."

Stan was pissed off. "I don't like being compared to a bantam rooster."

Jennifer sneered. "Just because they're small, right?"

Further exchanges between the two were cut off when Sam announced, "Tug plane three minutes out."

Everyone instinctively braced for the sudden acceleration. Hunter, in his pilot position, put both hands on the wheel as his feet worked the rudder pedals back and forth to warm the cold metal. He had already dropped the flaps for a quick climb.

Sam calmly informed them, "Tug plane two minutes out."

"Make sure your weapons and any loose gear are secured," Travis ordered. "We don't want any debris flying around in here to cause injuries."

"Yeah!" Jack agreed. "That includes bouncing people."

"Or heads," Stan added with a grin.

"Shut up!" Jennifer growled.

"I got to tell you, folks," Hunter added, "this baby is going to be stressed to the max."

"One minute out!" Sam said.

The faint growl of the approaching aircraft's engines could be discerned. The sound grew louder, until it seemed like a rolling explosion over their heads. Then in a neck-cracking instant, the interior of the glider turned violent.

The motorless aircraft was jerked airborne, forcing Hunter to fight the controls that rebelled against the instantaneous abuse. The pilot's head jerked back with such force that his hands came off the wheel. He fought against the centrifugal force of the yawing, rolling glider as he moved to grab the controls. He could see the needles of both the air speed indicator and altimeter spinning wildly. The vertical airspeed instrument was pegged to the fullest reading.

Then the tow hook broke off the front with a loud, nasty crack. The device was whipped away by the now rapidly disappearing tug aircraft. The glider slowed almost as violently as it had begun the wild takeoff.

"Shit!" Hunter exclaimed as they went into a flat spin.

Fiberglass ripped off the right wing. The real aluminum tubing buckled while Hunter pushed against the stiff controls in an effort to maintain some semblance of flight. They hit the ground with a hard bounce, then slammed down again and careened across the desert, sending up showers of rock and sand.

The glider suddenly stopped with a steep forward tilt. Everyone clenched their teeth, fully expecting it to flip tail-over-nose to an upside-down position. But the aircraft fell back with its belly on the ground.

Hunter took a deep breath. "We hope you enjoyed flying with Kamikaze Airlines. Please be careful when removing your belongings from the overhead bins."

"Cute," Travis said sarcastically. "Try again?"

"I don't think so," Hunter said. He pulled back and forth on the mushy controls. "This crate is no longer airworthy."

"Everybody out," the team leader ordered.

As the team members stepped outside, Jennifer went over to Stan, wound up, and punched him hard on the arm.

Stan looked at her and shouted, "Hey! What'd you do that for?"

"That's just my way of saying 'I love you.' "

"I know you do," said Stan, "but the next time you punch me you better be ready for action."

"Knock it off, you two!" Travis snapped. "We don't have time for any happy horseshit right now."

Sarah looked to the sky. "Hey! The tug plane is coming around again."

Hunter walked out to a visible spot and waited for it. As it approached he spoke through his helmet. "Tug pilot, this is glider pilot. Abandon the mission. The glider is bent."

Major Karlinski was not one to give up. "I read you. We look for landing area to pick you up, *da*?"

Travis broke into the communication. "Negative! Negative! Follow procedures and leave the area. We'll continue on our own."

The brave Russian persisted. "I will set down. I cannot leave you out here."

"No!" Travis barked. "It's too dangerous! No other choice!"

"Nyeschastniy," Karlinski said, expressing his regrets. *"Da skorig f'stryechyi.* See you later."

The Russian eased the An-24 over into a slow turn and waggled his wings in a combined signal of good luck and farewell, then climbed back up into the sky for his westward trip out of Kazakhstan.

Sergei checked his watch. "In two hours, at eight o'clock, Frateco Headquarters must send check-in signal to garrison. When it do not come, soldiers will go to see what the matter is."

"How serious will that be?" Travis asked.

"They have armored personnel carrier and Hind helicopter," Sergei said. "I think that is serious."

"Right," Travis agreed. "Well, folks, everyone get back into the auxiliary vehicle. It's a good thing we didn't destroy that puppy."

Sarah spoke up. "How about letting me man that machine gun, Travis?"

"Good idea," he said. "You're supposed to be a good shot, aren't you?"

"I sure am," Sarah said matter-of-factly. "I learned from the best."

Sam asked, "Your dad, huh?"

"No," Sarah said. "My grandmother. She was the women's state champion of Massachusetts for five years running." She noted the incredulous looks from the others. "Well, I never said she was the *typical* Jewish grandma."

"We'll make this an all-woman effort to start out," Travis said, continuing his orders. "Jennifer, take the wheel and head due south."

In less than five minutes, the team was back inside the vehicle as Sarah sat in the machine gun turret and Jennifer handled the driving. Travis called a planning session with Sergei, Jack, and Stan to discuss their options.

"So," Travis said, "here we are. Cut off and isolated in dangerous territory. I don't know about you guys, but this scares the shit out of me."

Jack nodded in agreement. "Sun Tzu says that the wise

commander recognizing changing circumstances will adapt to them with expedience."

Stan snorted. "Now ain't that food for thought."

"Well, let's hope I'm a wise commander," Travis said. "Okay! The first order of business is now underway. That is, we're getting the hell out of here. Now let's do some serious S-3 work and set up an operations plan. I think we'll all agree that going north is out. It's too far to reach safety in that direction."

Sergei added, "And it no doubt will put us in contact with more unfriendly forces."

"We sure as hell can't go east," Jack said. "I don't think the Red Chinese will exactly greet us with hugs, kisses, and bouquets of flowers, except maybe Sammy."

"What about south?" Stan asked.

Jack liked the idea. "That will offer us the best chance," he commented. "If we travel in a southerly direction we can reach either the Persian Gulf or the Gulf of Oman and link up with American naval forces. That means going through Turkmenistan, then crossing Iran."

"Turkmenistan?" Travis remarked. He turned to Eagle Team's naval intelligence officer. "Hey, Jen! What's the skinny on Turkmenistan?"

"It's a former Soviet republic," she replied, tapping the impressive store of information stored in her brain. "Poverty stricken with a chaotic government."

"Is true," interjected Sergei. "Very disorganized. If we play our cards—how you say—close to our chest, we might bluff our way through there." Then he added, "Or maybe no."

"We don't have a hell of a lot of choices in this mess," Travis said. He sent a signal via his battle sensor helmet up to the thirty-six-satellite constellation the TALON Force used for communications and global positioning. The exact positioning coordinates of their own location and the Persian Gulf were broadcast back to everyone else's helmet.

"It looks like a distance of around fourteen hundred miles," Jack said.

"Right," Travis agreed. "We'll start out on an azimuth of one-eight-zero degrees as the crow flies. Unfortunately we don't have any data that shows terrain features, villages, roads, military posts, and all that."

Jack was pensive. "What are the chances for an aerial pickup in Iran?"

Travis shook his head. "No can do. The Iranians keep a close surveillance on their air space. We'll have to travel overland all the way across the country."

"Oh, well," Jack said with a shrug. "Nobody said it would be easy."

"We have one thing in our favor," Stan commented. "At least the Iranians won't be expecting us. We're not even supposed to be there."

Travis yelled over at Jennifer, "How much speed can we get out of this thing?"

"According to the speedometer, a little less than seventy-five kilometers an hour."

Travis thought aloud, "Let's see. That'd be—"

"Forty-five or forty-six miles an hour," Sam interjected. "If we maintain top speed around the clock, we should reach our destination on the Persian Gulf in about—" His mind worked the figures. "—around a day and a half—about thirty-one hours."

"I figure a week and a half," Jack said. Then he added, "Worst case scenario."

Stan didn't agree. "Worst case scenario is that we don't make it at all."

"There he goes again!" Jennifer yelled over her shoulder.

"We'll make it," Travis said grimly. "But figuring contact with unfriendlies and rough terrain, we've got between two and three weeks to get through this exfiltration."

Stan chuckled. "We ain't exactly gonna set no speed records, are we?"

"Okay," Travis said. He leaned forward toward Jennifer. "Maintain a course of one-eight-zero. We'll check our exact position every half hour or so, depending on the situation."

"Roger!" Jennifer replied, making a proper adjustment to their direction of travel.

Travis turned to his battle sensor helmet and broadcast a brief but fully informative situation report to Brigadier General Jack Krauss at Task Force Headquarters. The rest of the team sat in silence listening to the one-sided conversation. Finally Travis ended the transmission. He turned a serious face to his comrades.

"Our plan is approved," he informed them. "General

Krauss isn't real happy about the situation but he figures there's no other choice."

"I'm not surprised," Jack commented. "This is a real sensitive area."

"Yeah," Travis said. "It's so damned sensitive that the situation has been classified as Condition Black. I say again—Condition Black."

The mood of the group turned somber. Condition Black meant no one was allowed to surrender or fall into enemy hands alive. Abandoned wounded would have to be killed. Imminent capture called for suicide.

"They've never hung us out to dry before," Stan said.

Jack agreed. "I never thought I'd see the day they wouldn't bust their asses to get us back. No matter what it took."

"It's because of the seriousness of ALAS," Travis explained. "If word ever got out . . ." He let the implications remain unspoken as he turned to Sarah. "You will install ipsiusmorsathol kits in the automatic trauma med packs. Now."

"Right," Sarah answered.

Ipsiusmorsathol was a drug Sarah had helped develop in a supersecret CIA lab. It caused instant, painless death.

Sarah climbed down from the machine gun turret to get the drug kits out of her gear. When installed, a push on the button took it out of safety mode for five seconds. Then the drug was automatically injected into the trauma pack wearer. There was no antidote. If the instrument was accidentally activated, the careless user had those five seconds to repush the button to put things right. If he failed, the curtain of life was closed forever.

Now, however, Travis had other things on his mind: "We'll organize ourselves into watches and take our turns at both driving and lookout with the machine gun. In the meantime, I suggest we situate ourselves as comfortably as we can and try to get in some shut-eye."

0700

Sarah was an hour-and-a-half into her watch. She sat in the turret, keeping a sharp eye on all points of the hazy desert

horizon as they rolled rather smoothly across the firm terrain. She didn't like the looks of the very visible tracks left
behind the vehicle or the resulting clouds of dust. These
were eye-catching conditions that could be discerned at
long distances.

A dot above the ground caught Sarah's eye. She dropped
down the battle sensor device on her helmet. It went into
a position over her left eye like a monocle. The laser pathway of the device generated a holographic illusion of the
thing she now viewed. The image and the data indicated
by the battle sensor device gave her immediate alarm. She
spoke into the transmitter receiver.

"Chopper on our six!" she yelled. "Three thousand meters and closing! Fast!"

The lady M.D. swung the machine gun around in the
direction of the approaching aircraft. She had to brace herself as Jen began evasive maneuvering, alternating sharp
veering motions with slower, unpredictable turns.

Down below, the others braced for the attack. "Shit!"
Stan said. "It's only a matter of time. They'll turn this damn
thing into a pile of molten metal with the first rocket."

"Maybe no," Sergei said. "Because of lack of funding,
no rockets for the Hind helicopter. Not much even to keep
it flying."

"Well, then, just what the hell do they have?" Travis
demanded.

"GSh machine gun," Sergei answered. "Thirty-millime-
ter. Big bullets and radar aimed."

"Shit!" Stan repeated. "That ain't exactly a popgun, is
it?"

Outside, the gunner of the Hind, sitting in a cockpit in
front of the pilot, had spotted the auxiliary vehicle on his
gun radar. He alerted his partner and they headed directly
toward the target as fast as they could.

Sarah gripped the handle and trigger as she aimed at the
approaching aircraft through the machine gun's sight. She
began pumping bursts of tracer rounds at the Hind, getting
a feel for the arc of the bullets. She ate up a fifty-round
belt, but now was confident of what she could do with
the DShK.

The air was shattered with incoming 30mm rounds that
snapped and banged off the vehicle. The sound was like

hundreds of ball-peen hammers to the people inside. Sergei risked a look through the plastic bubble of the navigational turret, then dropped back just as two bullets shattered it.

"No rockets!" he yelled. "But direct hits from GSh gun can punch through outer cover of vehicle."

The chopper passed over and maneuvered for another run. Sarah leaned inside. "Hey! Somebody give me another goddamned fifty-round belt and be quick about it!"

"Yes, ma'am!" Hunter responded. He passed up the ammo.

Sarah had just locked and loaded when the Hind came back for its second try at blowing them to hell. She was having trouble getting the target-leading alignment she wanted when suddenly Jen whipped the wheel to the left. Sarah instinctively knew she had the correct angle. Three long firebursts blasted out of the machine gun.

The chopper shook violently once, then the nose tipped up. In the next instant, the Hind's fuel and ammo exploded. The main fuselage disintegrated in the fiery blast. The front cockpit split off and whirled violently downward, throwing the gunner out. The unlucky man, still strapped in his seat, flew through the air in a lazy arc. He hit the ground hard, bouncing twice before coming to a halt.

"Got him!" Sarah shouted.

Cheers sounded from inside and shouted accolades for her shooting abilities gave Sarah an ego boost.

Sam cracked, "*Oy*! Grandma would have been so proud of you."

Sarah showed a slight grin. "Your Jewish accent needs a little work."

Sam looked at Jack. "What does she expect from a guy who grew up speaking Mandarin before English?"

Travis looked up through the now wide-open navigational turret and noted the smoke coming from the crashed Hind. "That took care of—" He grimaced at the sight of dust on the horizon. He turned to his own battle sensor device. "Armored personnel carrier!"

"What kind?" Jack asked.

"MT-LB," Travis reported. He turned to Sarah. "Look for a gully! A depression! Any kind of cover! We'll have to make a stand. They're faster than we are."

Sarah turned her attention to the direct front. Moments

later she dropped down into the interior. "Dry creek bed at ten o'clock."

Jennifer turned toward the natural trench and reached it within five minutes. She charged down into the terrain feature and the wheels sunk up to their hubs in the unexpected soft sand. Jennifer killed the engine.

"Well, we sure as hell aren't going anywhere now," she announced.

"Circle the wagons!" Travis ordered. They quickly exited the vehicle and took up team defense positions along the top of the gully. Travis continued giving his orders through his battle sensor helmet. "I don't want that APC damaged too bad. Let's draw those bad guys out into the open."

The APC came into view and everyone wisely let it close in on the team's position. It was obvious the attackers had spotted the auxiliary vehicle that was now out of their view. They had slowed down to relocate it. Because of their low-observable camouflage suits, the team members knew they were next to invisible to the renegade soldiers.

As soon as the MT-LB came close enough, its machine gunner fired several wild, ineffective firebursts that went over the team's heads.

Stan smirked. "Jesus! What a bunch of fucking amateurs."

Sergei explained, "They are not well trained. Spend most of time on guard duty or maintenance work."

"Stan! Jack!" Travis said. "Let's give those boys a bit of encouragement. I want you two to send some intermittent *ineffective* fire over their position. Make 'em think we're a bunch of frightened idiots."

The two team members quickly complied, firing sparse shots in the direction of the MT-LB without hitting it. Their shots whined off through the air, plowed up the ground, or ricocheted off rocks.

Shouted orders could be heard inside the armored personnel carrier, then the troops came out of the vehicle via the two doors in the rear of the hull. They formed into a ragged line of skirmishers and ran yelling toward the Force.

"Playtime's over," Travis said. "Shoot to kill."

The team cut loose with uncoordinated volleys of fire from their XM-29s. The 4.5-millimeter rounds slammed into the Russians, knocking them around like rag dolls before they collapsed in untidy heaps in only a matter of seconds.

A couple made an attempt at covering fire as they withdrew back toward the APC. One was kicked over on his back by incoming rounds. His buddy panicked and turned to run. He was unable to go more than a step before he, too, was cut down.

"Cease fire!" Travis ordered. "Alpha Team! Clear the vehicle."

"Let's go, kiddies," Jack said, leaping to his feet and charging over the side of the gully to level ground.

The rest of the team covered them as Jack, Sam, and Sarah approached the APC. Within moments, Jack gave the All-Clear signal. When the rest of the team joined them, he spoke to Travis. "There's some Russki uniforms inside."

"Yes," Sergei said. "They sell them to merchandisers for collectors in West. Probably stolen from Intendance Warehouse."

Travis looked inside and saw several large cardboard boxes filled with tunics and trousers. "We might just have use for these when we reach Turkmenistan."

"Yes," Sergei said. "I will take lead when we meet border guards."

"Then we'd better grab these AK-47s too," Sam suggested.

"Yeah," Travis said. "Go to it. Stan, siphon the gas from the auxiliary vehicle. I left my Texaco card at home." He turned to Jennifer. "Tired of driving?"

"Nope," she answered. "I assume we're going to take over this MT-LB."

"Correct," Travis said. "You can get your familiarization training on the way. Same course. Two-two-five. Turkmenistan, Iran, then some water that has American ships floating on it."

In short moments the team members were back moving across the desert. They left the sprawled, bullet-ripped bodies of the renegade soldiers where they fell.

Among the dead was Senior Private Yuri Koblenko. His young widow would be eating their extra rations alone that evening, and for many more to follow.

Chapter Five

Jen drove the MT-LB armored personnel carrier gingerly for the first five miles as she got the feel of the vehicle. With Sergei coaching her, she tested the two control sticks' effect on the treads and the resulting turn speeds and radii that she could expect from the APC. She continued her operation through acceleration and braking to get a further feel of her driving job. Eventually, Jen established a close working rapport with the thirteen-ton war wagon. Although she was pleased with the way it handled, she didn't like the sound of the engine.

"It's running rough," Jennifer complained. This was a Minnesota farm gal who had done her time helping daddy repair tractors. "This baby wants a tune-up and maybe a valve adjustment."

Sergei nodded in agreement. "They don't have extra parts needed for proper maintenance. They must make what you call improvisations. Also is shortage of proper tools, so they use what have got on hand."

Jennifer chuckled. "Back on the farm in Minnesota it's called using spit and baling wire."

Travis, sitting behind them, added, "In the army we call it field expediency."

Jennifer shrugged. "Either way, we're flying on a wing and a prayer. I just hope the oil's been changed regularly, not to mention replacing the filter now and then."

Sergei shook his head. "I don't count on it."

Travis spoke to Sam. "Contact General Krauss and let him know we're now in a stolen Russian armored personnel carrier. An MT-LB to be exact." Suddenly he noticed something and nudged Sergei. "Check out that canvas brief case beneath your seat."

Sergei hadn't noticed the container. He picked it up and sat it on his lap. He opened it and looked inside. "Maps. Ah! This indicates we are in command vehicle."

"Yeah?" Travis said. "Don't they have maps in all their APCs?"

Sergei shook his head. "Under Soviet system only commanders allowed maps. That way enlisted men can't find way to West to defect."

"Let's have a look at those maps," Travis said. "Maybe they'll help *us* find a way out of here."

Sergei went through the charts, checking each carefully. He found several to be in Arabic. He showed them to Travis. "I cannot read words."

Travis hollered, "Jack! Check out these puppies for us. They're in Arabic. Can you make heads or tails of 'em?"

Jack joined them and took the maps. He glanced at them and shook his head. "Nope. They ain't Arabic. They're Persian. Each one is a detailed section of the whole of Iran."

"What are Persian-language maps doing in a Russian APC?" Travis wondered.

"Are only maps of Iran available," Sergei explained. "Soviet military units in Asia always ready to roll into any nearby country."

Travis looked at Jack. "So? Do you know Persian?"

"I know a little bit," Jack replied. "Just don't expect me to indulge in any real deep scientific or intellectual conversation."

Sam, listening, said, "We don't expect you to do that in English."

"Ten thousand comedians out of work, and my little buddy is trying to be funny," Jack retorted. He looked through the maps. "Hey! I think these show military depots, fuel dumps, and other supply installations."

Travis wasted no time in calling a council of war with his two team leaders. They moved to the rear of the vehicle where they could sit together. The trio had to lay out a route that would avoid unnecessary contact with Iranian troops and police, yet have fuel, rations, and other necessities readily within reach.

By using the maps in combination with the positioning

gear in their battle sensor helmets, the three team members discovered they presently were on an arid plateau that extended into Iran from Kazakhstan through Turkmenistan. The terrain, cut by two small mountain ranges, was made up of loose stones and sand that merged into fertile soil along the higher elevations. The land was also dotted with numerous oases that dated back to time immemorial.

"Old caravan routes," Jack remarked.

"Looks good so far," Stan observed, looking over Jack's shoulder.

"Yeah," Travis agreed. "But check this out. There's a strip of inviting terrain to our direct front. Beyond that is one hell of a desert called the Dasht-e Kavir. It makes the Llano Estacado in New Mexico and Texas look like Hawaii. Gentlemen, it does not appear to be a particularly inviting place."

Jack gave the map a closer study. "What we have here is a salt desert about a hundred miles wide and two hundred and forty or so long. There's mud under the salt. That means in a lot of places there are marshes with the consistency of quicksand."

"Great!" Stan exclaimed. "All the makings of a horror movie, huh?"

"Oh, yeah!" Travis said, suddenly remembering. "I studied the Dasht-e Kavir during an intense area assessment a couple of years back at the Special Warfare Center at Fort Bragg. Legend says the place is the location of the ancient cities of Sodom and Gomorrah."

"The ones in the Bible?" Jack asked.

"Those are the only Sodom and Gomorrah I know of," Travis replied. "The Dasht-e Kavir is supposed to be cursed by God Himself. He turned what was once a fertile valley into all that salt and crap to punish the inhabitants for their sins and depravities."

"But I bet they had fun while it lasted," Stan said, sighing wistfully.

"Ha!" Hunter crowed. "You'd fit in perfectly with that crowd."

"Ah!" Stan said. "Now we hear from the witty fly boy."

"That ain't nothing to joke about," Jack said. "I don't like the sound of the place."

"What else can you glean from the map?" Travis wanted to know.

"Well, it looks like the only places you'll find people are on the edges of that awful goddamned salt desert," Jack said. He was obviously disturbed. "And that is a God damned place. Literally."

Travis began to realize that the area could play to their advantage. "Here's the plan," he announced. "We'll go into Turkmenistan using these Russian uniforms as cover. We'll swing to the southeast so we can enter Iran through the Dasht-e Kavir. It will serve us well because of its isolation and emptiness. When we need supplies, we'll hit one of those settlements along the edge of the desert. They're located in plush, fertile areas in the foothills."

"I don't know about going across that desert," Jack said with a strong tone of doubt in his voice. "There's a hell of a lot of places out there on those salt flats that won't support the weight of this vehicle."

Travis shrugged. "Then we'll abandon it and walk."

"Quicksand can pull people down too," Jack pointed out. "And a salt wasteland ain't exactly the best place for a stroll."

"That's not our only problem," Stan said. "This map shows the salt flats don't stretch all the way to the Persian Gulf. We're going to run into civilization before we get out of Iran. That means cops and troops."

"Then things are going to get real hairy," Travis observed. "This is going to be one hell of a challenge. Maybe the most difficult we've ever faced."

"I don't want you guys to think I'm crazy or a religious nut of some kind," Jack said. "But I'm not real anxious to enter some place that's had a curse put on it by the Almighty. It's a real sure sign He don't want nobody visiting it."

That was the first time any of them had ever heard Jack DuBois display any uneasiness about anything pertaining to a mission.

He explained, "This goes back deep into my roots. My great-grandmother was a voodoo woman in Haiti, and she taught me a lot about certain mysteries that us mortals cannot understand. One thing she really impressed me with was the spirituality of human beings and the things that rule us. *Unseen* things! I was pretty impressed by all that mumbo-jumbo as a kid. And I still believe in some of that stuff. What I mean to say is that there're things in this world beyond our control. And we shouldn't mess around with 'em."

Sarah, sitting nearby, agreed. "A lot of things we don't understand can't be explained by logic or science. The story of Sodom and Gomorrah is part of the Old Testament."

"You mean the After-Action Report issued by the ancient Hebrews, right?" Stan said.

"Yeah," Sarah said. "And the punishment God put on those evil people of Sodom and Gomorrah was a terrible one."

Stan shrugged. "What else can we do? Put wings on the APC and fly out?"

Jack smiled sardonically. "That might be easier than defying a holy curse."

Travis folded the maps. "Nevertheless, no matter what the Old Testament, New Testament, Koran, or my Aunt Fanny tell us, we're getting out of Kazakhstan and crossing Turkmenistan into Iran. And that'll include a little journey across the Dasht-e Kavir."

Jack took a deep breath. "In other words: out of the frying pan and into the fire."

Sam grinned. "Hey, Jack, doesn't Sun Tzu have anything to say about a situation like this?"

"Yeah, Sammy," Jack replied. "And I hope Travis pays heed to the advice. Allow me to paraphrase the Master: 'A commander who doesn't fully understand the dangers of the mission he plans for, won't be able to conduct a successful campaign.' "

"Now *that* is scary," Sam said.

"Hey," Stan said philosophically. "Shit happens!"

"Shut up, Stan!" Jennifer hissed at him.

Kazakhstan/Turkmenistan Border
2140 hours

Travis sat in the command turret of the APC, staring dully at the portions of the road illuminated by the vehicle's headlights. He wore his battle sensor helmet along with a Russian uniform adorned by epaulettes showing the rank of lieutenant. His eyes felt heavy with fatigue. He had been manning his post for ten straight hours.

Below and to his left, Hunter pulled his watch as driver. Jen had been reluctant to give up the job, and it had taken a direct order from Travis to get her to go to the rear of the troop compartment for some much-needed sleep.

Suddenly, a small, lighted area showed low on the horizon. Travis dropped down into the interior and signaled Hunter to stop. The unexpected halt brought everyone to an instant state of alertness.

"Lights ahead," Travis announced. "Looks like a border crossing station." He once more turned to the positioning device in his helmet for confirmation. "Yeah! We're on the Turkmenistan border." He nodded to Sergei. "Okay. Take over."

Sergei, dressed in a captain's uniform, climbed into the command turret. Stan Powczuk, because of his working knowledge of Russian, also came forward to see if he might give the Russian asset a hand.

"Listen up!" Travis said. "It's up to you two Russki speakers to bullshit us across the border."

"Aye, aye, sir," Stan said. He winked at Hunter. "Onward, Jeeves."

"Up yours, Swabbie," Hunter said as he put the transmission into first and stepped down on the accelerator.

They drove boldly and noisily up to the border station to give the impression they had every right in the world to be on that road at that particular time. The MT-LB pulled up to the crossing to find an elderly warrant officer and a moronic-looking kid private on duty.

Sergei and Stan hopped down to the ground and walked over to speak to the pair. *"Dobri Vyechyir,"* Sergei greeted them. "How are you this evening?"

The warrant officer mumbled something under his breath while the kid gave Sergei a vacant-eyed stare.

Sergei began the cover story. "We are a liaison vehicle sent to—"

The warrant officer suddenly stumbled backward and fell down to a sitting position. Sergei was alarmed by the action, and pulled his pistol. Nothing happened as the old man remained there, and the kid's head drooped. Sergei checked each closely, then looked at Stan. Stan understood what was going on. He grinned as they both walked back to the APC.

Travis looked at the strange sight. "What the hell's the matter with them?"

"They smoke hashish," Sergei said.

"Those two are stoned out of their gourds," Stan said.

"No shit?" Travis said. "I take it that discipline isn't too strict in the Turkmenistan Army."

"Standards fall since Soviet Union collapse," Sergei said.

"So much for the problem of crossing into Turkmenistan," Travis said. He jumped down from the APC to join Stan and Sergei. "Let's take a look in that guard shack and see if there's anything we can use."

A search of the file cabinet inside revealed official permits for entry into the country. There were also vehicle registration forms, and even authorizations to charge for fuel and rations at military installations.

"These are pretty weighty documents to be just sitting around at a lonely border crossing," Travis remarked.

Sergei explained, "This is quiet area and papers all date back to Soviet days. Turkmenistan is backward place." He pulled some of the forms out. "I can fill out papers to get us across country and get supplies."

"Then do it," Travis urged him.

It took Sergei a half-hour to prepare what they would need. He put official stamps and forged signatures with various names on the forms, then gathered them up. "Okay. All finish."

"Right," Travis said. "Before we go, let's sanitize the area. These two jokers aren't going to remember a thing about tonight."

When the team was ready to resume their journey, there was no sign of them having visited the place. Even the tracks of the MT-LB had been carefully wiped away with a couple of brooms found behind the small building. When the two border guards came out of their dope-laden haze in a few hours, they would not be aware anyone had even visited their station.

Now, seemingly proper and legal, the team rolled into the interior of Turkmenistan.

Turkmenistan
1130 hours

The people around the small village's well looked up in surprise as the APC drove off the rustic highway and came into the center of the hamlet. The male members of the team were atop the vehicle wearing their Russian uniforms. Jen and Sarah were out of sight inside the vehicle, with Jen once more doing the honors as driver.

The community's elders, sitting off to one side of the well, studied the new arrivals as the MT-LB came to a stop. The six old men were mildly curious about the presence of the Russian military. It had been close to a decade since Soviet troops had been in their midst.

Sergei climbed off the vehicle and walked up to the old-sters. "Greetings, comrades," he said politely. "I hope Your Honors are all in good health."

The senior man, a wizened old fellow named Mustafa, replied, "We are as well as Allah permits."

"Of course," Sergei said. "You speak excellent Russian, Your Honor."

"I fought against the Germans in the Great Patriotic War," Mustafa replied. "As did all my companions."

"If it would not trouble Your Honors, could you tell me the location of the nearest military facility?" Sergei asked. "We are here on official business and must contact them."

"There is a small garrison down the road on the other side of the village," Mustafa replied. "All you have to do is follow this road for five kilometers."

At that moment some soldiers in worn, faded uniforms pulled up beside the well in an old UAZ/GAZ-69 scout car. When they got out to fill their canteens, Sergei approached them and accepted their rather sloppy salutes.

"Good morning, soldiers," he said. "I am here on official business. I order you to take me to your garrison."

They were not particularly impressed by an order from a Russian officer as they would have been in the old days. But since they were on the way to their camp anyway, the request wouldn't trouble them. The soldiers acquiesced with more salutes. Sergei went back to the MT-LB. After climbing on board, he leaned inside to speak to Jennifer. "Follow scout car."

"Wilco," Jennifer answered.

They followed the vehicle down the crude highway until they drove through the gate of a barbed-wire fence. They pulled up in front of a mud hut that had a Turkmenistan flag in front of it. An officer who had heard their approach stepped out of the door. He was openly and rather angrily curious about their presence in his small garrison.

Once more Sergei dismounted. He pulled some of the forged papers from his tunic and handed them to the stranger. "We have authorization to draw fuel and rations."

"By what right?" the officer demanded.

"By the right afforded us by official orders from your government," Sergei said haughtily. "We are here to observe maneuvers to the west."

The officer protested, "All my supplies are stockpiled here for units in this district. We haven't much as it is."

"I believe the documents I have presented you will prove my authority in this matter," Sergei said. "This goes beyond your district, Captain. We are involved in international military relations here."

The officer looked carefully at each piece of paper, hoping like hell he would find something out of order. But to his disappointment, everything was carefully and accurately noted. Every stamp and signature was in its proper place on the forms. He turned toward the headquarters hut. "Sergeant!"

A noncommissioned officer emerged. He was a portly, sloppy fellow with an unbuttoned tunic. "Yes, sir?"

"This Russian officer has requisitions that must be filled. See to it."

"Yes, sir." The man turned toward Sergei. "Please come with me, sir."

Sergei turned and signaled. Jennifer gunned the engine, then slowly followed the two men over to the supply dump.

1500 hours

Even with the ventilation ports open, the interior of the MT-LB was close and stuffy. Boxes of rations, water cans, and people filled the troop compartment. Jerry cans of gasoline were lashed on the outside of the vehicle.

Although the uncomfortable situation was temporary and the load would lighten as machine and humans consumed the supplies, it was extremely dangerous for the team.

The strike of a single bullet could flash the fuel on the outside of the hull, and the resulting fire and heat would bake the flesh off the bones of those inside. Jen handled the vehicle's controls deftly and carefully with the help of someone topside to warn her of rough spots on the road.

Later that afternoon, Travis ran another position fix via his battle sensor helmet and announced a change in course to take them toward the salt flats of the dreaded Dasht-e Kavir. Jennifer made a twelve-degree turn that took them off the road and onto open terrain.

At that point Travis added another individual on lookout to make sure no unseen gullies or dry creek beds would trap them. If the APC rolled down a hill or into an incline, the team's mission would end even if no immediate injuries resulted. The gas cans would explode, leaving a mass of melted metal and charred flesh to excite official curiosity.

Later, after an afternoon of slow and evasive driving, Hunter was on lookout with Sarah. They had been moving slowly but steadily for a half dozen hours when Hunter suddenly called for a halt. Travis appeared at the commander's turret.

"What's up?" he asked.

Hunter pointed ahead. "Take a look."

Everyone came out and stood on top of the vehicle. The terrain to the front was a stark, glaring white. Travis checked his positioning instruments.

"Eagle Team," he announced. "We have crossed into Iran."

Hunter looked around. "What? No border crossings?"

"Evidently nobody thinks they're necessary," Travis said. "We are at the edge of the great Dasht-e Kavir Desert. Two hundred–plus miles of salt and mud lay before us."

Jack grimaced. "So we're looking at the land where the cities of Sodom and Gomorrah brought down God's curse on themselves."

Sarah added, "And where God turned Lot's wife into a pillar of salt when she turned to look back at the destruction."

Sam smiled nervously. "Hey, my doctor told me to lay off the salt. It causes hypertension, y'know?"

Hunter nudged him playfully. "C'mon, Sammy, aren't you real curious about the goddamned place?"

Sam admitted, "Well—yeah, I suppose."

"All right!" Travis said. "We're going to find out what hell is really like." In less than a minute the tracks of the MT-LB armored personnel carrier began tearing up the God-cursed Dasht-e Kavir.

Jack, remembering a Sunday school lesson from his boyhood, began speaking to himself under his breath. *"Yea, though I walk through the valley of the shadow of death . . ."*

Stan studied the stark, forbidding terrain. He was deeply impressed by its threatening desolation. "Those ancient dudes paid one hell of a price for all that wild partying."

"From the looks of the place, it's a debt that hasn't been paid in full yet," Jack commented.

"Yeah," Stan said seriously. "I hope like hell we aren't expected to make the last installment."

"Amen!"

Chapter Six

Travis walked slowly in front of the MT-LB, linked to the vehicle by a hemp rope. The line was tied around his belt with the other end attached to the winch on the front of the hull. It was his watch as pathfinder with the responsibility of picking a firm, safe route through the expanse of the Dasht-e Kavir. If he suddenly sank into the saline mire, the winch would be quickly activated to pull him free of the clinging muck.

The Green Beret struggled forward as his boots went down an inch or so into the soft soil of the desert with each step. He held a six-foot pole, poking it at the ground ahead of him to test the solidity of the terrain. This procedure had been developed after the first few hours of their journey across the salt-mud hell. Both the rope on his belt and the pole in his hand had been taken from the personnel tent they found rolled and stowed in the aft overhead compartment of the APC.

When the team first entered the wasteland the day before, they had driven the APC at about seven kilometers an hour with a couple of lookouts on top surveying the route ahead of them. It seemed to them that discolored or darker patches of ground would indicate marshy areas, and if these were avoided, they would be able to stay on ground firm enough to support the vehicle.

This was proved wrong during one of Stan's stints at the controls. He rolled slowly into a clean, white level area and suddenly felt the front of the APC settling downward at an alarming rate. At first he decided to charge through the muck, but when he increased the speed, the slippage grew worse and he felt the vehicle continue to sink. The Navy SEAL immediately threw the transmission into reverse and gunned the engine. The APC slipped and swerved, then bit into firmer ground in the rear and backed out to safety.

"This freakin' place is getting scary!" Stan had exclaimed.

"I told you it was cursed!" Jack had yelled up at him from the back of the troop compartment.

Travis, who had been on top, agreed. "We just rolled into some real pretty terrain that almost looked like a white Christmas. But the upper crust was thin as cardboard." He walked up to where they almost sank. "We obviously have to adopt new traveling procedures."

At that point, he decided someone detailed as a pathfinder would have to walk in front of the vehicle and test every foot of the ground they would traverse. That was when he had decided to use the tent's equipment. It was quickly untied, rolled out, and the rope and pole pulled from the canvas.

Jack had been the first to test it and found that the system worked well. Unfortunately, their speed slipped from seven kilometers an hour to a crawl of one-and-a-half.

Another decision had also been made. It was decided to conserve power in their TALON Force Battle Ensembles as much as possible since the exfiltration's time frame had now increased dramatically. They had begun Operation Sky Fire with a seventy-two-hour charge in their vital gear. This was actually better than it sounded, because they didn't run the systems on a continual basis. Each team member also carried three extra power cells, and Sam estimated everyone had seventy-seven to seventy-eight hours of running time. That would normally be more than enough, but crossing a wide stretch of Iran at a kilometer and a half per hour coupled with the very real probability of running into bad guys who would start fights with them, made it imperative to conserve as much system energy as possible.

The battle sensor helmets were not as much of a problem, but Travis issued orders they were only to be used when necessary. The pathfinders, of course, needed to employ their positioning data continually while on duty to maintain the correct course. Without this electronic aid, it would be very easy to wander off into the wrong direction, especially when the situation grew confused because of the constant changes in direction.

The low observable camouflage suits, however, were not to be used at all. The greedy outfits could drain the system in only six hours. Travis put out the word that those garments were not to be turned on without his specific authorization.

Now, as Travis took his turn on pathfinder duty, he continued to tread forward, moving slowly, poking at the ground. Suddenly the pole went into the earth like the salty mud was pure liquid. He started to step back, but found he was stuck. Movements to free himself caused him to begin sinking.

Jack and Stan were on top of the hull, and they yelled at him to stand still. Jen, driving inside, yelled out to find out what was going on.

Jack answered, "Travis is in the muck and sinking. Hold it up!"

Stan jumped down to the winch and pulled back on the lever. The motor whined and the drum rolled slowly, taking up the slack in the rope. Travis began to be pulled toward the APC.

Stan laughed. "I caught a big one!"

Jack grinned. "Want me to gaff him?"

"Naw," Stan answered. "Let's hit him with a hammer and stun him."

Travis grimaced as the rope tightened. He could feel himself being wrenched out of the quicksand. His feet stuck for an instant, causing him to sit down in the salty mud. Then he went over on his back as Stan continued with the winch. Both he and Jack howled in merriment at the sight of their leader being dragged through the mess.

Then Travis was back on firmer ground, and Stan turned off the winch. The mission commander, covered with salt and mud, struggled to his feet. He turned and gave Stan and Jack an enraged glare that cut short their laughter as they retreated back to their positions on top of the hull.

Travis, not wanting to waste time, went immediately to the left, looking for firm terrain. After going twenty yards, he gave it up. He moved into the opposite direction, and found the ground solid only a couple of paces away from where he'd gone in. He took a quick positioning reading

for a new azimuth and stepped out once again with the
MT-LB following slowly behind him.

Up on the top, Stan sighed and glanced over at Jack.
"Care to join me in a chorus of 'I'll Be Home for
Christmas'?"

"Christmas?" Jack remarked. "Hell, at this rate we'll
probably still be out here this time next year."

1745 hours

The wind whipped a hard, powdery spray of salt against
the APC. The team, caked in the white stuff, sat inside the
vehicle to wait for the storm to subside. Travis checked
his watch.

Sam asked, "How long have we been sitting here?"

"A little over three hours," Travis answered.

When the storm first hit, Jack had been on pathfinder
duty. After the initial stinging by the flying grit, he stopped
long enough to don gloves and a covering made from one
of the Russian uniforms for his face and neck. That helped
a bit, but as the bad weather increased, visibility dropped
to nothing. Even the battle sensor device was useless when
its thermal viewer could pick out no images in the tempera-
ture-neutral environment of the desert's whiteout.

After a quarter of an hour, Travis saw the uselessness of
the Marine's efforts. He called him back into the MT-LB
to wait out the tempest.

Hunter brushed some of the salt off his trousers. He
glanced at Travis. "How're we doing on supplies?"

Jen interjected, "We've got plenty of gasoline. We aren't
exactly burning up fuel with this crawling pace we're doing."

"Water might be a problem in a couple of days," Sarah
reported. "And the rations are starting to run out." She
looked at Jack. "Some of us eat a lot."

Jack grinned. "I'm a growing boy."

"If you grow any more, we'll have to get a trailer for
you to ride in," Stan joked.

Sam grinned. "I estimate we'd get another five gallons
per mile if Jack walked instead of rode."

Jack moaned. "Thanks, Sammy." He shook his head. "It
sure is good to have friends."

Travis brought the conversation back to a serious level. "We're going to have to raid a ration dump. But at this point we can't afford a pitched battle. This is going to call for a bit of finesse."

"What do you mean—*finesse*?" Stan asked, as if the word wasn't in his vocabulary.

"We won't be able to drive the APC over to the target area," Travis said. "Too noisy."

Jennifer agreed. "We'll have to go on foot to the ration dump, then carry supplies back here."

"Another problem is that if we're careless and get compromised, the Iranians will figure out that troublemakers are in the area," Jack pointed out.

"There're plenty of opposition groups in Iran," Stan said. "The university students have been restless lately."

"Yeah," Hunter said. "Or we can even make it look like common bandits did it."

"That would be a big help," Travis said. "We don't want the locals mobilizing a large force to seek out foreign infiltrators."

Jack looked at one of the Iranian maps. "I think we're near a garrison." He checked his helmet's positioning device. "Yeah! There's one only thirty kilometers due north of here. It's located a short distance out of the desert."

"Is it army, police, or what?" Stan asked.

Jack carefully noted the words in the flowing Persian alphabet. "Paramilitary. An ayatollah's personal guard or something."

"Really?" Sarah said. "Aren't those the bastards that go around harassing women who don't wear the veil?"

"The same," Jack said.

"All right," Travis said. He glanced upward at the sound of the salt spray slapping across the top of the hull. "As soon as this storm subsides, we'll consider visiting the place."

Stan was pleased. "That'll break the monotony of the trip."

Jack gave him an incredulous look. "You're *bored*?"

"This whole mission is turning into a real bummer," Stan said. "I wish we could get a bit more excitement."

"There's an old saying that especially applies to you," Sarah said. "Be careful what you wish for. You just might get it!"

1915 hours

Occasional gusts whistled and buffeted the MT-LB. Hunter went to the command turret and lifted the hatch for a quick look. He dropped it and turned back to the interior.

"It's dying down," he reported. "The sky to the east is starting to clear. These desert storms go away as quickly as they appear. The thing will probably blow itself out in Turkmenistan."

Travis checked his watch, noting it would soon be 2000 hours. "Listen up. As soon as we can after dark, I want to send a recon patrol to that paramilitary facility we noted on the map. We can ease over toward the edge of the Dasht-e Kavir, and the scouts can move across normal terrain."

"Who're the lucky recon folks?" Stan asked.

Travis replied, "Jack and Stan."

"Say," Stan said. "You're not mad at us for laughing when you got stuck in the quicksand, are you?"

"Yeah," Travis replied bluntly.

"Just wondering," Stan said with a weak grin.

Travis motioned them to join him. The two crawled over the others to settle in next to the mission commander. He gave them the map. Stan looked at it and was disappointed.

"It doesn't show any buildings," he complained. "Only a big dot where the installation is located. You can't tell what the post is really like."

"That's why I want a reconnaissance," Travis explained. "We need you guys to get up close and cozy to scope the place out. I don't expect you two guys to bring anything back."

"I take it we'll pull a full-blown raid with the full team later," Jack said.

"Right," Travis said. "And remember! It's rations we're after. Preferably the field variety. So don't look for sides of beef or fresh vegetables. We can't exactly stop out here and cook gourmet meals."

Jack understood. "I think it's best if we look for warehouses or other storage facilities."

"Right," Travis said. "And I'm authorizing you to power up your camo suits."

Stan laughed. "I don't think we'll need to worry about camouflage." He indicated their salt-encrusted uniforms.

"You'll be out of the desert for this mission and probably into some greenery," Travis cautioned him. "You'll have to be chameleons and change colors as the terrain changes. So turn 'em on."

"What about water?" Jack asked. "Should we try to locate some wells or tanks while we're onsite?"

"Forget it," Travis said. "We'll replenish our cans at oases. We'd never be able to lug water over that much distance on foot."

"And fuel?" Stan asked.

"Make a note of it if you see a dump," Travis said. "When we reach the point we need gas, things are really going to get hairy. If we're discovered trying to swipe gas, we'll have to fight for it."

Jack got off his seat. "Stan and I might as well get ready now and move out at dark."

"Right," Travis said. "And I want to emphasize that this is a *recon* patrol, not a *combat* patrol. Do not make contact with the bad guys. If you do, make an immediate withdrawal. And, for the love of God, don't lead them back here to our Winnebago!"

"Understood," Stan assured him. "And we'll avoid capture."

Sarah gave her teammates an encouraging wink. "Go get 'em guys! I don't want to have to go on a diet."

0200

Jack peered through his battle sensor device into the garrison on the other side of the barbed wire. He and Stan were in concealment behind some thick brush near the target area. They had stalked around one side of the paramilitary post until reaching an area that appeared to be a place where a large amount of supplies were stockpiled.

Suddenly the heat outline of a sentry appeared around the building to the direct front. Stan saw the man and sounded a whispered warning through his helmet's commo device. "Watch it! Guard!"

Jack spoke softly. "Right. I see him. Let's wait until he

goes around to the other side. Then we can crawl in under the wire fence."

"Roger," Stan acknowledged. "What about taking cover behind those boxes to the left?"

"Good idea," Jack said. The guard disappeared from view. "Let's go!"

It had taken the two-man scouting patrol two hours to reach the garrison from the vehicle at the edge of the desert. They had moved slowly through a scattering of mud huts and cultivated fields before reaching the road they sought. Only the braying of donkeys, bleating of goats, and the barking of a dog acknowledged their presence in the area. The few people who lived in the area were inside their crude homes, sleeping peacefully.

Now, with the guard out of sight, Jack and Stan silently rushed to the fence and rolled under the lowest wire to gain entrance to the garrison. They jumped to their feet and went to the stacked boxes. Ten minutes later the guard reappeared, walking his rounds. As soon as he was once more out of sight, they rushed to the building to their direct front.

The door had a large, old-style padlock on its hasp. Stan took a close look at it, then turned to the master key shafts in his gear. He had the device opened in less than two beats. Jack led the way in.

"Bingo!" he said.

Stan studied the boxes stacked in the place. "Hey! These are U.S. Army rations!" he said. He checked the labeling on the containers. "They hold twenty-four meals each. That's enough for one person for eight days if we eat three squares a day."

"You can forget that," Jack said. "When Travis—" He stopped speaking when the sounds of voices could be heard outside. He signaled Stan to squat down in the shadows as he eased over to a window to look out.

A sergeant with another man stood talking to the guard they had first seen. Jack's initial alarm at the sight subsided as he realized the man on duty was being relieved.

"What's going on?" Stan asked as Jack returned.

"Changing of the guard," Jack told him.

"I hope they won't notice the open lock on the door," Stan said.

"They're over at the side of the building, nowhere near it," Jack said. "As soon as the new guy starts his rounds, we'll haul ass."

"Aren't we going to take any of this with us?"

"Negative," Jack said. "We couldn't carry enough between us to do much good, and it'd be risky. Travis said we'd all come back tomorrow night for an unauthorized requisition."

They went to the door and listened. The new guard followed the same route as his buddy. They heard him walk past the door, then go around the side of the building. They eased outside, then Stan relocked the entrance.

The recon duo had hardly taken one step toward the fence when the guard suddenly reappeared. He had obviously now remembered to check the door. He blinked his eyes at the near invisible shimmering of the two TALON Force troopers in their low-observable camouflage suits. The militiaman's confused consternation was plain on his face.

Jack felt for Stan's arm and silently led him a few steps away from the puzzled guard. Within a couple of seconds they had completely disappeared from his sight. The Iranian shook his head, then went back to walking his guard post, wondering what sort of tricks his eyes had been playing on him.

Jack and Stan moved back to the fence, brushing away any telltale traces they might have left on the ground. Then the pair was under the wire and moving silently back through the dark of night toward the APC.

Chapter Seven

The interior of the MT-LB contained two neatly stacked boxes of rations taken from the warehouse the night before. Restraining straps fastened to buckles on the bulkheads kept the food from being toppled by the motion of the vehicle.

The entire team had revisited the paramilitary warehouse under the cover of darkness. Once more the low-observable camouflage suits stymied the paramilitary guards. By exercising care and a good deal of coordinating maneuvers, the team was able to loot the warehouse almost at will.

The food turned out to be vintage 1970s American C rations, and the team, used to the modern Meals-Ready-to-Eat, did not particularly enjoy the outdated cuisine.

"C'mon, folks," Stan said, defending the food. "Remember these were sent over here in the days when the Shah and the CIA were buddy-buddy. So naturally the chow is a bit old, all right?"

"These rations were outdated crap the Iranian Army shipped over to the paramilitary," Hunter said. "They sure weren't going to give up the best of their field fare."

Jennifer made a face. "Listen, pal, this stuff tasted like shit when it was fresh."

"Let's look and see what we have here," Sam said, pulling out some cans. "Pork sausage patties—lima beans—fruitcake—not to mention peanut butter that sticks to the roof of your mouth like cement."

Jack nudged Stan. "If I'd known they were going to bitch so much about the food we found for them, I'd never have told them about it."

"Yeah," Stan agreed. "I told them there wasn't an A&P in this town."

"If no one appreciates the effort," Jack said, "this is the last time we'll go out shopping for this bunch. Let the ingrates starve."

"Oh, don't be so damned sensitive," Hunter said. He took a bite of a pork sausage patty. "God! This is horrible! It may be good enough for the Marine Corps and the Navy, but it doesn't meet the high standards of Air Force cuisine."

Jack sneered. "Who cares what candy-ass fly boys dine on?"

Even dour Travis Barrett got in on the joking. "What we really need is a box of roadkill helper."

Sarah grimaced. "God! Pardon me while I hurl!"

By the next day, the grumbling gradually decreased as the team consumed more of the meals. They began getting used to the old food very quickly. They even found the fruitcake somewhat tasty, although no one liked the greasy pork sausage patties.

1115 hours

Stan moved forward as he prodded the ground to his front with the tent pole. He had been on pathfinder duty for two hours and had managed to stay on solid ground.

Hunter stood on lookout duty atop the APC's hull. In accordance with Travis's energy-conservation program, he used a set of binoculars found in the vehicle in lieu of the battle sensor device as he scanned the horizon.

Stan was suddenly jerked by the rope attached to his belt. He turned to notice that the APC had stopped and that the engine wasn't running. Hunter was down on his belly talking to the people inside.

"Hey!" Stan yelled out. "What the hell's the matter? Why did we stop?"

Hunter popped back up and looked at him. "The engine overheated."

Within moments, everyone but Jennifer and Travis were outside on a defensive perimeter per the mission leader's orders. Inside the vehicle, Jennifer removed the engine cover that sat between the driver's seat and the machine gun turret. Steam puffed out of the radiator cap.

"Don't burn yourself," Travis cautioned her.

"Right." She waited a while for it to cool down a bit, carefully loosened the hot cover with a rag, then took it off. A cloud of steam rushed up and out the turret. "We can't keep moving this slowly for so long. The engine is starting to overheat. If we're not careful, the damn thing will seize up."

Travis shrugged. "We don't have a hell of a lot of choice about it."

"Maybe not," Jennifer said. "But this engine isn't designed to crawl at a low RPM. And it's not doing the transmission and clutch any good either."

Travis picked up a jerry can. "Restart it and I'll add some water to the radiator."

Jennifer got the engine chugging as Travis slowly added water to the cooling system. She watched the needle on the temperature gauge slowly ease back to normal.

"This baby is gong to start drinking water like a thirsty camel," she advised him. "We're gong to have to lay in a good supply unless you can find some Prestone back there somewhere."

"I'm afraid you're right, Jen," Travis said in agreement.

When the engine had completely cooled down and began to run smoothly, she turned off the ignition. Travis led the way outside through the machine gun turret. "Stan! Jack! Front and center!"

The two team leaders joined him and Jen. Travis briefly explained their new predicament while he powered up his helmet for a position check. Then he turned his attention to the map.

"There's an oasis some seventy-five kilometers from here as the vulture flies," Travis informed them. "Unfortunately, the terrain in that direction is this same crap we've been plodding through. We've got to get out of this muck. I figure if we head due east, we can reach a rather good highway that will make the trip to the water a quick one."

Jack shook his head. "That's pretty dangerous, Travis. Some real unpleasant and curious folks might see us."

Stan was in agreement. "That's more of a probability than a possibility."

"There's nothing else to do," Travis said. "This exfiltration is going to get a hell of a lot worse before it gets better."

"That's getting to be the theme song of this operation," Stan said.

"We need to use a cover," Jennifer said. She thought a moment. "How about if we come on as an international geological survey? We could hide the machine gun and re-arrange things to make us look like a civilian outfit using an unarmed military transport to do our work."

"Not bad!" Stan exclaimed. "It's a plausible story." He looked at Jennifer. "You're pretty smart for a girl."

She kicked his shin, causing him to hop back in pain. "And you're a jackass, for a Polack."

"Hey! I was just complimenting you."

"Stan, even from you that's no compliment," Jen said.

"It *is* a great idea," Travis said. "Except for Hunter, we all speak foreign languages. Sam could be a Red Chinese, Stan a Pole, etcetera." He let out a loud whistle to get everyone's attention on the perimeter. "Come on in, Eagle Team. There's a new game plan about to be put into high gear."

1005 hours

The team in their APC rolled boldly up the hard-packed surface of the dirt highway toward the village that con-tained the oasis. The group wore Russian uniforms with all insignia and epaulets removed. The lack of military adorn-ments gave the TALON troopers the look of civil-service workers and technicians. Everyone, with the exception of Stan who was driving, lounged very civilianlike on top of the vehicle. Even Sarah and Jennifer were in plain sight, as would be the case of foreign women geologists.

All-in-all, they created a most unthreatening appearance.

When they reached the small hamlet, Stan steered the APC down a narrow lane between the mud huts and came to a stop at the brick-walled oasis. Local women, properly veiled and wearing the customary *fustans,* gossiped while drawing water for their household chores. The females looked up in surprise at the unexpected visitors. Several

men who had been lounging in the shade of a palm tree
got up and walked slowly toward the vehicle.

Jack jumped down from the hull and greeted them in his
Pidgin Persian. "Hello, friends. How are you this day?"

"Thanks to Allah, we fare well, stranger," the oldest man
replied. "What brings you to our village?"

"We petroleum survey," Jack replied as best he could.
"We in desert long time. Look for petroleum. Look at
rocks and dirt. Long time. Now need water."

One of the men, noting his difficulty with the language,
asked, "Where do you come from, stranger?"

"I from Rwanda in Africa," Jack said. "Other friends
mine from everywhere. China. Poland. Norway. Other
places. Many places. Iran government put us on contract."

"We welcome you to our village," the elder said. "The
Prophet has written that one is blessed when he shares with
others in need."

"Many thanks I offer you," Jack said. He turned to
Travis and spoke in Spanish. *"Me dijo que esta bien que
agarramos agua de sus oasis."*

"Bueno," Travis acknowledged.

He signaled to the others and each grabbed a couple of
water cans and hopped down to fill them. They carried on
their roles, conversing in the foreign languages they knew
to each other, taking care to speak absolutely not one word
in English.

As they worked, a trio of women appeared with trays of
rice cakes and thick hot coffee in silver urns. They poured
the brew in tiny cups and offered the refreshments to the
team members. Thanks were expressed in the several languages, and the food and hot drinks gratefully consumed.
After days of C rations, the meal hit the spot.

A half-hour later, the team was back on the hull of the
APC, waving good-bye to their new friends. Sam remarked,
"They're nice people."

"Yeah," Sarah agreed. "Too bad politics and shithead
leaders make enemies of decent folks."

Travis made a quick command decision to continue along
the highway. "It's worth the risk to make some distance
after all the slow plodding we've put up with these past
days."

"Right," Jennifer said. "And making some speed might blow the gunk out of this abused motor."

Stan continued to drive, traveling at a steady clip of forty-five kilometers an hour. They passed through several more small villages. The locals waved greetings at them as they went by.

Jennifer, enjoying the change of actually being outside the hull with the fresh wind whipping past her, leaned over the hatch opening and glanced inside. "Hey, Stan. How're you doing? Not tired, are you?"

"Naw," he replied. "I'll do the driving today. You deserve a break."

"I appreciate it," she said, surprised at this sudden chivalry. "How far have we come since leaving the desert?"

"Let's see," Stan said. He studied the odometer. "About fifty kilometers."

Sam, overhearing their conversation, said, "That's a little more than thirty-one miles. Not bad."

Hunter, keeping an eye to the rear, suddenly announced, "Looks like some dust on our six. Another vehicle is closing in on us. They're either in a hurry or want to make contact."

Travis, the only one with his helmet powered up, flipped down the battle sensor device. "Looks like an official car. Yeah. Red lights on top. A policeman."

Sarah sat up. "Want me to remount the machine gun?"

"No," Travis said. He tossed his helmet inside for Stan to conceal. "Everybody just keep their cool. I'll play this one by ear." He looked at Jack. "You'll have to do the interpreter duties."

Within ten minutes the police car, a small blue-and-white Fiat, had come up alongside. A driver and another officer occupied the vehicle. The man in the passenger's seat motioned them to pull over. Stan complied, coming to a stop. As the policemen got out of their car, Travis and Jack jumped down to the road.

The first policeman was a grim-faced, portly officer with a big belly. "We were told about you by the villagers at the Kaderian oasis. You are petroleum engineers?"

Jack nodded. "Yes. We look for the oil. Contract with government."

"We know nothing of your presence in this area," the policeman said.

Jack answered, "We in different district. Come look for water. Now go back."

The policeman frowned. "Go back where?"

"Desert," Jack said.

"You mean the Dasht-e Kavir?" the cop asked.

"Yes."

"Impossible," the policeman said. "Show me your papers."

"I tell chief engineer," Jack said. He translated the exchange into Spanish for Travis.

Travis thought fast. *"Dile que nuestros papeles están en Tehran con nuestra compañia."*

"My chief say papers in Tehran with our company," Jack said.

"I must talk to my headquarters," the policeman said. He pulled a hand transmitter-receiver off his belt and put it to his ear.

Travis, in a casual movement, raised his hands as if stretching and aimed his RF Field Generator on his wrist at the communications device. He spoke loudly, complaining, *"Estoy bien cansado."*

His voice activated the generator via his micro-biochip transmitter, sending a short but intense burst of RF energy at the policeman's radio.

The policeman made several attempts to get the now damaged transmitter-receiver to work. Then his partner made several futile tries.

"We have schedule," Jack said. "No can stay long."

"You'll stay as long as I demand of you!" the first policeman snapped.

"Impossible!" Jack protested.

"Don't tell me what is possible or impossible!" the policeman shouted in a rage. "I have become very suspicious of you strange people."

"You crazy man," Jack said, deciding to try a bluff. "My company tell your captain you bad to us." He turned and took Travis by the arm to lead him back to the APC.

The policeman pulled his pistol. "I order you to stay here or I'll shoot you. Maybe I'll put a bullet in you anyway, you rotten pig of an infidel!"

Stan had seen what was going on through the side slit of the driver's position. He quickly retrieved one of the silenced .45 pistols from its hiding place and carefully eased it up through the machine gun turret.

Jennifer saw the weapon and took it. She stuck it in her trousers' pocket and got up nonchalantly to go to the side of the hull. The two policemen looked up and noted a mere woman looking down at them. Gorgeous, but still a lowly female. They turned their full attention back to Travis and Jack.

Jen quickly drew and fired twice. One bullet each struck the Iranian lawmen. The fat cop staggered backward into the car and rolled to the hood before sliding down on the road. His friend doubled over and went down on top of his head before sprawling out into a most undignified position.

"Nice going!" Travis said, looking up at Jennifer. "Things were just about to get completely out of hand."

Jack checked out the policemen to make sure they were dead. "Damn! Why'd those villagers rat us out? I kind of thought we had made friends with them."

Travis shrugged. "It was probably the headman's duty to inform officials of visitors to their little one-camel town." He thought a moment. "I think I know how to avoid that little glitch in the future." He turned to Hunter and Sergei. "You two guys get down here and put on those cops' caps. You can drive ahead of us in the car and make it look like you're our official escorts."

"Good idea," Hunter said as he and Sergei dismounted the vehicle.

"Wait a minute!" Sarah said. "Hunter looks like a tanned, blond Southern California surfer dude."

"Yeah," Travis said, looking at the Air Force pilot. He called out, "Hey, Stan! I want you guys to—"

Jen interrupted, "I can take care of that. You're forgetting I was a makeup artist in Hollywood. A bit of darkening gel blended into his hair, a fake mustache, a pair of shades, and a policeman's cap can make him easily pass for an Iranian."

"Go to it," Travis said. He turned to Jack. "Pick up the cop's hand transmitter-receiver. You can use that to monitor their net since you're the only one of us that understands any Persian. Maybe we can avoid any more nasty surprises."

"Uh, boss, we fried the cop's radio," Jack reminded him.

"Give the damn thing to Sam," Travis said. "He'll fix it."

"Right," Jack said. He walked over to pull the device from the dead man's belt.

Travis called over to Stan and Sergei. "You two guys take care of the dead cops."

Within twenty minutes the two dead Iranian policemen had been interred in the bushes some fifteen yards from the highway. After finishing their grave-digging chore, the duo made a close inspection to make sure no clues would lead to the graves.

By then Hunter's appearance had been changed under Jennifer's skillful applications. When he donned the police cap and sunglasses, he was ready to go.

"Take along a helmet in case you need commo with us," Travis said. "But take it off when you come across villages or other traffic on the road."

"Right," Hunter said, catching one that Stan tossed to him. "This way no more villagers will be calling the real fuzz down on us."

The team got into the two vehicles to resume their journey that would hopefully eat up more critical distance. This time, with the red light on top of the Fiat rotating and flashing, they were a column of two, moving rapidly along, looking very legal and official.

1345 hours

Hunter eased the wheel of the cop car to the left as he drove through a cut in the hills that cradled the highway. They emerged back into open country, showing an immense scrub plain ahead of them. Sergei pointed through the windshield.

"Look! Village!"

Hunter slowed down as he exchanged the cop hat for the battle sensor helmet to communicate the news to Travis via his implanted micro-biochip.

"Roger," Travis acknowledged. "We see the place now.

Slow down and drive past like a good police escort should. We'll stay right behind you."

The two vehicles traveled slowly past the villages. The inhabitants looked up out of curiosity, then went back about their individual activities without showing any further interest.

As the journey continued, they passed two more Iranian hamlets without alarming the villagers. It had been a critical test of the impression they were making on the local people. Travis felt confident and optimistic as he ran a position check, then found the coordinates on the map.

"Hey, folks," he announced. "We've made more than fifty miles today."

Jack remarked, "Not exactly the world land-speed record, but better than a kilometer or two an hour we'd been making in that damned desert."

Travis received another report from Hunter that a village lay directly ahead. Travis ordered him to proceed as before. The usual mud huts showed up ten minutes later, and the team gave the little community only casual glances. Suddenly Jack sat up straight and grabbed Travis's arm.

"Hey!" he said. "That building in the center of the place has a sign on it that says it's a police station." He put the repaired police transmitter-receiver to his ear.

Jack listened to the police radio traffic on the device. "I don't hear any chatter about us."

"Maybe they're asleep in there," Sarah said. "These are country cops, y'know."

"Wait!" Jennifer said, glancing back at the bucolic headquarters. "There's a couple of cops lounging in the shade at the side of the place."

"Wave to 'em," Travis ordered.

Everyone complied, and the cops waved back. Sam grinned. "Piece of cake."

"Uh-oh!" Jack said, monitoring the transmitter-receiver. "They're calling the car Hunter and Sergei are in."

"Well, Hunter can't hear 'em, so he won't be answering," Sarah said.

A few minutes passed as Jack kept listening in on the police net. "Damn!" he swore. "Sounds like they've put in calls to a police unit ahead. They're probably pissed off about the other car ignoring them. I think they're mounting a pursuit. Estimated time to engagement—ten or fifteen minutes."

Travis called ahead, ordering Hunter and Sergei to halt, then leaned down to tell Stan to pull up beside them. When the two vehicles were together, the two bogus policemen abandoned their caps and vehicle to rejoin the team.

"Everybody inside," Travis said. "Button down! Sarah and Sam, remount that machine gun! Jen, take over the driving! Stan, you come up here with me and let's put these grenade launchers to use."

Jack announced, "I'm not sure, but I think they're planning on closing up the highway both behind and in front of us." He quickly disappeared inside the vehicle.

"They're on our six!" Sarah yelled. "Coming fast."

"Same situation on our twelve!" Jen called back from the driver's seat.

Within moments the police vehicles were in view to both the front and rear of the armored personnel carrier.

"Open fire!" Travis commanded.

Sarah adroitly squeezed the machine gun trigger, sending out three equally spaced fire bursts of six rounds toward the rear. The first police car exploded and rolled over in a ball of flames. The two behind it came to a stop and the occupants rushed out to take up positions alongside the road.

A car and a truck filled with policemen at the front moved up to within twenty-five yards before halting to the APC's direct front. The well-trained squads poured out and formed skirmish lines in the brush.

"Let's give 'em an education," Travis said to Stan as he raised his grenade launcher. "I'll fire at the truck and the left side of the road. You hit the car and go right."

The first two high-explosive grenades they launched hit the vehicles. The car's doors flew off as it was kicked over on its side in the flash of detonations that turned it into a blazing shell.

When Travis's projectiles hit the truck, the heavy vehicle bounced from the concussion of bursting grenades, turning over on its side before erupting into flames. The other six grenades Travis and Stan shared between them landed among the cops in the bushes. The explosions sent body parts catapulting through the air. The rest of the policemen got smart and pulled back.

"Inside!" Travis yelled to Stan.

When both were safely in the troop compartment, Travis tapped Jen on the shoulder. "Head for the salt!"

"Roger!" she replied, gunning the engine and turning back toward the hell of the Dasht-e Kavir.

"I guess our days of speed and luxury are over," Sarah remarked from her machine gun position.

"Only temporarily," Travis said grimly. Then he added, "At least it better just be for the interim. We can't afford to spend a lot more time out on that fucking salt."

"They're not pursuing us," Jack told Travis. "They've just broadcast orders—I think to stand fast."

"Ha!" Stan crowed. "We scared the hell out of the bastards!"

"Maybe," Travis said. "Maybe not. They seemed to over-react to seeing us."

Jennifer drove on as she spoke. "I think the raid on that warehouse has given the locals a bad case of the jitters."

"It's a sign they've had troubles out here before," Travis agreed. "That's our bad luck."

The APC bounced as it raced through the brush. A quarter of an hour later, the ride smoothed out as they closed in on the desert. Then they ran slower as the soft, salty soil grasped at the treads.

"Welcome back to the Dasht-e Kavir," Sarah announced from her vantage point in the turret.

"Okay," Travis said. "Everybody into your battle suites. Don't power up 'til I give you the word."

They quickly donned their advanced fighting apparel. Sam relieved Sarah and Stan took over from Jennifer to give the women a chance to slip into their own combat gear. When they had changed, the two women went back to their posts.

"Fuck!" Jack said, his ear to the police commo instruments. "I believe they're calling in a chopper. An *army* chopper."

"Oh, God!" Sam moaned. "That won't be like the Hind back in Kazakhstan. This bird is going to have rockets."

Jennifer wrestled the steering levers as the APC continued to plow through the desert terrain. Then they came to a sudden and most unexpected halt, throwing everyone forward. Sarah bounced off the rim of the turret and fell inside.

"Shit!" Jen yelled. "We're stuck!"

The MT-LB's front suddenly went down.

"Stuck, hell!" Stan said. "We're sinking!"

"Everyone!" Travis yelled. "Out! Now! Move it!"

"You mean we're abandoning ship?" Stan asked. His sailor instincts made him rebel against the action.

"Out, goddamn it!" Travis bellowed at him.

Everyone exited through the turret and ran off the back of the hull to leap to the ground. Then the sight of an approaching French Aerospatiale 341 fighter helicopter with Iranian markings appeared on the horizon.

"Turn on your systems!" Travis ordered. "Full power camouflage!"

Chapter Eight

The MT-LB rocked with the impact of the first rocket, sending out sheets of flame from openings in the hull. The blazing jolt from the second projectile pushed the vehicle another couple of yards into the soft salty earth. The team, under the cover of their electronic camouflage, watched helplessly as the destruction of the armored personnel carrier continued.

The attack helicopter came in again, unleashing yet another air-to-ground missile. This time, the fiery wallop into the hull made the rear of the APC lift to a vertical position. It settled back into a steep 45-degree incline as it rapidly slipped beneath the surface of the Dasht-e Kavir like a ship sinking at sea. The heat from the battered hull made the watery salt and mud boil and give off a noxious cloud of steam.

The team watched the demise with a sense of loss. They were painfully aware of the physical difficulties they now faced, but there was also an emotional side to this new situation.

Stan, the sailor, rendered a salute. "We've just lost a comrade-in-arms. Like an old friend."

"Roger that," Travis agreed. "She served us well."

"Let's get practical," Sarah said. "We have to give some thought to our present problem in lieu of a funeral service for an APC. Sorry. But I'm just not the sentimental sort."

But Jen had bonded with the vehicle. "We abused the old girl and damn near burned out her engine, but she stayed faithful to the end."

Sarah rolled her eyes. "Puh-lease!"

Meanwhile, the helicopter crew had taken note of their target's disappearance. Now they were interested in finding any people who might be in the vicinity. Travis ordered everyone to stay motionless as the enemy aircraft went into a hover in a position almost over their heads. The pilot swung his chopper back and forth as the gunner scanned the ground. The team, blending like chameleons into the color of the desert, was invisible to him.

Sam gazed at the airborne threat. "He's confused because there's no trace of a crew. Maybe they'll end up thinking we went into the muck with the APC."

"That's the idea," Travis whispered. "If they think we're goners, they won't send out search parties to scour the countryside for us."

The helicopter went into a more nose-down attitude, slipping into forward flight. Then it flew away from the location.

Stan grinned. "I guess the SOB thinks his job is done."

"Yeah," Hunter said. "He's probably heading for a two-martini lunch at the officers' club."

"Muslims don't drink alcohol," Jack reminded him.

"Remind me not to bother to loot one of their clubs," Hunter shot back.

Sarah exclaimed, "Wait! He's coming back."

The helicopter had turned and was making another run toward the team. Suddenly the machine gun in the nose flashed and bullets began splashing about their position.

"How can he see us?" Stan yelled out. "Is somebody's suit malfunctioning?"

"He turned on his FLIR," Sam said in a matter-of-fact tone. "Pretty clever of him, ya gotta admit. He suspected we were hiding here someplace and Forward Looking Infra-Red seemingly has proved his suspicions."

"Christ!" Stan exclaimed. "If you admire his smarts so much why don't you send the guy a letter of commendation?"

"We may be only shimmering images, but he knows it's us," Travis said. "Return fire!"

Eight camouflaged XM-29 rifles opened up, sending dozens of combustible, armor-piercing rounds into the front of the attacking aircraft. The glass in the gunner's position shattered first, quickly followed by that in the pilot's cockpit. The helicopter spun quickly and violently. It lost altitude and hit a solid piece of ground, then bounced over to land upside down in the marshy area where the APC had sunk. Within moments, the chopper—crew and all—were nestled in the depths of the salt swamp.

"Looks like the MT-LB is going to have company for about an eternity or so," Travis remarked. "I hope that chopper crew's headquarters thinks everybody—including us—is dead."

"They might assume so," Jack said, "but since there's no physical confirmation you can bet your ass they'll mount a search anyway."

"Right," Travis agreed. He stood up. "On your feet! We'll head out across the desert for the next twenty-four hours or so to put as much distance between this location and ourselves as we can. Then we'll have to move into more populated areas."

Jack reloaded his rifle. "That means a bigger chance of getting captured."

"Can't be helped," Travis said. "It is impossible to cross the Dasht-e Kavir on foot." He signaled to the rest of the team. "Everyone will keep their camo suits on full—I say again—*full* power." He signaled with a swing of his arm. "Move out!"

0345 hours

The sky above the Dasht-e Kavir was cloudless, and the full moon looked down on the desert like a giant reflecting disk, washing the terrain in an eerie, yellow light. It was all surreal and a bit disturbing.

Jack and Sarah shared a guard post while the rest of the team slept. Jack yawned and stretched.

"Hell of a day," he said flatly.

"Yeah," Sarah agreed. "I've had better."

"I figure we walked thirty miles to make fifteen," Jack said.

"It was all those marshes," Sarah pointed out. "For a while I was afraid we'd never find our way through them." She glanced eastward. "This is a strange land. The moon is high, yet you can see daylight on the horizon."

"False dawn," Jack pronounced. "It can do that in absolutely flat terrain sometimes." He flipped down his battle sensor device and looked out across the desert. "My God! I've finally lost it!"

Sarah looked at him closely. "What are you talking about?"

"Is that a woman out there?"

Sarah used her own battle sensor device. "It sort of looks like one. But she's not moving."

Jack got to his feet. "It wouldn't be Lot's wife, would it? Standing out there for a thousand years as a pillar of salt?"

Sarah continued to study the apparition. "Wait a minute. It's a shadow on a small knoll."

Jack peered at the image. "Yeah. You're right."

The 3-D aspect of the battle sensor devices could give an illusion of depth and wholeness to flat objects at times. This was especially true at night.

Sarah took a deep breath and slowly exhaled. "The fact that we're exhausted added to the illusion."

"It's this weird desert," Jack said. "I'm surprised we're not all hallucinating." He took a deep breath. "People aren't supposed to be out here."

"I think you're right," Sarah said. "This place is as alien as Hunter ordering blintzes in Ratner's Delicatessen. And as hostile as the waiters." She checked her watch. "Time to sound first call. We have a busy day ahead of us."

The pair woke up Travis first, then went to each individual member of the team, shaking them until they were awake.

"Cold camp," Travis called out. "No fire. No smoke. Eat your rations and be ready to power up your cammos and move out in twenty minutes." Everyone had odds and ends of C rations in their packs. Travis got out a can of peaches and began slurping down the fruit as he walked among the others. "Listen up! We're going to move to the edge of the Dasht-e Kavir for all of today's travel. There's no way in hell I want to repeat yesterday's activities. That means security has got to be tight. We'll put out a point, rear guard, and flankers in a modified diamond formation. Right now the Iranians don't know our exact location. Let's take advantage of the situation as long as we can."

Sam bit down on a C ration cracker smeared with peanut butter. "It looks like we're stuck traveling on foot for a while. Maybe the rest of the way to the coast, huh?"

Travis shook his head. "Only if absolutely necessary. We're going to have to get our hands on some vehicles sometime. On foot, we're like ants on a bare white tabletop."

"Yeah," Stan said. "Especially when these power packs start to flicker out."

Hunter put the final touches on his gear. "Why not steal an aircraft? That means going farther and faster."

"Too vulnerable to AA defenses," Travis said. "I'm afraid we're going to be stuck on ground transport."

Sergei was ready to go. "We can hijack airplane, *nyet*?"

"I don't think so," Travis said. "That generates a lot of publicity. If we start flying around in some aircraft we've hijacked, then our own side will shoot us down."

"As if we don't have enough troubles," Stan remarked.

"C'mon, folks," Travis urged them. "We've got to get moving."

0945 hours

The terrain was a strange mixture of fertile earth and barren salt. Stan and Hunter walked side-by-side, maintaining a distance of ten yards between them.

They were on point, leading the team in its southwesterly trek toward the faraway sea. The two were required to make periodic checks with Travis to make sure they maintained the correct azimuth on the long journey.

The view to the north showed a gradual but steady improvement. The ground elevation increased and greenery could easily be discerned growing on distant hills. A look to the south, on the other hand, revealed nothing but a vast wasteland.

Suddenly Hunter stopped. "Hold it!"

Deep tracks of several wheeled vehicles crossed the soft dirt to their direct front. Stan walked up to them and knelt down, studying the indentations.

"I can't tell what direction they're going," he remarked.

Hunter pointed to the smashed brush off to the side. "They're heading out into the desert. See the direction those bushes have been pushed over?"

"Right," Stan said. He went into commo mode. "This is

the point team. We've come across the tracks of several wheeled vehicles headed into the desert."

"Military or civilian?" Travis asked.

"Can't tell," Stan said. "Could be tractors, but I don't think anyone would drive out to a salt waste to do any farming."

"I'll hold everyone up," Travis came back. "You and Hunter check 'em out."

"Roger."

Stan and Hunter followed the tracks, keeping a close eye on the horizon to make sure no nasty surprises were sprung their way. After a short five minutes, they picked up images on their battle sensor devices. Both men slowed down and made a stealthy approach toward the location. A few moments later they heard the faint sound of conversation.

"Whoever it is isn't too concerned about intruders," Hunter whispered.

"Then let's intrude," Stan suggested in a soft voice.

They continued until they could see the people and vehicles without using the battle sensor devices. It was a temporary bivouac set up around three armored cars.

Stan got back on commo. "We've got three wheeled scout vehicles with a dozen men who seem to have stopped for a midday break."

"Roger," Travis replied. "Stand fast. I'll have everyone hold up. Sergei and I will be up to join you. Out."

A quarter of an hour later, Stan and Hunter gazed at the vehicles in the company of the mission commander and their Russian asset. Sergei knew exactly what they were looking at.

"Are BRDM-2 armored cars," he told them. "Soviet Union sell many to Third World country. Mostly Arab." He studied the men around the vehicles. "I don't know what are their uniforms."

"Me neither," Travis said. "They're probably some sort of paramilitary outfit. I'm sure they're not army or police."

Hunter spat. "Troops of the radical ayatollah?"

"Yeah," Travis said. He turned back to his helmet for communications. "All personnel. Rally to this location. On the double, but be quiet as hell."

Stan grinned. "Do we have transportation now?"

Travis flashed a rare smile. "Does Raggedy Andy have cotton balls?"

1030 hours

With the low-observable camouflage suits on full power, the Alpha Team moved forward toward the target area under the cover of Bravo's weapons.

Travis and Sergei situated themselves in the center and slightly to the rear of both teams. They stood fast during the maneuvering as Travis directed the attack with brief exchanges of commo with Jack and Stan.

When Jack was in position, he was able to take a closer look at the men around the armored cars. He contacted Travis, reporting, "These guys are not regular army men. And they're not—I say again—*not* Iranians."

"Who the hell are they then?" Travis demanded to know.

"A paramilitary outfit," Jack informed him. "From Algeria. I can tell by the insignia sewn on their sleeves."

"Okay," Travis said. "Iranian-sponsored terrorists. They're probably in training for some operation, like slaughtering innocent villagers back in their own country."

"No shit," Jack replied.

"Are you in position to attack?" Travis asked.

"Roger."

Stan broke in the transmission. "Bravo's ready too."

Travis smiled grimly. "Then let's rid the world of some assholes." He took a deep breath and whispered, "Fire!"

The half dozen XM-29 rifles of Alpha and Bravo Teams spit steel-jacketed, anti-personnel bullets into the lounging group of Algerians. One fellow, standing up drinking from a canteen cup, staggered backward when three rounds simultaneously slammed into his body. He went over on his back, flinging the contents of the cup into the air.

Most of the others who had been sitting and reclining in the area jerked crazily under the impact of the fusillade, dying instantly as they rolled and collapsed into positions of death.

One man who had miraculously escaped any wounds turned and began running wildly. This caught everyone's attention, and he was quickly in the sights of all six weapons. The fifteen bullets that struck him blew off one arm and sent his head rolling in front of his body, which continued to run some eight yards on reflex alone before sprawling onto the salty terrain.

"Cease fire!" Travis ordered.

The team moved in cautiously. They made sure all three vehicles were clear of other personnel before relaxing. Travis and Sergei quickly joined them. Stan checked out the turrets of the vehicles.

"There's two side-by-side machine guns in each one," he informed the others. "A fourteen point five millimeter and a seven point six two. Not exactly cannons, but formidable in their own way. And there's plenty of ammo for both types of weapons. These guys were ready for war."

"They were probably on a live-fire training exercise," Travis said. "That would mean full combat loads."

Jennifer had examined the rear-mounted engines. "What we have here are water-cooled V-eights. And they've had good care taken of them."

"I know vehicle pretty good," Sergei said. "It can do hundred kilometers in one hour on road."

Sam, once more using the instinctive calculator of his brain, added, "That's over sixty miles per hour."

"Another thing," Sergei said. "Maybe important. They are going in both water and on the land."

"You mean these puppies are amphibious?" Sam asked.

"If that mean they work on land and water both, yes," Sergei said.

"That's what the man said," Jack happily replied.

Sarah had gotten down inside each vehicle for her own look-see. The news she had was not good. "There's less than a quarter of a tank of gas in each one. More like an eighth of a tank."

Travis spat. "I don't suppose we should look gift horses in the mouth, but that really pisses me off."

"We'll be lucky if we can get fifteen miles on that," Jennifer said. "I'm sure this engine will absolutely slurp gasoline. We'll be running on fumes within an hour."

"Okay," Travis said. "That's something to work on. First thing we have to do is examine these SOBs laying around here."

The team went to the corpses and turned their pockets inside out. Then they checked the bloodied clothing for marks of some sort. But there was nothing to ID them.

"They're absolutely sterile," Stan announced to Travis. "The only thing they had on them were these Algerian sleeve insignia."

"Mmm," Jen said. "Maybe they're really not Algerians."

Jack interjected, "They're Algerian. I could hear them shouting a couple of times during the attack, and it was in Arabic. And the bumper markings are in Arabic too. Religious slogans and stuff from the Koran."

"That's a good indication they were getting ready for some real sneaky operation," Travis said. "Maybe a suicide mission."

"Probably," Jack said. "They fit the profile. Which means we'd better bury the bastards."

"Right," Travis said. "And obliterate any trace of the graves. If somebody comes looking for 'em they'll see the tracks that came in here and the ones leading back out. It'll seem our late Algerian friends went off somewhere else to practice for their pending acts of political or religious murder."

"Good idea," Jen said. "That'll buy us some time."

The team went to work scooping out graves. The ground crust was firm, but the muddy soil beneath made for easier digging. It was tough to keep the sides from collapsing, though. A mass grave was excavated that went some six feet deep. When it was done, the corpses were tossed in, then covered up. While Alpha Team began removing traces of the digging, the Bravos went around turning the soil over on spots of blood that had soaked into the ground.

"Dust on the horizon!" Hunter Blake yelled. He leaped up on the hull of the nearest armored car, flipping down his battle sensor device. Suddenly he began laughing.

Travis growled, "What's so goddamned funny?"

"It's a gasoline truck!" Hunter said. "I swear to God! It's a gasoline truck and it's coming directly toward us."

"The Algerians not only stopped for lunch but were also waiting to be refueled," Sarah said.

Sam said, "Aw! They just wanted the free steak knives with each fill-up."

"Get out of sight!" Travis yelled. "We sure as hell don't want to spook the guy."

Ten minutes later an Iranian Army gasoline tanker pulled up. The driver looked around and was obviously puzzled when he didn't see anybody. He opened the door and stepped to the ground. As he walked toward the nearest vehicle, Travis rose up and pointed his silenced .45 at him. The driver didn't have time to protest before taking a bullet straight into the skull.

"C'mon!" Travis said. "Plant this guy, then gas up!" He walked over to the gasoline truck and noted the gauge by the pump. "Hey, folks! We've got over seven thousand liters in this baby. We'll take it along for at least two or three refuelings."

Stan and Jack began working on the Iranian's grave while the others gathered around Travis. The commander continued his organizing activities.

"Okay! Here're the vehicle assignments. Number one will be Sergei driving and I'll man the machine gun." He looked at Jack. "You'll ride along with us."

"Right," Jack said. "I'll monitor their radio net."

"Exactly," Travis said. "Jen can drive number two with Hunter as the gunner. Sam will drive number three and our champion skeet shooter Sarah will handle the gunnery details."

Stan, busy tending to the driver's grave, stopped his work and looked up. "What about me? Am I supposed to walk, or what?"

"We're gonna leave you here!" Jen said with a laugh.

Stan smirked. "In your dreams, Olsen!" He turned to Travis. "Well?"

"You're driving the gasoline tanker," Travis said. He nudged Jack and Hunter. "You two guys finish up Stan's work there. He's got to open his filling station for business."

The drivers went to their assigned vehicles and started the engines. Within moments they were in a line at the tanker. Jennifer was the first waiting to be served. She grinned at Stan.

"Fill 'er up, please."

"Yes, ma'am," Stan said. "Check your water and tires?"

"No, thanks," Jennifer said. "But clean my windshield

and check the oil, please. By the way, I left my credit card in my other camouflage suit. Can you spot me 'til next payday?"

Travis overheard the banter but he was in no mood for humor. "Knock it off, you two! Fill up the goddamned gas tank! We've got an exfiltration to get done here."

Stan began pumping gasoline.

Chapter Nine

The convoy moved down the dirt highway at a steady clip of thirty-five miles an hour. The armored cars could have gone much faster, but because the big tanker truck could not keep up, Travis slowed the pace to keep everyone together.

Travis, Jack, and Sergei occupied the interior of the leading vehicle. There was very little communication among the cars. A high degree of alertness kept everyone tense and ready for whatever situation the Fickle Finger of Fate would flick at them.

Travis stepped down from the machine gun turret to settle between Sergei and Jack. "We're not attracting much attention," he remarked. "I've noticed that people on the road hardly give us a second look."

"Is true," Sergei said. "Same in villages. Nobody look upon us."

Jack moved the earphones to uncover one ear so he could converse with his companions. "It's the Algerian markings. Foreign vehicles from friendly nations mean we're not an unusual sight around here. There must be a lot of activity involving all sorts of military vehicles."

"I'd say so," Travis said. "That means either a large government installation or several small ones. Has there been much commo?"

Jack shook his head. "Not really. And what I've picked up has sounded like routine stuff. Seems like nobody has missed those Algerians or the gasoline truck yet. It could be they were out on a training operation that was to last a week or so."

Travis nodded in satisfaction. "This has turned into a blessing. If our luck holds out, we'll be far, far down the road before trouble catches up with us again."

"Could be," Jack said. "Or maybe we'll just get real lucky and end up driving all the way to the Persian Gulf."

"Ha! Ha!" Sergei laughed. "Maybe Travis forget to say for us to be halting and we drive into the sea."

The two Americans looked at him in confusion. The Russian's humor was not coming across very well in his fractured English.

Sergei said, "Is joke! Ha! Ha! Not to worry. Armored car go in water. Remember? Ha! Ha!"

Jack grinned. "Real funny, Sergei. You're a regular Yakov Smirnov."

Sergei looked confused. "Who?"

"Never mind," Travis said. "Anyhow, let's keep our fingers crossed." He climbed back up into the gunner's seat.

An hour later the traffic increased slightly with mostly civilian vehicles. But none of the other travelers paid the convoy any particular mind. Things might have been peaceful, but Travis's initial optimism gradually faded away, and he called a halt. As the four vehicles pulled over, he hopped down to the road and went to the car occupied by Jennifer and Hunter.

"Take a five-kilometer recon down the road," Travis ordered them. "Don't be obvious about it. Just take a casual look around."

"What are we looking for in particular?" Hunter asked.

"Road blocks, large concentrations of police or troops, things like that," Travis answered.

"Right," Jen said. She shifted into first and stepped on the accelerator and went out into the middle of the road, picking up speed as she began the scouting mission. Hunter sat in the machine gun turret to observe their surroundings from a better vantage point.

The others had to wait only twenty minutes before the vehicle returned. Hunter opened the top of the turret and stood up. "Nothing much to report. Traffic has increased a little. But from all appearances, this is a normal afternoon for this part of the world."

Jen spoke from the interior. "We even went past a couple of those little police cars parked on the outskirts of a village. They didn't as much as give us a second glance."

"Okay," Travis said. "Maybe we can start enjoying this little vacation of ours."

"Everybody else already is," Hunter said. He grinned. "Come on, dude!"

Travis looked up at him somberly. "Yeah. Right."

They resumed the journey, maintaining a steady but cautious speed. After a half hour of easy travel, Jack suddenly reached over and grabbed Travis's shoulder. "I'm beginning to monitor other languages besides Persian!" he exclaimed. "Wait!" He listened some more. "Arabic! Yeah, and Chinese. I swear it's Chinese. Hold it!" He continued to listen over his headphones. "And here's some Russian. What do you—oh, shit!" Jack gave Travis a look of astonishment. "I may be finally cracking up, but I'm certain I heard somebody say the word *Frateco.*"

Travis immediately ordered a halt. "Sergei! Take over those earphones!"

Sergei stepped from the driver's position and joined Jack to assume monitoring duties. After only a few moments, he took a deep breath. *"Proklyatie!"* the Russian cursed. *"Is* Frateco. Talk of launch site and Chinese Long March Rocket." He handed the earphones back to Jack.

Travis stared at him. "Did you say a launch site? *A launch site!"*

Sergei nodded. "Yes. Same like cosmodrome. Shoot rockets in space. Here they got Chinese Long March Rocket."

"For the love of God!" Jack exclaimed under his breath.

Travis contacted Sam in vehicle three. "Quick! What do you know about a Chinese rocket called the Long March?"

"It is their main launch vehicle," Sam replied. "Not as reliable as others in the world. They had a hell of an accident on a launch pad a few years back. Big explosion. Huge! Their complex and a couple of villages were wiped out. A lot of dead and injured."

Travis mulled over the information. "Would it be unusual for one of those Long March gizmos to be here in Iran?"

"Uh, yeah, boss," Sam replied with a snide chuckle. "You can't do much with a rocket without a launch pad."

"Suppose I told you we've just found out there's a complete operational launch complex near here?" Travis remarked.

"Damn!" Sam said. "Really? If that's so, could be their vehicle is a Long March Rocket. The Red Chinese and Iranians are partners in crime on several projects."

"We can't let this slide," Travis said. "It'll have to be checked out. Thoroughly! After hearing that the Frateco is around here, I'm beginning to think there could well have been a second ALAS after all."

Jack held up his hand. "The Arabs got back on the net. And I heard the word *sawarikh*—rocket. And again the Esperanto word Frateco."

Travis got back on the team commo system. "I want everyone to search your vehicles for documents, maps, letters, anything that may give us some information on what's going on in this district. Hurry up! Turn your cars inside out if you have to."

Fifteen minutes and three negative reports were given as every corner of the interiors, seats, and storage areas were ransacked. Surprisingly, it was Stan in the gasoline tanker truck who found something. He went to Travis's vehicle and climbed up, looking down through the machine gun turret.

"I found a map," he said. "It looks like a plain old road map. I think it's in Arabic."

He dropped it inside where Jack could pick it up. The Recon Marine quickly scanned the document. "It's a road map all right, but somebody's made notations on it. There's a launch site noted in one area. Somebody's drawn a big square around it. So it's probably some sort of new complex."

"Don't that beat all?" Travis remarked. "Here's a top secret rocket launch site that's hidden from the world, and some dickhead truck driver marks down its location on his road map. Like the Union soldiers who found General Lee's battle plans for Antietam wrapped around three cigars."

"It's carelessness that compromises security more than anything else," Jack said. "Sun Tzu said to take advantage of such a situation. He said that one who purposely remains ignorant of his enemy's activity is no general. He does not serve his sovereign well, and is no master of victory."

"In that case, I shall strive to become a master of victory," Travis said. He took the map and turned on the positioning device in his helmet. "This is about twenty-five klicks back in the direction we came from." He spoke to the other vehicles. "We're heading back folks. There is a strong possibility that the Frateco and ALAS are still in full operation."

1630 hours

The three armored cars were parked in a row beneath some olive trees. Travis ordered Stan to put the gasoline truck at another spot a hundred meters away. If the team came under fire and the tanker was hit, he didn't want the fuel carrier to explode in their direct vicinity.

The olive grove was located in a narrow valley, out of sight of the surrounding countryside. The two teams were spread out along the crest, occupying advantageous positions that offered both cover and excellent fields of fire.

Travis, Jack, and Sergei occupied a spot between two trees. They had a good view of the flat terrain spread out before them. A narrow road led off the highway to a guard station. Although there was no fence around the place, barriers and trenches extended out from the position. Before leaving the armored car, Jack had taken out the vehicle's radio and attached a portable battery case to it so he could continue listening in on the bad guys.

"Any radio traffic, Jack?" Travis asked.

Jack nodded. "Affirmative. The number of foreign languages has increased. That's a real international operation out there."

"I notice the guards aren't real inquisitive of visitors passing through the gate," Travis remarked, as he surveyed the area through his battle sensor device.

"They have no reason to be," Jack said. "As far as they're concerned, everything is hunky-dory. These vehicles we're driving around in evidently haven't been missed yet."

Travis flipped up the battle sensor device and turned his attention to Sergei. "Are there any other groups of the Frateco besides those in Kazakhstan?"

"Maybe so," Sergei replied. "But I not know much. Once

I hear that Frateco make deal with Arabs to use ALAS against Israel sometime. No give warning to nobody. Hit Tel Aviv. To be paid for by Arabs. Would mean Iranians too."

Travis was thoughtful. Now his years of experience and training channeled his concentration down several avenues of possibilities. "There probably was another ALAS all along. That bullshit about there being only one was just a ploy. They wanted to keep any anti-Israeli operations secret."

Jack agreed. "Yeah. And this launch site has been established primarily to hit Israel. It was bound to be discovered through satellite imagery, but the Chinese and Iranians could claim it was for commercial launches only. Those two groups have been butt buddies for a long time."

"It's all coming together now," Travis said. "The Frateco obviously had at least a couple of ALASes. They never would have risked just one. Especially since they had to pull a dangerous trick and sneak it aboard a Russian rocket in place of an American satellite."

Jack pointed. "Truck approaching. There're some guys sitting in the back."

The three used their battle sensor devices to scan the vehicle. Sergei almost jumped up in excitement. "I know some of them. They are Frateco technicians!"

"There're Chinese in there with 'em," Jack pointed out.

"Well, shit!" Travis said in disgust. "Then our mission most definitely was not accomplished." He spoke into the Interforce commo system. "Each team leave one person up here for security. The rest of you meet me down in the olive grove."

Five minutes later the team gathered around Travis beneath the trees. He gave them the bad news that their mission of destroying ALAS and the Frateco's operations had not been completed as they had thought.

Sarah was not too upset. "It's a delay, that's all. Hell, we're at the right spot to finish the job. *No problema*, right?"

"*Problema grande*," Travis countered. "We're going to have to go in there and destroy that launch complex. And folks, there's a good chance we won't be getting out alive."

"It doesn't look that dangerous to me," Hunter said.

"We'll be attacking more than the personnel," Travis said. "The rocket itself will be our main target. ALAS is on top of the damned thing."

"Travis!" Sarah exclaimed. "That means the rocket is going to explode too."

Sam raised his eyebrows. "Everything within a radius of a half mile is going to be glowing like charcoal at a Texas barbecue. That means us too, folks!"

"Then nobody in the world will know what we did to save Mother Earth," Sarah remarked.

"Come on, Sarah," Jen said, "we never expected to have our pictures in *People* magazine, did we?"

"All right," Travis said. "Here's the plan. After the armored cars are gassed up we make a simple, direct attack on the complex. Stan takes command of vehicle two and Jack honchos number three. Those two guys, along with me, will be grenadiers. The drivers will use their rifles. Sarah and Travis will man the machine guns in their vehicles."

"I assume we don't spare the ammo," Hunter remarked.

"No reason to," Travis said. He continued. "We'll drive right up to the guard gate. From that point on, everything is going to be simple, quick, and final. You drivers put the pedal to the metal and head straight for the rocket. When we're in position, we'll hit it with everything we've got. Machine guns along with armor-piercing rounds and grenades from the XM-twenty-nines."

"Maybe it will take out the rest of the Frateco," Sam said.

"An added bonus," Travis remarked. "Just as long as the ALAS is destroyed."

"What time do we go in?" Sarah asked.

"Right now," Travis said. "We don't know their launch schedule. They may be planning on getting that hellish thing up in orbit within the hour. So let's gas up, then rock and roll!"

Frateco Launch Site #2
1700 hours

The sentries in the guard station at the entrance to the launch site looked down the road at the three armored cars approaching their post. They noticed the markings on the vehicles.

One spat in the dirt. "Is not that the Algerians?"

"Yes," the second said with a snicker. "I thought those offspring of African donkeys and camels were out on a two-week training exercise."

"Open the barricade and motion them through," the first said.

"Let us make them dismount and identify themselves," the second suggested. "It is amusing to hear them try to explain themselves."

But his partner shook his head. "I've no desire to hear Algerian offal try to speak the beautiful Persian language. My ears would prefer the barking of a desert hyena."

Travis Barrett, in the machine gun turret of the first car, noted the quick signal to enter the complex. "Drive on," he ordered Sergei.

Jen, just behind the first vehicle, followed closely. "We're going in, but we're not coming out," she said under her breath.

Stan, sitting beside her, heard the remark. "Sure we are. We're not suicidal. We've always got a chance."

Jennifer showed a slight smile. "Since when are you the eternal optimist?"

"Well, babe," Stan replied. "I always take a positive— well, dumb *and* positive—attitude toward our operations."

"I suppose," Jennifer conceded. "But I agree with Sarah. I'm really bothered that if we're blasted into bits, nobody will ever know what we accomplished. We'll just be part of the trash when they clean up the mess later on."

Stan nodded. "Yeah. But notice there's no hesitation on anybody's part."

"Nope," Jen said. She grinned in a resigned fashion. "Do or die. That's us."

"Correction," Stan said. "Make that do *and* die."

Jen frowned. "God, Stan! Do you have to *die* an asshole too?"

"I try to stick to what I'm good at," Stan said.

Jen frowned. "I wish you hadn't said that."

Sam occupied the machine gun position in the third car. He peered through the viewing slit at the different areas of the facility. Suddenly he spoke into his commo device to the first vehicle. "Halt! Travis! Call a halt!"

Travis responded instantly, then asked, "What's up?"

"Look at that building over there on the left," Sam said. "That's the LCC. The launch control center. It's a well-built bunker. Even the blast from the rocket won't harm it or anybody in it."

"I get you," Travis came back after studying the structure. "The hard-core Frateco types in there will survive. But we can't hit both places without alerting everybody."

"I can get in there," Sam said confidently. "Easy."

Travis continued to survey the building from his vehicle. "How? There're two guards on the door to the place."

"Correct," Sam responded. "But check out who is going in and coming out of the place."

Travis took a couple of minutes to monitor the visitors. "Hey! No Frateco goons. They're all Chinese!"

"Right," Sam said. "They are, no joke, a bunch of rocket scientists. Remember, the Long March is from Red China."

"Mmm," Travis mused thoughtfully. "Could it be that you have a plan?"

"Of course," Sam said. "Let's talk."

Sam opened the hatch in the hull and climbed out. After dropping to the road, he walked as nonchalantly as he could up to the first vehicle where Travis waited.

Chapter Ten

Sam Wong had exchanged his TALON Force low-observable camouflage suit for the Russian uniform he wore when they crossed from Kazakhstan into Turkmenistan. Now, after some minor alterations to the tunic, he walked from the armored cars across the road toward the launch control center looking very much like a Chinese Communist bureaucrat. The clipboard he had found in his armored car enhanced the effect.

Sam was ready to put his plan into operation. If he failed to return from the bunker within twenty minutes, it was to be assumed that he failed. At that point, Travis would shift back into the original attack plan against the Long March Rocket itself. Meanwhile, Sam would have pulled out his .45 for a do-or-die gunfight with the Red Chinese launch crew.

Sam walked boldly toward the LCC in confident strides with his free arm swinging to give the appearance of a busy man with something important on his mind. The Iranian sentries at the door, noticing he was Chinese, only nodded to him as he approached. Sam barely acknowledged their presence as he entered the bunker.

His appearance elicited looks of curiosity and suspicion from the Chinese staff sitting at the three rows of computers that filled the room. Sam played on their conditioning of years of totalitarian rule and rhetoric by giving them a look of superior authority. Then he pulled out a pen and scribbled a few lines while giving everyone a deep frown. This brought looks of apprehension from the people.

"Are you on vacation here?" he demanded in fluent Mandarin. "Do you loaf about, staring at everyone who walks in here?"

Completely faked out, they quickly turned back to their

individual tasks over their keyboards and CRTs with heads bent low in signs of diligent socialist labor.

Sam remained stern, demanding in a loud voice, "Who is the chief engineer?"

A plump little man on the far left side of the room stood up in front of his console. "I have that honor, Comrade. I am called Li-Chien."

Sam wrote the name down, then strode purposely toward him. "Comrade Li-Chien, what is the condition of the people's rocket?"

The chief engineer was confused. "The condition?"

"Yes!" Sam snapped. "The condition. Its status, if you will."

"It is fully fueled and ready for launch, Comrade," the chief engineer answered. "We are well into the countdown to launch."

"How long until that launch?" Sam asked.

"Two and a half hours," the chief engineer responded.

"Mmm," Sam said in a disbelieving tone. "When is the next automatic countdown hold?"

"Not for two hours."

"So! Launch in approximately two and a half hours. Excellent." Sam said. He gestured to the people in the room. "And who are these people? Are they all experts in their individual fields of science and disciplines?"

"Of course!" the chief engineer insisted. "Excuse me, Comrade. Who—"

Sam interrupted, "I want a list of their names before I leave."

"Of course, Comrade," the chief engineer said. "Let me assure you they all received their educations and training in the Marxist Socialist environment of the People's Republic of China."

"Very impressive," Sam said in a sarcastic tone. "Were they on duty when the rocket blew up in nineteen ninety-two wiping out two villages and an elite crew of rocket scientists and technicians?" He sneered. "Of course not! That gaggle of incompetents and reactionaries are all dead. As they should be!"

The chief engineer's face reddened with fear at the reminder of a catastrophe that everyone had been forbidden to discuss or even mention casually. He wisely made no reply.

"And why are you sitting back here?" Sam asked. "Don't you think it might be a good idea for the chief engineer to walk around and see what his subordinates are doing? Or do you blindly trust them, giving no consideration to the safety of the People's Republic and its property?"

"Of course, Comrade," the chief engineer said. "I was just getting ready to do that when you honored us by your presence."

"Go to it then!" Sam barked.

As the chief engineer scurried to tend to the task, Sam strolled over to the man's console and sat down. He quickly deciphered the main control board and noted the digital timer that clicked through hours, minutes, seconds, and tenths of seconds. Sam made sure he was unobserved, then nonchalantly reached over and pressed down the advance button, running the timer past the automatic countdown hold to put the actual blast-off of the rocket to within ten minutes. Then he stood up and walked toward the door.

"Chief engineer!" Sam called out. "Please step outside with me."

"I would be honored," the man replied, hurrying over to obey.

They left the bunker and strolled back toward the road and the armored cars. The chief engineer, now without witnesses to any insubordination on his part, suddenly lost his meek demeanor.

"I wish to see your official identification and credentials, Comrade," he said in a surly tone.

"Do you doubt me?" Sam snapped. "What else would I be doing in this wretched Iran?"

"I have every right to see your papers! I am the chief engineer on this launch project!"

"Of course," Sam replied, suddenly cheerful and polite. "I am glad you demanded these of me, Comrade. I was about to note that you failed to have me identify myself." He pointed to the vehicles. "All my documentation is there."

When they reached the cars, Sam climbed up onto the hull of number three. He turned, reaching down to offer his hand to the chief engineer. It took skinny Sam a great deal of effort to pull the plump fellow up onto the armored car. His plan was to open the hatch and shove the man down into the interior. But when he lifted the cover, the engineer caught a glimpse of Sarah and Jack.

"What is this?" he yelled. He turned toward the guards at the bunker and screamed out in Arabic, "*Gasus! Gasus!* Spies!" He spun back around and hit Sam, knocking him to the ground, then jumped down after him.

The guards immediately rushed toward the cars. Sarah was up with her .45 in her hand. She capped the two guards, blasting the heavy rounds into their upper torsos. As they sprawled onto the road, Sam got to his feet and rushed after the chief engineer, who fled back toward the bunker. Sarah took quick aim and fired again. The engineer's skull exploded, sending brain and blood into Sam's face.

Sam turned, a little shaky. "Thanks a lot, Annie Oakley!"

"Messy, but effective," Sarah said. She grimaced at him. "You, uh, might want to wipe off your face."

By then the rest of the team was on top of their vehicles. Travis looked toward the guard post at the entrance to the site and noted that one of the sentries was speaking into a handheld radio.

Sam rejoined them, climbing back up on his vehicle. He waved at Travis. "Everything is groovacious. I've advanced ignition." Suddenly a roar of the engines sounded from the launch site. "Uh-oh! We've got about a minute to get out of the explosive radius of that damned rocket!"

As Sam, Sarah, and the others dove back into their armored cars, Travis issued orders to haul ass. The convoy fired up their engines and turned toward the entrance. The gate guards ducked back inside their shack as the vehicles sped their way.

Travis, in the first machine gun turret, hosed the small structure, sending wood and glass splinters flying. One of the sentries, riddled by bullets, staggered out into view and fell. Sergei showed no hesitation as he ran over the man's body and crashed through the barricade.

Sam literally shrieked over the commo net, "Close down the hatches! That rocket is going to explode any second!"

Just as all three armored cars had reached the highway

and turned south, a tremendous, deafening, all encompassing detonation rolled over them. The concussion of the shock waves rocked the vehicles violently. All three drivers fought the twisting and turning steering wheels as the cars careened on the road. Then the concussion waves quickly subsided as a tremendous amount of superheated air made the metal in the vehicles' interiors hot to the touch.

"Halt!" Travis ordered.

The three vehicles were braked to quick stops. Everyone took care not to burn themselves as they climbed out on the hulls to look back at the launch site. The entire complex was nothing but a large, burning crater. Even the ground around the armored cars was scorched and charred.

Sam grinned proudly. "See what happens when you have ignition two hours early and skip the automatic countdown hold?"

"All I care about is that ALAS is no more," Travis said.

Jennifer spoke everyone's thoughts when she remarked, "Mission accomplished."

"Amen," Travis agreed. "However, I'm afraid those guards at the gate got the word out on us before the explosion. I suggest that we move on down that lonesome road."

As soon as everyone was back in their places, the drivers put the cars into gear. Travis stayed in the open turret looking back at the destruction that gentle, intelligent Sam Wong had created in saving at least half the world's population.

He shook his head as he settled down and once more pulled the hatch closed. Then he spoke into the commo system. "Sam?"

"Yes?"

"Thank you."

"You're welcome, boss."

1845 hours

Travis shared the vehicle with only Sergei now, so he manned the machine guns. He felt like a World War II armored force commander as he led his column down the highway.

Stan, now rid of the gasoline truck, commanded vehicle two with Jennifer driving and Hunter as gunner. Back in vehicle three, the situation was slightly different. Sam drove while Sarah manned the weapons and acted as commander. Jack had to continue listening to the bad guys on the radio to keep Travis appraised of what was fast becoming a very fluid and dangerous situation.

They had been traveling for fifteen minutes when Jack spoke over his helmet's communication system. "Travis! An armored car platoon is deploying ahead of us and another is closing in on the rear."

"Roger," Travis acknowledged calmly.

He knew a platoon normally consisted of four to six cars. That meant the team was outnumbered four to one in a worst-case scenario. To make things more unsettling, he really didn't have room to maneuver. He couldn't go out on the treacherous Dasht-e Kavir because of the quicksand. On the opposite side of the road were rolling hills that did not allow any great speed. If he took the cars to that higher country, all the Iranians would have to do would be to come in with rocket-armed choppers. It was also impossible to leave the vehicles and try to continue the exfiltration on foot. They needed them for both transport and defense.

"Listen up," Travis said to the team. "We are going to fight."

He ordered vehicles two and three to draw up beside him with number two on the right and number three on the left, forming a mobile skirmish line across the road as they headed toward the battle. He knew the Iranian cars would most likely be in a column and this would be the best way to meet them.

"When we sight those bastards, pour all your firepower straight into the front car," Travis instructed the team. "When he's blown away, do the same thing to anyone stupid enough to follow him."

It was a bit over ten minutes when the Iranian column appeared around a bend ahead. All three vehicles cut loose with both machine guns in each car. A combination of armor-piercing 7.62-millimeter and 14.5-millimeter slugs splattered the first enemy vehicle. The car burst into flames and spun wildly off the road, coming to a burning, smoking halt off to the side.

The second was also riddled, with a good many of the rounds going into the unwise driver's open hatch. The man died instantly as bit and pieces of him flew back to splatter the rest of his crew. They went off the road and rolled into a ditch, settling upside down. The car exploded, sending up a ball of roaring flame into the sky.

When the third caught hell from the team's armored skirmish formation, it came to a complete stop. Then, in less than a beat, it simply exploded. The top turret opened and a badly wounded man wrapped in flames came out and fell to the hull. The team mercifully put him out of his misery with quick salvos.

The fourth crew, who evidently had a powerful belief in the advantages of caution, turned and fled out toward the deadly salt flats. Bad choice.

"Keep going ahead," Travis ordered. "No sense in chasing the stupid bastards. They'll be ten feet under salty quicksand within five minutes."

The convoy continued down the highway as Jack monitored the Iranian commo net. "Travis!" he exclaimed. "The other platoon has reached the wrecks of their buddies. It sounds like they've got a real gung ho leader. I think he's ordered them to press on."

"Roger," Travis said. Then he noted a cut in the hills to their right. "Hold it!" They came to a dust-spewing halt. "Stan, move your car over to the far left side of the road and park it sideways as if it had some kind of trouble. Then you and your crew get out and join the rest of us in that open area on the opposite side."

"Wilco!" Stan yelled, setting the order into motion. When he'd complied, he led Jen and Hunter over to the others, who were now out of their own vehicles.

"We're going to have an ambush here," Travis said. "Stan, Jack, and I will use our grenade launchers. HE projectiles. The rest of you load up with armor-piercing rounds in your XM-29s. Nobody fires until I give the order. Find concealment with good fields of fire. Move out!"

They settled into their individual positions just in time to hear the approach of the other cars. Instead of using a bit of discretion, the Iranian commander had them speed up to Stan's seemingly wrecked vehicle. The leader, a very young lieutenant, came out of his armored car and charged Stan's vehicle alone, armed with only a pistol.

"Fire!" Travis bellowed.

The kid lieutenant was buffeted by the fusillade that kicked into his slim body. He went down like a stack of boxes, folding over in the middle. The nearest car turned its turret toward the source of fire. Travis aimed and sent a 20-millimeter grenade flying at it. The explosive hit in the gun ports. Flames spewed out of the open hatches. The car next to it started to maneuver for an escape, but Stan's grenade knocked off one of the front wheels. Armor-piercing bullets from XM-29s slapped through the hull, ripping the flesh of the crews inside.

The men in the surviving car wisely leaped out, planning on making a foot attack against the ambush. The raking fire from the team studded the skirmish line, toppling the men to the dirt. There was one very lucky exception. The survivor quickly threw down his AK-47 and held up his hands in surrender.

"Cease fire!" Travis bellowed.

The team crossed the road to the prisoner. He was a big, muscular fellow with a huge handlebar moustache. His bare head was shaven and his face had a rugged look about it. He was obviously frightened, but not cowardly.

Travis called over to Jack, "Hey, I want to interrogate this guy."

The man looked in astonishment at his captors. "What is this? Has America invaded Iran? Thanks be to Allah!"

Travis studied him. "So, you speak English."

"Of course, sir," the prisoner said. "I am Ramin Kahnjani. I drove a cab in Washington, D.C., for ten years. I came back to Iran for the funeral of my dear father and was denounced as a spy and blasphemer. They put me in jail and only the influence of a cleric uncle saved me from a death sentence. He got the authorities to give me a choice of life in jail or life in the army. Of course I took the army. But they took away my American passport so I cannot go back."

Jack walked up, sneering. "Nice story."

"It is true!" Kahnjani insisted. "Please to allow me and

I shall show you my Social Security card and my taxi license. I drove my own cab. I was a businessman."

Jen walked up and took the man's wallet from his shirt pocket. The naval intelligence officer pulled it out and found the documents. Both looked authentic, but she had experience with forgeries in the past. As an expert in disguise and subterfuge, Jennifer Olsen had been exposed to the best in bogus paperwork.

"We'll check you out, Kahnjani," Travis said. He turned to the team. "Let's mount up, folks. I think we need to put a bit of distance between us and our latest social discourtesy."

1950 hours

The grove of trees ended abruptly where a vast area of thorny brush took over the terrain like a creeping plant army. Beyond that was the barren salt expanse of the Dasht-e Kavir.

The three armored cars were well hidden within the trees with the concealment augmented by the camouflage netting each vehicle carried in its equipment and tool boot. Everyone in the team was on the defensive perimeter established around the area. The exceptions were Travis and Jack. The Iranian Ramin Kahnjani sat cross-legged in front of them as he ate from a can of C ration peaches.

Travis squatted down, looking at the prisoner. "Do you know the area around here?"

"Of course," the Iranian answered. "I grew up here. And I know where are the police and army. And I know where are back roads and places to hide."

"That's very interesting," Travis said.

"I am most happy to help you," Khanjani said hopefully.

Jack knelt down and joined them. "So you drove a cab in D.C.?"

"My *own* cab," Kahnjani replied. "I work for myself. I don't hack for nobody else."

"Tell me something," Jack said. "Let's pretend I'm in Washington. I'm at Fourteenth Street and New York Avenue, okay?"

Kahnjani stopped eating as his mind pictured the location. "Okay."

"And I have my wife with me," Jack said. "And she's pregnant and about to give birth."

"Praise Allah," Kahnjani said. "May you be blessed with a male child."

"Whatever," Jack said. "And you come driving by in your cab—your *own* cab—and I hail you."

"I am pleased to serve you," Kahnjani assured him.

"So I tell you that we have to go to D.C. General Hospital," Jack continued. "How would you get us there?"

"To D.C. General?" Kahnjani said. "From Fourteenth and New York? Easy! I go south on Fourteenth to Independence Avenue. Turn east. Go to Nineteenth and turn south. Halfway down the block and turn left into the hospital."

Jack nodded. "Right on."

Kahnjani grinned. "So I get big tip, right?"

Jack grinned in spite of himself. "Yeah."

Travis got to his feet and walked to the other side of the grove. Using his helmet, he got on the TALON Force net and made contact. From there he was routed directly to Brigadier General Krauss. The general was not in a good mood.

"What the hell are you up to?"

"Were you aware there was another ALAS?" Travis asked.

"Shit!"

"Not to worry," Travis said. "We destroyed it. Along with a Red Chinese launch site in Iran."

"Say again," Krauss requested.

"We located a Sino-Iranian rocket launch complex here in Iran," Travis reported. "We destroyed the goddamned place!"

"My God!" Krauss gasped. "How'd you find it?"

"A gasoline tank truck driver had marked it down on his road map," Travis explained.

"I can't wait to read your full report, Barrett," Krauss said. "It must be full of little surprises."

"In the meantime, we've got to get the hell out of here and join the fleet," Travis said. "I think we may have obtained another asset. We had an encounter with a couple of armored car platoons and ended up with an Iranian prisoner."

"Is there any way to check him out?" Krauss asked.

"Yeah," Travis said. "On your end. His name is Ramin Kahnjani and he claims he owned his own taxi in D.C." He pulled out the prisoner's Social Security card and taxi license, reading the numbers off to Krauss.

"Okay," Krauss said. "I've just passed the info off. They can check it out PDQ." He paused. "Now listen up, Travis. I don't like telling you this, but it's something that's got to be faced up to and dealt with."

Travis said nothing, knowing what he was about to be told.

"If you can't make it out of there," Krauss continued, "you're personally going to have to eliminate the team if capture is imminent."

"You've already established Condition Black," Travis replied in a calm voice.

"This is *complete* elimination," Krauss emphasized. "That means more than personnel. Equipment too. We can't have a shred left. Not even a rag of brilliant suit. That means you don't use ipsiusmorsathol. You've got the ultra-destruct kit, so you'll have to activate it with them all around you. Or at least within a twenty-five meter radius. That includes any corpses."

"Wilco."

"And I can't emphasize—" He stopped speaking for a moment. "Here we go. My dossier guy just handed me a printout. Ramin Kahnjani checks out. He is a widower who lives with a sister over in Rockville, Maryland. He has two kids. One named Ibrahim and the other Ali. Ages seven and five. Question him on personal data. If he can supply that information quickly and accurately, go with him."

"Roger," Travis said. "Out."

He walked back to rejoin Jack and Kahnjani. He looked down at the Iranian. "What is your wife's name?"

"She is dead," Khanjani said. "She passed away five years ago. After that I lived with my sister."

"I see," Travis said. "Do you have any kids?"

"Oh, yes," Kahnjani replied proudly. "Both boys. Seven and five years of age. My pride."

"Names?"

"Ibrahim and Ali," the Iranian answered.

"Tell me, Kahnjani," Travis said, "would you be interested in an all expense paid trip back to the U.S.A.?"

Chapter Eleven

Ramin Kahnjani wasted no time in proving his worth to the TALON Force's Eagle Team. He took the road map that Stan had salvaged from the gasoline truck and picked a surreptitious route that would take them from the danger of populous areas to much more secure environs out in the hinterlands.

Ramin sat with Travis on top of the lead armored car. His directions were passed down to Sergei at the steering levers. After a couple of hours of driving around roads that were little more than dirt tracks, they ascended to higher elevations where no villages existed. The journey ended up in the highlands where a forest offered some badly needed concealment.

Ramin had brought them deep into the Elburz Mountains. This was a forested area nestled between the Dasht-e Kavir Salt Desert and the Caspian Sea. The Iranian suggested they go far enough into that wooded terrain to set up a well-hidden bivouac that would offer the security and concealment they needed.

"The longer you are exposed in the open, the easier you will be to find even in this remote area," Ramin warned Travis. "Unscheduled and spontaneous helicopter patrols are always a possibility."

"Your knowledge of the army in this area will prove invaluable," Travis said. "We'll take your advice and stay out of sight for the time being."

"I swear by Allah we will all be safe," Ramin promised. The mission commander chose an easy opening in the forest, then had Sergei turn into the thick vegetation, with the others following. Jack, Sarah, and Sam in the last vehicle stopped long enough to sterilize the entrance spot, then came after the others.

They crawled along in four-wheel drive for twenty minutes. Then Travis called a halt next to a small clearing and ordered everyone to dismount.

"Seventh inning stretch," he announced as everyone climbed down from their vehicles. They all sank gratefully down to sit on the soft, mossy earth of the forest floor.

Travis surveyed his command, taking careful note of their appearance. "We need a break. Even though we're all in fantastic physical condition, and have received periodic boosts from our medi-pacs, we've reached a point where those inner supplies of energy and enthusiasm have to be recharged."

Sarah looked at Travis. "You aren't exactly a bundle of zeal and eagerness yourself."

"I'm tired," Travis admitted. "I'm good and tired. And like you, I'm getting careless and sloppy. Ramin did a good job in finding us a secure spot. I'm sure most of you don't know that Iran is only twelve and a half percent forest. That means that the other eighty-seven and a half percent of this country is pretty wide open."

"Very true," Ramin added. "When you leave these woods, you will be exposed mightily until you reach the marshlands along the coast. Even there you will have to squat down to hide in the brush."

Travis continued, "That means our little foray is going to become even more dangerous. That's one reason I want us to take a bit of a break. Our mental processes need to be recharged too."

Ramin gestured to the trees around them. "There are deer in here. Maybe we go hunting? Fresh venison will help build strength faster than rations in cans."

"All right!" Stan said enthusiastically.

Travis wasn't so sure of the idea. "Gunshots will attract attention."

Ramin disagreed. "There are no people near here. That is why I chose this spot. If you hear vehicles or aircraft, then cease hunting until they go away."

"What about foot patrols?" Jack asked.

Ramin shook his head. "Never happen. Not worth it. Nobody comes here."

Stan laughed. "Only crazy bastards like us."

"Okay," Travis said. "In that case we'll get some fresh meat." He chose Stan. "I'm appointing you as our official hunter. Go get us a deer."

"Sure," Stan said. "But I'm going to need some help." He looked at Sarah. "C'mon hotshot. What do you say?"

"I'm your gal," she replied.

"You guys don't have to go right away," Travis told them. "Take a load off your feet for a while."

"I think we need some of that meat," Stan said. He gestured to Sarah. "Want to go now?"

"Sure," she said, reaching for her rifle. "We can rest up with full bellies after we bring back some fresh venison."

During that first day of R&R in the woods, Eagle Team learned many things about Ramin Kahnjani. The Iranian was a much more complicated and colorful man than they realized.

When he was younger, Ramin had been an active and successful wrestler in his native country's athletic program. Wrestling was a popular and traditional sport of Iran. Although he had won no major championships, he had twice been an alternate on their Olympic team. Later, after his retirement from active competition, he coached several excellent regional teams that won national honors. Even after immigrating to America, he donated time to the Iranian community, coaching in the sport.

During their idleness, Ramin took advantage of the situation by working out. He did push-ups, squat jumps, and chinned himself continually from the branches of trees. He could do twenty-five repetitions of behind-the-neck pull-ups in fifteen seconds, then rest while hanging from the branch before repeating the set of exercises.

Travis and Jack were also physical fitness fanatics. They went through their own demanding regimens, and Ramin impressed both of them with his level of conditioning.

"Jesus!" Sam said. "I thought we were supposed to be taking a break."

"You relax your way, Sammy," Travis said between deep-knee bends, "and we'll relax ours."

After two solid hours of almost violent exercise, the trio, sweating profusely, knocked it off and replaced their jackets. Jack grinned at the Iranian. "You do look like a tough dude, Ramin."

Ramin shrugged. "Maybe. To me you have the appearance of a wrestler. You ever play the sport?"

"Nope," Jack said. "Football was my thing. Both in school and the Corps." He thought a moment. "But y'know, I wouldn't mind seeing just how good you are."

Ramin grinned. "You want to wrestle with me?"

"If you're up to it," Jack replied.

"I love to wrestle," Ramin said. "It is my life!" He stood up and stripped off his shirt. His pectoral, deltoid, and trapezius muscles bulged in hairy magnificence as he swung his arms around to warm up.

"Hey!" Sam exclaimed. "Aren't you guys ever going to take a break?"

"What for, Little Buddy?" Jack said. "You only rest up when you're tired." When he took off his uniform jacket, his smoother physique was just as impressive as Ramin's. He did some deep-knee bends and toe touches to get his own blood flowing again.

Sam was on communications watch with his battle sensor helmet, but he joined the others to watch the match. He kept his ears tuned to the net as the team gathered around for the spectacle they knew would be something to remember.

The bout started with the two brawny competitors warily circling each other. The six-foot, six-inch Jack towered over Ramin's compact height of five feet ten. Now and then they reached out or feinted to test the other's determination and reflexes. Ramin suddenly burst into a charge, then stopped just as quickly as Jack sprung back out of harm's way.

"I got my eye on you, man," Jack assured him. "Don't you try sneaking up on me like that."

Ramin grinned and said nothing, but continued moving as he made quick little dips and twists as if preparing to spring another attack.

Then Jack moved in and grabbed Ramin around the waist, lifting him high. Ramin's hands clapped down on his adversary's shoulders and he pushed back with a kicking and twisting motion that forced Jack to let go. Once more they went back to circling each other, waiting for an opening.

Travis, sipping a cup of C ration coffee, studied the two men with a professional soldier's appreciation. He noticed that Jack was the enthusiastic athlete, enjoying the competition and challenge as he went back to looking for an opening. Ramin, on the other hand, was the cold perfectionist, calling up a wealth of knowledge, experience, and skill while approaching the match with the same quiet determination a mathematician would use in deciphering a complicated problem in calculus.

Jack began to move like a linebacker along the line of scrimmage. He shuffled sideways and hunched his thick shoulders to give illusions of charges that never materialized.

Then he attacked.

Ramin took advantage of his own shorter stature by going even lower to the ground as Jack closed in like a runaway locomotive. Then the Iranian grabbed the taller man around the waist and stood straight up. Jack went over his head while Ramin, still holding on, fell to his back.

Now Jack tried to turn to take advantage of his upper position, but Ramin had already twisted like a cat and rolled free. He was on his feet in a flash and dove down on Jack who now desperately tried to escape. Ramin pulled him to his feet and threw him down, turning him over and pushing his shoulders to the ground.

"I'm pinned!" Jack said more in astonishment than anger. "Damn my black ass! How'd that happen?"

Travis showed a rare grin. "You'd better give up wrestling along with Ping-Pong, Jack."

Jack chuckled. "You could be right."

Both competitors got up and shook hands. Ramin well appreciated his opponent's sportsmanship. "Thank you for the wrestling match."

Jack dusted the grass and dirt from his trousers. "You're better'n me, Ramin. I'll own up to it."

"Yes, I beat you," Ramin said. "But with experience. You know, Jack, you are a talented man. If I was your coach I could make you champion in the Olympics. It would be a matter of the student surpassing the master."

"I'll take that as a compliment," Jack said. "Thank you."

At that moment Stan and Sarah walked into the clearing.

Stan had a small deer over his shoulders while Sarah carried both their rifles.

"Meat for the elite!" Stan announced.

The others turned toward the duo with sincere appreciation. Fresh meat was just as good as rest to renew their spiritual and physical strength. Stan dropped the deer and took his rifle back from Sarah.

Sarah looked at Ramin and Jack replacing their shirts. "Did you guys have a disagreement or something?"

Jack shrugged. "A test of skill. Ramin pinned me in a wrestling match."

"Go on!" Sarah said.

"My friend Jack was a most worthy opponent," Ramin said.

Stan made ready to dress out the deer carcass. Sam, still on commo watch, sat off to the side of the clearing monitoring the TALON Force net. He wasn't expecting any contact from Joint Task Force Headquarters and when the call sign came through the internal earphones, he was so startled that he leaped up. He listened to the transmission, then alerted Travis that Brigadier General Krauss wanted him on the net.

Travis took his own helmet and walked away from the others who had gathered around the deer. He acknowledged the contact with, "This is Barrett, over."

Krauss's voice came over calm and businesslike as usual, but there was a tinge of tension in it. "This is Krauss. Are you sitting down? Over."

"Negative," Travis said. "I'm squatting down in the trees looking like I'm about to take a dump. Is that good enough? Over."

"Roger," Krauss said. "Our inquiry about Ramin Kahnjani has produced some very interesting intel. I should add *surprising* and interesting. Over."

As Krauss spoke, Travis, now astounded with each word he heard, sank down into a sitting position.

Travis removed his helmet and walked back through the trees to the clearing. He had been gone so long that the team had already begun cooking the deer. Hunks of flank venison, impaled on sharpened sticks stuck in the ground, roasting over an open fire.

Jen looked up as the team leader rejoined them. "You've been yakking over there for an hour. Big news?"

"Yeah," Travis replied. "There's always something going on." He went over to Ramin who was helping with the butchering task. He tapped the Iranian on the shoulder. "A word with you."

"I am most happy to oblige you," Ramin said agreeably.

The two walked back into the trees away from the clearing. Travis stopped and turned. He waited a moment then said, "What lives in the winds of Iranian freedom?"

Ramin paled, looking in disbelief at the American. Then he recovered and replied, "The spirit of Persian patriotism and courage." He cleared his throat nervously. "Where did you get our challenge and passwords?"

"I've just been speaking with our headquarters," Travis said. "We know all about you."

Ramin said nothing.

"When you immigrated to America you did not start your own cab business," Travis said. "It was all set up for you as a cover."

Ramin remained silent, waiting for the other to continue.

"You're in the Iranian Resistance," Travis said. "My organization has made contact with your organization. We know that you *truly* did return to Iran for your father's funeral. We also know that you *truly* were denounced as a heretic and imprisoned and your uncle did get you released to the army."

Ramin chuckled a bit. "Cover stories are easy when they're true."

"And we know that you are now active here in Iran with the Resistance since your induction into the military," Travis said. "You are part of the counter-revolution against the present government in Iran."

Ramin nodded. "They did not live up to their promises. The Islamic government is as repressive as that of the Shah."

"You've helped get several important dissidents out of the country," Travis continued. "You could get out yourself, anytime you wanted. But you've volunteered to remain in the army and continue operations against the present government in Iran. At least for as long as you can be useful and effective."

"Since you were given the correct code words to make official contact with me in the name of the Resistance, am I to assume you have been given orders concerning me?" Ramin asked.

"A correct assumption," Travis said. "You are now under orders to not only get us the hell out of here, but to accompany us."

"They want me to leave my advantageous position in the army?" Ramin asked.

"You are nearing a point where you could be compromised at any moment," Travis said. "The Resistance has recently found that out."

Ramin shrugged and sighed. "Ah, well! In that case, I shall obey those orders with the greatest of pleasure. I am anxious to return to my children in America."

Travis studied him for a few moments. "Tell me, Ramin. If we hadn't made this arrangement, what would you have done where we're concerned?"

"It depended on what the circumstances dictated to me," Ramin said. "I wanted to escape from you and return to continue my duties. Frankly, I do not know how you've managed to come this far. You and the others have been both fierce and cunning. Nevertheless, I would have broken contact as soon as possible so as not to be compromised. Then I could get back to the Resistance. However, it now appears we are comrades with the same mission."

Stan's voice sounded from the clearing, "Chow call!"

The two walked from the trees back to the clearing. When they joined the others, Travis explained that Ramin would become instrumental in the continuing exfiltration. Everyone looked at the Iranian with a new respect.

Jack took a bite of venison and chewed thoughtfully. "So how you going to pull this off, Ramin?"

"It will not be easy with so many of you," Ramin said. "Our escape and evasion net is designed for maybe one or two people at a time. And they have also always been native Iranians who can fit into the local population."

Travis added, "It's going to take a great deal of effort and concentration on our part. I want to emphasize that Ramin is putting himself in harm's way through his efforts. It is as dangerous for him as it is for us. Perhaps more so."

Hunter fetched another piece of the roasted meat. As an

Air Force pilot, he had participated in several escape and evasion operations. "What does your E and E net consist of?"

"We have safe houses, of course, and transportation of many types such as automobiles and trucks," Ramin answered. "And there are guides and other helpful people scattered along the way. Documents are available to aid cover stories. All that, along with money, travel tickets, and whatever else is needed can be provided."

"What are we up against in the way of unfriendlies?" Sarah asked.

"Patrols and checkpoints by police and paramilitary," Ramin replied. "Also public transportation includes inspections and checks."

"What about the army and air force?" Sam asked.

"Very little," Ramin said. "The Iranian economy is hurting because of international boycotts. The military has been provided very little operating funds since there is no war. Our garrison lost a helicopter somewhere and has no other for this district."

The TALON Force troopers looked at each other, knowing the aircraft was beneath the salt of the Dasht-e Kavir. But since Travis didn't mention it, they didn't either.

"Well," Travis said impatiently, "we've got to get this thing rolling ASAP."

"Right," Ramin agreed. "First thing. No more armored cars. These attract too much attention and the army *will* get involved if it looks like a foreign military force is loose in the countryside."

"They may already think that," Travis commented.

"I pray to Allah they do not," Ramin said.

Jennifer asked, "So what do we do? Simply walk out of these woods?"

"I will walk out," Ramin said. "You all will wait here. I must meet with my organization to make solid plans."

"I'll send someone with you," Travis said.

Ramin shook his head. "*No!* That cannot be allowed. We want you to have minimum contact with our people. Understood?"

"Makes sense," Travis conceded.

"You may not know it," Ramin said, "but I have spoke in truth with Travis. My friends, you have already come as far as you safely can. With luck you might have made another twenty or twenty-five kilometers before strong forces descended upon you."

Jack folded his bulging arms across his massive chest. "Then if something happens to you and you don't get back with us, we're in deep yogurt, huh?"

"You are doomed," Ramin said seriously. "Okay. We talk enough. I must get to my people and have them place you in the net. Right now the authorities search for you on the roads. Eventually they will go out into the countryside. When they do that, they will come to these woods. But not for a long time."

"How long will it be before you get back?" Travis asked.

"Three days," Ramin said. "Four at the most. Stay quiet and hidden." He grabbed a piece of the venison and began walking toward the edge of the woods. "Allah willing, I will see you soon."

The Americans watched the Iranian as he penetrated the trees and disappeared from view.

Chapter Twelve

Jen lay hidden in the concealed guard post at the edge of the forest. It was a peaceful, almost soothing spot. A gentle, intermittent breeze wafted through the trees. Birds twittered while an occasional insect buzzed among the flowers.

But the tranquility of her surroundings was lost on the young woman. Her nerves vibrated with concentration as her eyes scanned the terrain in front of her. Jennifer waited anxiously for signs of Ramin Kahnjani's return. This was the third day since his departure and Travis had decreed that if he wasn't back by the end of the fourth day, the team would have to assume he was compromised by capture or death. That would mean resuming the perilous exfiltration on their own. And Ramin had warned them that the dangers they now faced would make the operation impossible. The circumstances had deteriorated and the Iranian authorities would enjoy all the advantages from now on.

Jennifer was well camouflaged, but not with the power-hungry low observable camouflage suit. Instead she used the conventional methods of cut vegetation and a large piece of netting taken from her armored car to cover herself. The effect was successful. With green and brown face paint from her makeup kit smeared on her face, she was practically invisible.

Back in the clearing a dozen yards away, the rest of the team lounged about the campsite. They were well rested to the point they were antsy and craving some sort of activity or action. Stan idly whittled a stick of wood while Jack and Hunter watched him without any particular interest. Everyone's ears were cocked to the one-sided conversation that Travis was having with Brigadier General Krauss via his battle sensor helmet.

"Roger. Over.—I don't like the idea. Over.—That can't be all that necessary. Over.—Goddamn it! You're stripping us down to nothing! Over—Understood, but if we go down the tubes, I want it to be in a blaze of glory, not a cloud of despair. Over.—Wilco. That's it then, goddamn it! I understand orders are orders. I'm breaking off this commo now. *Now!* Out."

Travis abruptly ended the commo session, then took off his helmet and angrily threw it across the clearing. "I won't need that anymore."

"What the hell's going on?" Jack asked.

"The ground rules of this exfiltration have changed," Travis reported. "If Ramin makes it back, we'll be moving straight into the Resistance's E and E net. That means we'll be under their direct authority with no recourse but to obey their every whim and order."

Hunter shrugged. "We wouldn't have much choice anyway. We're in their ballpark now and the rules are theirs. Anyway, they know what it takes to make the thing work."

"There's a hell of a lot more to it than that," Travis said. "All TALON Force gear is to be destroyed. We're to dig a hole and throw every single item in it. Helmets, RF field generators, Trauma med packs, the whole works. Even the XM-29 rifles. Nothing is to be left that might be found in case our little escape turns to pure shit."

Sarah looked up. "What're the chances of that?"

"Damned certain without the Resistance's help," Travis admitted. "Even with them calling the shots, it's going to be risky." He sighed. "Oh well. At least they'll let us keep our forty-fives."

"There's nothing special about the pistols," Sarah said. "So no sense in keeping them away from the bad guys."

"They've probably got the same model pistols in their own arsenals," Hunter said.

"What the fuck?" Stan snorted. "Burying the TALON Force gear is sure as hell not gonna destroy it."

"We're to shoot two or three phosphorous grenades into the hole containing the equipment then bury the whole bit," Travis said.

Sarah raised her eyebrows. "That crap will burn for a

week, even under all that dirt. They aren't kidding when they say they don't want anything left for curious eyes."

"Yeah," Sam interjected. "I think the real significance is that Task Force Headquarters doesn't have a lot of faith in Ramin's net."

"How can they?" Travis said. "Even Krauss admitted that they don't know as much as they should about the organization. The Resistance may have a smooth-running operation, but on the other hand, the thing may be a cluster fuck."

"What kind of clothes are we supposed to wear during the E and E?" Jack asked.

"Are you worried you won't be stylish enough?" Stan asked.

"I like to look good for the ladies," Jack said.

"We'll wear whatever the net provides us," Travis replied. "I assume it will be civilian attire. Meanwhile, we'll switch to basic fatigue uniforms." He got out a packet of C ration coffee to brew a cup. "At least this is the last of that crap."

"I'm on my final can of lima beans," Hunter said.

"Thank God! I'm tired of smelling your lima bean farts," Stan remarked with a glare at the pilot.

"Air Force shit don't stink," Hunter retorted. "And our farts smell like roses." He took several more quick bites of the beans. "Just a minute. I'll prove it."

Sarah winced. "Please don't, Hunter!"

Travis set his cup on the coals of their campfire. "We'll be split up into twos and threes at the Resistance's discretion. All the necessary cover stories, documentation, and other goodies will be provided to back up the roles we're to play."

Hunter saw the Resistance's side of the situation. "Remember," he reminded his friends. "Those people are going to be putting their asses on the line for us. Any sign of noncooperation on our part, and we'll be eliminated as fast as Palestine terrorists at a bar mitzvah."

"You're right," Travis said. "And they're going to have to coordinate things so that all our teams arrive at the safe houses in the city of Bushehr at the same time. For those whose knowledge of Iranian geography is a bit weak, the place is located on the Persian Gulf."

"Ah!" Stan exclaimed. "That wonderful magic place where the United States Navy is located."

Further conversation was interrupted when Jennifer suddenly appeared in their midst with Ramin. The Iranian wore cheap civilian clothing and showed a wide, smug grin.

"The army has listed me missing and presumed dead," he announced with near glee. "I can now be anybody I want to be."

Travis was not interested in idle talk. "What's the story on the Resistance's net?"

"They are getting ready for us to be inserted into the system," Ramin informed them. "A truck will arrive on the road on the other side of these woods just before dark. It will take us to a safe place to organize for our escape and evasion."

Sergei Mongochev, who had been quieter than usual, glanced up through the trees at the sky. "Sunset will come soon. We must make rush."

Ramin looked at him. "You are in a hurry, my friend?"

Sergei replied, "Like you, I have family to see again."

"Come on, folks," Travis said. "Let's get some shovels out of those armored cars and dig a nice hole. Six by six by six."

The group set to work on the project. After watching them get in each other's way, Travis became irritated. "Jack! Stan! You dig."

"We dig," Jack said as he and Stan began stabbing into the dirt with their shovels.

They quickly worked their way through the soft forest earth until the excavation was complete.

"Strip down and toss it in!" Travis ordered.

Jen was brought up to date on the latest events as they peeled off their TALON Force attire until everyone was in a basic fatigue outfit with boots. They packed their .45 automatics in holsters on belts. Within a few moments all the TALON Force gear was tossed into the hole. Travis took his XM-29 and loaded a white phosphorous grenade into the launcher. He fired it into the pile of outrageously expensive cutting-edge equipment. The team leader followed it up with two more grenades, then tossed the rifle into the white-hot glow.

"Cover it up!"

Stan and Jack dutifully shoveled dirt until the hole was refilled. They tamped it down. "Damn!" Jack said. "I can feel the heat through my boots."

"Yeah," Stan said. "That shit's gonna burn for three or four days. Maybe even a week."

The next item of business was to get the armored cars deeper into the woods. When that was done, they were covered with cut brush and tree limbs with dirt thrown over the camouflage for good measure.

Stan didn't see the reason for the effort. "These are gonna be found someday, y'know."

"But we'd prefer that didn't occur until far into the future," Travis said. "Hopefully by some archeologist searching for signs of the ancient Persian Empire."

When the job was finished, the vehicles were invisible at distances greater than five meters.

Ramin checked his watch. "Okay. Now we go to the edge of the forest and we wait for our ride." He grinned at his new friends. "We are about to start a grand adventure."

"Really?" Jen said. "I thought we were already in the middle of one."

1930 hours

Sunsets don't last long in mountainous terrain. When the bright disk in the sky reddens and begins to dim, its descent behind the peaked western horizon does not take long.

A pink glow and long shadows dominated the area as Kahnjani and the members of the TALON Force Eagle Team sat just inside the treeline that looked out on the poor excuse for a road that ran past the place. No one spoke as each sank into his or her own thoughts.

The very real fact that their group was about to begin the most perilous episode of the entire mission was foremost in their thoughts. They would no longer operate in an independent manner in which they could rely on their own cunning and skills. Instead, they would be at the mercy of people they did not know, in a hostile country they had never visited before. To add to the tension, they were in the midst of an indigenous population who looked very different from all of them.

Ramin, on the other hand, was completely at peace with the world and himself. Ever the wrestler, he kept himself occupied by performing innumerous push-ups at a slow, steady, and very quiet cadence. Sergei Mongochev watched the Iranian's exercise regimen without really observing him. Sergei's thoughts were on his wife and daughter waiting for him back in Brighton Beach. His family was under the impression that he was on a business trip for a Russo-American commercial enterprise. Suddenly Sergei sat up.

"Vagonetka!" he whispered loudly, then caught himself and repeated the word in English. "Truck! Lorry! Listen!"

Ramin stopped in mid push-up as the others tuned their ears to outside noise. The sound was faint, but a truck engine in low gear could be heard moving toward them. Ramin motioned his companions to stay under cover as he made his way to a good position to observe the narrow road.

Within a few minutes an ancient Ford stake truck came into view, growling and complaining. The engine began to sputter and choke, then stopped.

"Oh, great!" Jennifer growled. "The damned thing's broken down."

"Don't worry," Ramin assured her. "This is part of pick-up plan."

The driver got out and went around to the front and opened the left hood cover. That was the signal Ramin was looking for.

"Come on!" he urged them. "Be quick!"

As the driver simulated checking the engine, Ramin led everyone from the trees around to the rear of the old vehicle. They clamored onto the back under a canvas top. The space was empty and everyone scrambled to settle down. In a few moments, the sound of the hood slamming shut startled them. Then the engine was fired up and the truck lurched back into motion.

The ride through the countryside was forty minutes of bumping, grinding, and careening down the rustic road. Everyone grabbed onto whatever they could to keep from being tossed around in the bouncing truck bed. Stan, who had tried sitting down, was given a violent bump that slammed him painfully on his tailbone.

"Ow! Don't they know what shock absorbers are in Iran?" he growled at Ramin.

"Shocks are luxuries here," Ramin explained. "And this truck is strictly for working."

"This truck is strictly for bruising my ass," Stan shot back.

Then the sound of the tires on a firm surface hummed back at them. After a bit more than an hour of what was imagined to be highway travel, they abruptly slowed down. Several automobile horns being honked by angry drivers informed the passengers that they were now out of the country and into a more urban environment. In only short minutes, the shouts of irritated pedestrians increased as the truck's speed decreased to a crawl. Ramin chanced a quick glance outside. He turned back to the others with a wide grin.

"I am pleased to welcome you to the city of Tajrish, which is located just north of Tehran," he said.

The truck moved slowly for another quarter of an hour before making a turn. It rattled on for twenty minutes then came to a squeaky stop. A grinding of gears announced the driver shifting into reverse. The vehicle chugged backward then abruptly halted.

"Follow me!" Ramin said.

He stepped from the truck onto a loading dock. The others followed as he led them into the interior of a dark, musty warehouse. The place was dimly lit and filled with crates of various sizes. They threaded their way through the cargo area until they reached a freight elevator on the other side of the building. Ramin motioned them inside, then joined them. A press on the button and they descended to a basement. An armed man stood to their direct front as they reach the lower floor.

"*Koshamadid!*" he welcomed them, pointing to a door down twenty feet from the elevator.

Ramin nodded to him, saying, "*Salaam.*"

He took his companions to the door and led them to a set of rickety stairs that brought them down one more level. When they reached the bottom, they found a well-lit area with partitions. A dignified looking man wearing a fatigue uniform was waiting for them. He nodded a silent greeting and shook hands with Ramin.

Ramin introduced him. "This is Dow. That is not his real name and in Farsi, it means Two. So he is Number Two. Understand?"

Dow responded, "And I speak English, my friends. How are you?"

Travis stepped forward. "I'm the team leader," he said, purposely omitting his name. "I trust you are prepared for us."

"Indeed," Dow replied. "We have been well informed, at least as much as is our business to know about you. Our only concern is to get you safely through our escape and evasion net so that you may leave Iran. Are you ready to begin the operation?"

Travis nodded. "We are *anxious* to begin the operation."

"Fine," Dow said. "I am going to break you down into teams according to the information supplied me." He pulled some notes from his pocket. "Team number one will be the mission commander, the Russian asset, and Ramin Kahnjani."

The three formed up together.

"Your cover story," Dow continued, "will be that you are foreign oil workers going on company-sponsored vacations to Italy. Ramin is Turkish, the mission commander is Spanish, and the Russian will be logically Russian."

Sergei said, "But look at us. We are dressed in generic military fatigues."

"You will be supplied with appropriate civilian attire, luggage, and items to carry with you," Dow explained. "That will include passports, visas, work certificates, and other documents normally carried by people in your situation."

Travis was pleasantly surprised. "Very professional!"

Dow smiled. "As you Americans say, you are now in the Major Leagues." He turned his attention back to his list. "Team number two will be your explosives man and your pilot."

Stan and Hunter presented themselves, rolling their eyes at being teamed up with each other. Stan started to make a wisecrack, but thought it not appropriate under the circumstances.

Dow pointed to Stan. "You are Polish and your friend is Irish. You are engineers at a desalination plant on the

Caspian Sea. You are on your way to the city of Bushehr to report progress of your work to company management." He looked up and spoke to the group. "By the way, everyone's destination will be Bushehr."

"What about escorts?" Travis asked.

"You will be met in that city by someone who will take you to different safe houses," Dow said. "At the right time you will be brought together at a secluded spot on the coast. Arrangements will have been made by then to take you to a specific U.S. Navy ship."

Stan asked, "Will the Navy be ready for us?"

"Of course," Dow said. "We are in constant contact not only with U.S. Naval Intelligence, but also the intelligence services of other nations with ships in the area."

"What if a team is delayed or late in arriving in Bushehr?" Jennifer asked. She made no mention of the fact that she was a U.S. Navy Intelligence officer.

"I am sorry to tell you they will be on their own," Dow said. "We will abandon them completely and disavow all knowledge of them. So please follow our instructions most explicitly." He paused and cleared his throat. "Now to continue. The black man, the Chinese, and the two women will make up team three."

Jack, Sam, Jennifer, and Sarah stepped forward.

Dow pointed to Jack. "You are a Saudi prince." Next he nodded to Sam. "And you are his Filipino servant."

Sam protested. "I am *Chinese*. I don't even look Filipino."

"No one will question you here," Dow assured him. "All Asians appear the same to Iranians."

"And to Americans," Sam added.

"But you will be a Moslem, understood?"

Sam nodded affirmatively. "Hey, big guy," he said to Jack. "Don't ask your servant for any crazy shit, okay?"

Jack snickered but nodded.

"What about us women?" Sarah asked.

"You are wives of the Saudi prince," Dow informed them.

Jennifer shook her head. "Figures. And how the hell are two white chicks going to convince any native Mid-Easterner that they're home girls. I don't have my makeup kit anymore."

"You and your friend will be completely covered and veiled," Dow said. "No one will speak to you while you are in the company of your husband. And remember. The women of Saudi Arabia do not even carry identification cards. Iranian passport control officers will be courteous enough to ask you no questions since you are the wives of a Saudi prince."

Jack grinned, the implication of being a wealthy prince sinking in. "A Saudi prince? Cool! Do I get a Rolls-Royce?"

"No," Dow answered, "but you get first-class accommodations on the national railway." He smiled at Jack. "By the way, Saudis are notoriously poor tippers."

Sam laughed. "You picked the right guy for *that* cover story! You won't even have to act, Jack!"

Dow smiled. "The two engineers from the Caspian Sea will also travel first class on the train. But not in a private compartment like the prince."

"Hell! That's fine!" Stan exclaimed.

"What about us oil workers?" Travis asked.

"Bus," Dow replied. "Sorry. We don't want all three teams together."

"Right," Travis said.

"Come with me," Dow said.

He led them across the wide expanse of the room to another door. Inside were neatly stacked piles of clothing and various types of luggage. All was laid out according to cost and gender.

Hunter was amazed. "Where did you get all this?"

"Tehran International Airport," Dow replied. "Baggage handlers there are notorious about conveniently losing things. Some are members of the Resistance while others are professional thieves." He gestured to the loot. "Pick out what you need. And remember, you'll have to have something inside that luggage as well."

After the team, Sergei, and Ramin were outfitted, the next step in the procedure was taking passport photos for the various documents. The team members were taken to a special room where a photographer and his camera awaited them. Within moments, they were seated for the portraits necessary for their E&E paperwork.

When the preparatory procedures had been taken care

of, there was nothing left to do but wait as the documents were prepared by the Resistance's teams of experts. Most of the papers they had were authentic. Changes were skillfully made to alter names and attach photographs and seals. When necessary, master forgers were available who could produce ID that could only be detected if sent through high-tech scanners. And such devices were rarities in Iran.

The escapees were taken to another part of the building where simple but comfortable living quarters were available for them. They had a healthy meal of fruit, vegetables, and chicken along with strong coffee and sweets. They were in a good mood as they ate. These were the first real creature comforts they had enjoyed since leaving Desertville in California. But Travis dampened their spirits somewhat.

"I just want to remind you that even though we're all sterile with these IDs we're to be furnished, it's still Condition Black," he said. "Do not fall into enemy hands. And don't let anyone else suffer that fate. You know what you must do." He belched contentedly. "Pass the grapes, please."

Tajrish, Iran
0830 hours

The team and their two assets sat around the table in a small conference room just off the main area in the subbasement. All had donned their escape clothing and now enjoyed hot tea and rice cakes that had been set out for their breakfast. Stan glanced over at Sarah and Jennifer wearing their veils and costumes as a prince's wives. He winked at Jen.

"Jen," he said. "You're so mysterious. You look sexier than you did in that receptionist role back at the Pentagon."

"I'll tell Angela you said so."

"That'd be just great," Stan said. "I'll get through the dangers of an Iranian E and E net only to be murdered by my wife."

Jennifer lifted her veil and treated herself to some hot tea. "One of these days, Moslem women are going to raise up and storm out into the streets and start kicking every man they see in the balls."

Jack shuddered. "I hope I'm far away when that happens."

The door opened and Dow came in with an assistant who carried a cardboard box. The container was set on the table.

"Passports, identification, work permits, etcetera, etcetera," he announced.

The documentation included wallets, industrial ID, driver's licenses, and even photos of loved ones. Each team member was given his or her proper papers. Then Dow pulled travel tickets from his inside jacket pocket.

"Here are first-class railway accommodations with private compartments for the prince and his entourage," Dow announced. "First class for our desalination engineers." He turned to Travis, Sergei, and Ramin. "Sorry about the bus. You will have to buy your tickets at the depot."

Travis shrugged. "I don't suppose we'll be going Greyhound."

"I fear not," Dow said. He walked to the door and opened it as his assistant left. He turned to those in the room. "And at this point may I remind you that nothing— *nothing*—is perfect. So! As we say in Farsi, *'Movazeb baash!'* Roughly translated, means 'Watch your ass!' "

Dow made a quick exit. Everyone sat unmoving for a couple of moments, then Ramin stood up.

"Let's go."

Chapter Thirteen

The travelers in the dusty station glanced toward the street as a long, white limousine pulled up to the curb. A small, thin Asian man stepped from the front passenger seat. He was dressed in a trim, cream-colored suit and moved briskly as he opened the large door in the rear of the automobile. He seemed worried and agitated as he waited for his companions to exit the luxurious vehicle.

The first person out was a tall, imposing black man dressed in the white *jellaba* and *kaffiyi* of an Arabian prince. He stood straight as a ramrod and wore gold-rimmed sunglasses, glaring through them disdainfully at the crowd of curious onlookers. Within a moment two heavily-veiled and cloaked women joined him.

A half dozen eager porters rushed forward as the flustered Asian man snapped his fingers at them. The driver of the limousine opened the trunk to allow the luggage to be removed. The Asian barked, *"Dirk balak!"* at the porters as they struggled getting the suitcases out of the trunk.

When all was ready, the imposing prince grandly led his entourage across the waiting room and out to the platform where the train awaited them.

Over in the first-class waiting room, Stan and Hunter watched the procession go by. Both men wore rather stylish business suits and had expensive Corinthian leather luggage with them.

Stan chuckled and leaned close to his companion, speaking softly. "Jack is really playing it up, isn't he?"

"Right," Hunter agreed. "And don't try to tell me he isn't enjoying it. The guy looks like he's ready to order half the people in the depot beheaded for even looking at him."

"The sad thing is that the crowd will never know how hot Sarah and Jen are under those outfits," Stan remarked. He was thoughtful for a moment. "Y'know, I bet a lot of these women here would look really nice in miniskirts and low-cut blouses."

"Stan, you're such a pig, though you're probably right," Hunter said. "But don't stare too closely at them. It's considered bad manners in a Moslem nation."

"What's to see?" Stan asked with a shrug.

The train's conductor appeared at the door of the waiting room. He spoke politely to the well-to-do crowd. Everyone got up and walked out toward the coaches as he repeated his announcement several times.

"C'mon," Stan said. "I think he just said 'all aboard.' "

A porter appeared as if by magic and picked up their two suitcases. He followed them to the first-class car. The interior was quite pleasant. The seating was spacious and comfortable, and the passengers were all well-dressed and neatly groomed. They were obviously upper class and would accept nothing less than the finest in service and accommodations.

Stan tipped their porter, then sat down across from Hunter. A steward appeared, offering them coffee, sodas, and snacks.

Stan took a can of Bon Aqua sparkling water and settled back. "This is going to be a really nice trip."

Hunter, already munching a bar of rich Swiss chocolate, nodded. "Yeah. I think we've finally reached a point where we can relax and enjoy the sights."

Downtown Tajrish
1100 hours

Travis stood in the second floor window of the seedy hotel where he shared a room with Sergei and Ramin. He gazed down at the narrow crowded street below, studying the tumultuous scene. The people shouted and pushed their way along the trash-strewn thoroughfare. Travis turned back to his companions.

"We aren't exactly in the best part of town, are we?" he remarked.

Sergei frowned. "So much noise. Everybody all the time shouting. All cars got honking horns."

"The Iranian people are noisy," Ramin admitted. "We have much exuberance about life. Religion. Politics. Our emotions run high."

Travis took a careful look below. "I don't see the guy that's been tailing us." He was speaking of a man who appeared during a casual sojourn they had taken out in the streets the evening before. He quickly showed an obvious interest in the trio.

"He's probably in the lobby," Ramin said. "Don't worry. He is a police agent, but it is only routine procedure to keep outsiders under surveillance. The authorities are suspicious of all foreigners."

The three were dressed in casual shirts and slacks that made them look like living advertisements for the Gap. Jogging shoes finished off the outfits and their luggage was made up of three small scuffed and cheap suitcases. But they gave the exact impression they desired: semi-skilled foreign oil field workers.

Sergei scratched his armpit. "I am bit by bugs all night," he complained.

"Me too," Travis said. "This place needs to be fumigated."

Ramin laughed. "Now you know why I gave the beds to you two and I slept on the floor."

Travis growled, "It really pisses me off to think of how those other two teams are traveling."

Sergei shrugged. "We couldn't all go together, so somebody had to travel cheap, *nyet*?"

"Yeah, I guess," Travis said. "But I wouldn't have minded a coach seat on an airliner." He checked his watch. "Well, it's time to head for the bus station. Is everybody ready? Good. Let's get the hell out of here." He snorted, "I'm really in no mood for a long bus ride."

Ramin laughed. "You don't know what is a long bus ride until you take one in Iran."

"It's a lesson I'm not looking forward to learning," Travis said.

Sergei frowned. "Me too."

They picked up their sparse luggage and left the room, going down some rickety stairs to the tiny, dusty lobby on the first floor. Ramin had been right. Their plainclothes cop was sitting along the wall in a shabby overstuffed chair. The clerk was not particularly friendly either. He treated them to a silent, almost hostile greeting. He obviously was not fond of foreign infidels. He could tell they were checking out by their appearance. He pulled their bill from under the counter and added it up.

"Bist-o-shesh-zaar," he said. Then added in several languages, *"Yirmi altu bin. Vente-seis mil. Ishrin sitt aelf.* Twenty-six thousand rials."

The three travelers acted like typical working stiffs settling a bill. They pulled out their wallets and got the money together, feigning an argument about who should pay what and how much. After the brief, animated exchange, they laid a wad of rials down in front of the clerk. He scooped them up without thanks, and went back to glaring at them as they headed for the door. The police agent stood up to follow after the three departing guests, making no pretense about his intentions.

Travis and his companions went outside into the crowded street. Ramin led the way with Sergei in the middle. They bumped and pushed their way through the throng. Travis noticed some shady characters lounging off to the side. They apparently had nothing to do as they scanned the people passing by. These were obviously a pack of greaseballs who were up to no good. One stepped out as they passed by and bumped into Sergei. Travis saw the man picking the Russian's pocket.

"Ladron!" he yelled in Spanish and grabbed the pickpocket.

The man struggled against Travis's grip until the American tripped him and threw him to the street. The thief began yelling and shrieking while his buddies moved in to help him. A crowd immediately gathered around the scene, and their collective mood turned ugly as they noticed that Travis and his friends were foreigners. Several men moved menacingly toward Travis. One took a swing at him and Travis kicked him hard on the knee.

Another became threatening and Sergei slammed the

heel of his hand into the guy's chin, snapping his head back and knocking him unconscious to the street.

Now the angry mob had the undeniable intention of beating and kicking the foreigners to death. Ramin quickly jumped between the Iranians and his two friends.

"This man is a pickpocket," he yelled out loudly in fluent Persian. "The miserable wretch tried to rob my two friends!"

At that point, the crowd, many of whom had had their own pockets picked in the past, turned their anger on the pickpocket and began pummeling him. As the situation quickly reversed itself, Ramin grabbed both Travis and Sergei, pulling them away from the fray. After another glance at the street criminal who was trying to get away from the punches and kicks, they resumed their trip to the bus station.

Travis noticed the plainclothes police agent was showing no interest in the crowd's antics. Instead, he continued to give him, Sergei, and Ramin all his attention. Travis felt a flash of alarm. Ramin had obviously come out of his cover when he spoke in fluent Persian to the crowd. It was in direct contrast to his appearance as a foreigner.

When they reached the Tajrish Bus Station, they went inside, going straight to the nearest ticket window. They each bought a ticket to Bushehr by gesturing and saying the name of the city. From there they went to a corner of the waiting room and took the far end of one of the hard wooden benches. They had just settled down when the plainclothes agent came in with two uniformed policemen. The cops looked around the depot, then spotted the three evaders.

The man and the officers came up and motioned the trio to get to their feet. Something was said in Persian. Travis and his two companions smiled apologetically and shrugged to show they didn't understand what was being said to them.

This angered the cops, who grabbed the trio and pushed them roughly toward a door at the back of the building. The group entered a small room that held a battered desk, table, and a few mismatched chairs. This was a room set aside for the convenience of the police.

"Pasportamra!" the man from the street demanded.

Travis and Sergei understood the passport sound in the word and produced their identification. Ramin hesitated, knowing it would be to their advantage if he could communicate with their captors. He spoke in a contrived Turkish accent.

"I no understand you."

"You don't speak Farsi?" the police agent asked in the language.

Ramin shrugged. "I Turk. No speak much Farsi."

"I heard you speaking the language perfectly out in the street," the agent insisted. "You had no accent. You are an Iranian!"

Ramin shrugged. "No, I Turk. Maybe you hear not good in noise of crowd, eh?"

"I heard everything just fine," the agent said. He gave their documents a close scrutiny. He glared at Ramin. "Why don't you have Iranian papers?"

"I Turk," Ramin again insisted.

The agent noted they were oil workers heading for a holiday in Italy. He spoke to Sergei, who did not understand him.

"Ya ne ponimayu," Sergei said with another shrug and smile.

The agent suddenly slammed his fist into the Russian's ribs. Sergei gasped and staggered back, hitting the wall.

The other two policemen tensed themselves for any sign of resistance. The agent spoke again and still Sergei made no reply. The agent turned his attention to Travis, speaking to him.

"No comprendo," Travis said in Spanish, wanting to kick the Iranian's ass up between his ears. Instead, he shrugged and repeated the apologetic smile.

The agent kicked Travis hard in the shins and gave him a short, but powerful punch to the midsection. Travis's strong abdominal muscles took the blow, but he gasped loudly.

"Please," Ramin said. "No to hit my friends. They no understands you."

The agent spoke rapidly in Persian for several moments, glaring in angry suspicion at the three. "I don't know what is going on here, but I think we have some funny business."

"Our papers are in order," Ramin said, continuing his accent.

"I am not impressed by papers," the agent said. Then he made a gesture that indicated they were dismissed.

When they got back to the bench, they sat down. Travis rubbed his throbbing shin. The other travelers eyed them with curiosity and suspicion. Travis asked, "What the hell is going on?"

Ramin answered in a soft whisper. "We are in trouble. The policeman heard me speak Persian in the street."

"I was afraid of that," Travis said with tension in his voice.

"I am sorry, Travis," Ramin said. "But I have not the experience that you do. And you two were in great danger. More danger than you know. The crowd would have killed you."

"Forget about it," Travis said. "It's too late to get upset about it." He took a deep breath. "What else did that guy tell you?"

"He is going to telegraph our names to every bus depot between here and Bushehr," Ramin explained. "We must check in with the police at each stop. I am sorry, but if we are careful we shouldn't have much trouble other than a few punches."

Travis thought for a moment. If Ramin's optimism proved wrong, there was every chance the trio would be compromised. And the mission was still Condition Black. Now, with the poison in the trauma pack no longer available, it would be difficult to obey that somber order.

Ramin noticed the serious expression on Travis's face. "Are you worried?"

"I was just thinking," Travis said. "That son of a bitch isn't just going to let us get on the bus and go our merry way. He'll plant somebody to follow us to see if we try anything."

"Of course," Ramin agreed.

"Yes," Sergei added. "That is what Soviet KGB would do."

"I have a feeling that we'll be getting a lot of punches and kicks before this trip is over," Travis said. "We pulled a lot of shit out on the road. I'm sure the authorities are seriously alarmed. Foreigners are going to get a lot of unpleasant attention."

"Just don't go crazy," Ramin advised. "Our papers are in good order, so eventually I think they will let us loose."

"I just hope we don't get delayed too much," Travis said. "That would mean we'd have to get out to the Navy on our own."

Ramin frowned. "That will be dangerous, will it not?"

"Yeah," Travis said. "There's a good chance we'd get wasted by our own side since they wouldn't be expecting us."

A door opened and a bus driver stepped into the waiting room, making a loud announcement that included the word "Bushehr." Ramin grabbed his suitcase and stood up. Travis and Sergei followed suit and trailed after him toward the door.

Iranian National Railroad
1215 hours

Sam, in his cover as a Filipino servant, rapped politely on the compartment door. He balanced a serving tray of coffee and rice cakes against the rolling of the train. A moment passed and he knocked again.

"Dakhal," Sarah said as she had been taught.

Sam entered and bowed politely. *"Sabahil kher."* He shut the door and put the tray on the table between Sarah and Jen. "This is so embarrassing," Sam said as he sat down with the two women. "Everybody thinks I'm a houseboy."

"No, it's better than that, Sammy," Jennifer said as she removed her veil. "Everybody thinks you're a *castrated* houseboy." She laughed.

"What!" Sam exclaimed.

"That's right," Sarah interjected. "Only eunuchs can attend the wives of the master. We could do that dance of the seven veils and you wouldn't even be able to become aroused."

Sam groaned. "Please don't!"

Jennifer took a bite of rice cake. "By the way, how is our lord and master getting along?"

"Okay, I guess," Sam said. "Jack usually doesn't drink

much, but he would kill for a cold beer right now, I mean *really* kill someone, but Muslims aren't allowed alcohol."

Jennifer pulled up the hem of her robe and stretched out her legs, revealing the Levi's she wore beneath the garment. The jeans had been with the clothing in the basement warehouse back in Tajrish. "I think we can all breathe easier now. The rest of this mission is going to flow as smooth as a deep river."

"Seems so," Sam said. "Y'know, I've given this Iranian Resistance some thought. I'll bet anything that the organization is funded by the CIA."

"No doubt," Sarah agreed. "They seem to have a lot of money to run their operations. It's got to be extensive."

Sam stood up. "I get back to Prince Jack, chop chop. Even houseboy *sans* balls not supposed to dally long around master's wives."

He left the compartment backward, bowing and scraping sarcastically, and stepped back into the coach. As he walked toward the quarters he shared with Jack, he passed the seats where Stan and Hunter sat. They paid no attention to him other than a casual glance.

On the bus
1400 hours

Travis and Sergei sat packed together in the double seat while Ramin occupied the floor at their feet. The bus was crammed with men, women, children of various sizes, and an assortment of livestock. Goats bleated among the cackling of chickens and the snorting of pigs. In spite of open and broken windows, the air inside the vehicle reeked. Its shock absorbers were shot, and the ancient vehicle swayed and bounced violently.

Ramin leaned toward his companions and spoke only loud enough for them to hear. "I'm sure Travis is correct. We are being followed by a police agent. I think we should try to spot him. When we know who he is and where he is sitting maybe we can do something about him."

Travis stood up as if to stretch. As he twisted his torso, he glanced at the other passengers in a quick but efficient manner. He spotted a particularly interesting man wearing an old worn suit and a blue T-shirt. Travis sat down. "I think I've made the guy."

Sergei said, "I lived in Soviet Union. I got instinct to spot secret agents. I look and see if we suspect same guy." The Russian stood up and placed his suitcase on the seat and opened it. As he acted like he was looking for something, he let his eyes furtively scan the appearances of their fellow travelers. He sat down. "Is man in suit with blue T-shirt. I am sure of it."

"Yeah," Travis said. "That's the guy I picked out."

"Why we don't get pistols and put in our pockets?" Sergei asked.

"Bad," Ramin argued. "We are now under constant surveillance. Carrying concealed pistols is against the law even if they have no proof of who we are. Then they arrest us for sure in Bushehr. Right now, we at least got fifty-fifty chance of whether we meet others in time to go to the U.S. Navy with them."

The three settled down for the trip as the bus continued on its bouncing, dust-billowing way down the highway.

Chapter Fourteen

The bus rattled into the town of Saveh and the sudden activity of passengers gathering up luggage, children, and animals in preparation to disembark shook Travis, Ramin, and Sergei out of their individual reveries.

Travis looked out the bus window as the vehicle came to a stop. Three policemen walked rapidly and purposefully toward the door. He gestured to Ramin and Sergei.

"Our reception committee awaits us," Travis observed.

Ramin took a look. "Yes. Get ready for some more rough treatment, my friends."

"Let us stay here so they can come in and get us," Sergei suggested. "Why make it easy for them, eh?"

"I agree," Travis said. "That's what innocent men would do. After all, we're supposed to ride this rattletrap all the way to Bushehr." He looked back toward the rear of the bus. "Blue T-Shirt is still sitting back there."

The departing passengers and animals struggled off the bus, giving the lawmen nervous glances that faded away when they noted they were not the objects of the officers' attention.

Travis and his two companions remained in their seats. The cops stepped aboard the bus and immediately spotted them. They signaled for the three travelers to get off.

"But we go to Bushehr," Ramin protested in his pseudo-Turkish accent. "We not supposed to get off in Saveh."

The policemen, irritated by this show of noncooperation, wasted no time. They rushed up the aisle and swarmed over the three, punching and slapping them. The evaders did not resist the mistreatment except for covering their heads against the storm of blows.

After a minute or so of the punishment, the cops wrestled them out of their seats, and dragged them down the aisle to the door. Once outside, the policemen quickly snapped handcuffs on the prisoners. Some more punches were given out, then one of the cops commandeered a frightened porter to take the prisoners' luggage. The arrested men endured additional pummeling while being pushed toward a waiting van.

The policemen put them in the back seat, while they took the front. As the van was driven off, Travis whispered to Ramin, "What do you make of this?"

"It is because of the telegrams from Tajrish," Ramin deduced. "These guys must cover their asses and show they received the message and performed their duty properly."

"Do you think we'll just be given the usual roughing up then sent along our way?" Travis asked.

"I think so," Ramin said, then quickly added, "I *hope* so."

One of the officers in front noticed they were talking. He turned toward them and growled a guttural expression. Travis and Sergei correctly assumed it was an order for them to shut up.

Within a couple of minutes they pulled up in back of the police station. The three captives were dragged out and shoved inside by two of the men while a third brought in their luggage. Travis was seriously concerned that they might find the pistols hidden in secret recesses of the traveling gear. But when they got inside the building, the suitcases were tossed aside while the prisoners were thrown into a large cell.

Travis quickly determined this was the local lockup for petty criminals. There were no cells other than the one they had been thrown into. Although the place was filthy, insect-ridden, and stunk from the one latrine bucket in the far corner, the three were not separated. They sat down on one of the benches mounted along the back wall. There was graffiti and crude sexual drawings all over the place.

Sergei surveyed the scene. "Why no other prisoners I am wondering."

"This is a small city," Ramin said. "No major crimes I think. Probably all the people arrested last night have paid their fines and been released after seeing the judge this morning."

Suddenly a door leading toward the outside opened and two burly cops stepped inside. They looked at the prisoners for a moment, then chose Travis. They opened the door and motioned him to come with them. The moment he stepped outside the bars, they began the customary kicking and punching as they led him out of the confinement area.

Travis was taken to another part of the building and shoved into a small room that held a table and chair. He was roughly forced to sit down, then his escorts stepped back. A policeman who showed more rank insignia than the others stepped inside. He yelled at Travis and snapped his fingers.

Travis didn't understand the words, but assumed the man wanted to see his papers. He quickly produced them with a polite nod of his head and laid them on the table.

The man barked some more words, and when Travis didn't understand, the two men behind him gave him hard slaps. Travis protested in Spanish.

"No les entendio! Por favor, no me pegan! Yo soy español!"

The fact that he spoke in words they couldn't fathom earned him further blows. This time the pair used their fists, and the punches to his face were heavy and painful.

The senior officer yelled and the beating stopped. He pulled a printed form from his pocket and laid it on the table in front of Travis. He gave him a pen and yelled again.

Travis knew he was expected to sign the paper, but that was something he most certainly was not going to do. He couldn't read the document and thought it might be some sort of confession. Instead of signing, he shrugged and pointed at the paper to indicate he couldn't understand it.

The officer yelled again and his subordinates gave Travis another series of punches. But Travis shook his head and stubbornly refused his signature. A renewal of the beating began but suddenly stopped when the door opened. All three cops sprang to the position of attention and the senior one saluted.

The new arrival wore a flashy uniform indicating an even more superior rank. He looked down at Travis's battered features and began bellowing at the three. Their faces showed the discomfiture they felt, and Travis surmised that beating the hell out of him was something they shouldn't have been doing.

But he quickly found out that wasn't the case. They pulled him up to his feet. One stepped to his direct front and now concentrated on Travis's body, throwing punches to his ribs and stomach. The commanding officer had given them orders not to put any more visible bruises on his face.

He refused to sign three more times before the ranking man issued an order. The ordeal stopped and Travis was immediately dragged from the room.

He was taken back to the cell by the two ass kickers. They opened the door and threw him inside, then beckoned for Ramin to step out. Ramin stood up and feigned being nervous.

"Please to have mercy in the name of Allah," he said.

The policemen laughed and wasted no time in launching into another punching routine, throwing hard punches into Ramin's tough body.

Sergei watched them drag the big Iranian away, then turned back to check out Travis. "How you feel my friend?"

"Like I just took an accelerated Ranger course at Fort Benning," Travis said. "But I'll live."

"Now they beat on Ramin," Sergei said. "Next they beat me."

"Stupid bastards!" Travis said. "They don't have the slightest idea of what's going on with us. As far as they know, we're oil workers. But they'll kick our asses in hopes that they might—just *might*—discover something. And all this because of one suspicious cop back in Tajrish."

"Is Ramin's fault for to talk Persian," Sergei said.

"He did what he had to do," Travis said.

Sergei sat down on the bench in the cell. "I am wondering if we can be trusting Ramin."

"I don't think he'll betray us," Travis said. "He's got too much to lose. He wants to get back to his family like you do."

"I am thinking he won't, how you say—rat us out—I am thinking he might sneak away from us," Sergei said. "He could easy get back to his Resistance and they then could get him out by himself."

Travis shrugged. "Anything is possible. If he does, we're going to have a heavy load to carry. It'd be tough for two foreigners alone in a crowded coastal area where there are plenty of armed forces and police."

The door opened and Ramin reappeared with the two policemen. The luggage was also with them. Travis and Sergei stood up to take a look at their companion.

"Are you okay?"

Ramin nodded. "The captain said to turn us loose to get the next bus to Bushehr. He don't want to talk to us no more. He say it is a waste of time." He grinned at Sergei. "You don't get no ass kicking, my friend."

"I feel shame," Sergei said.

Travis put a hand on his shoulder as the cops opened the cell door. "Don't be silly. C'mon. Let's get the hell out of here." He looked over at Ramin. "What was that document they wanted signed?"

"Simple thing," Ramin said. "It was for to acknowledge we had been in custody here. I sign it. No big deal."

Travis spat. "And I took a battering for that?"

"Too bad you didn't know Persian," Ramin said.

Five minutes later they sat on the back of the same van that had brought them to the police station. Ramin made sure the Iranian cops weren't listening, then he whispered, "They don't know nothing about us, but made a good show for interrogation when police commanders come around." He took a deep breath. "I think maybe we are out of all this shit now."

Sergei was encouraged. "Maybe we will be on time to join others."

"Unless something happens to them," Travis said.

Ramin grinned. "Cheer up!"

The Persian Gulf
1845 Hours

The Royal Navy Gazelle HT-2 helicopter buzzed at an altitude of a thousand feet over the waters of the Persian Gulf.

The lone passenger, Brigadier General Krauss, gazed down at the various American, British, and French warships the aircraft flew over.

After ten minutes, the chopper slowed and nosed up to a prelanding hover. Now Krauss could see the British ship directly below them. A landing signal petty officer, standing on the helicopter platform on the stern, waved instructions up to the pilot.

Krauss's photographic memory called up some facts he knew about the Royal Navy vessel he was about to land on. She was an Amazon Class frigate with a complement of 11 officers and 150-plus ratings. She had been of a class that was first propelled by all gas turbine propulsion and was a well-armed, superior warship with an efficient, dedicated crew.

As soon as the chopper touched down, Krauss jumped out to the deck. He wore a nondescript set of camouflage fatigues bearing only the insignia of a single star pinned on each collar and the cap. He didn't even sport a name or service tape above the pockets.

A crisp British officer stepped forward and saluted. "How d'you do, sir? I am Commander Nigel Huntington-Smythe. Intelligence staff of Her Majesty's Gulf Battle Fleet. I believe you would be Brigadier Krauss."

"That's Brigadier *General* Krauss," he grumpily replied.

"Sorry, sir," the Brit said.

"It's all right," Krauss said. "Just a simple matter of protocol."

"Follow me, if you please, sir," Huntington-Smythe said, leading the way forward toward the bow.

The usual courtesies of an introduction to the captain were omitted as the two officers headed below decks. This was a covert visit that everyone involved was supposed to forget. They stepped into a small office area where two men waited. The commander quickly introduced Krauss to Major Alistair Lee of the Royal Marines and a man called Hashuli of the Iranian Resistance.

Krauss sat down in a chair offered him. "Report?"

Hashuli spoke in a businesslike manner. "Two escape and evading teams are on the train heading for Bushehr. Everything is fine with them. The third team, traveling by bus, has been delayed."

Krauss showed no emotion. "What happened to them?"

"Our operatives observed them being taken from the bus to the police station in the town of Saveh," Hashuli said. "We do not know why."

"Did it appear they are compromised?"

Hashuli shrugged. "It is a strange situation. They did not stay there long and were taken back to the depot and put on the next bus to Bushehr. They are not exactly behind schedule as far as we know, but any overnight stop in jail could seriously jeopardize their chances for coming out with the others."

"Were they formally arrested?" Krauss wanted to know.

"It appears they were not," the Iranian replied. "Perhaps they inadvertently made a *faux pas* where the traditions of Iran are concerned. That would include staring at some-one's woman or drinking alcohol. All law in the country is based on Islam. Even if their transgression only appears to be minor, they could be delayed enough to create a problem."

"Who was on that team?" Krauss inquired.

"Our Iranian, the Russian, and your team leader," Hash-uli said. "We sincerely regret this incident and are com-pletely confused by the situation."

"Understood," Krauss said, "but this is going to have to be dealt with." He looked at the marine officer. "I take it you are supplying the boat for the pickup?"

"Yes, sir," Major Lee said. The Royal Marine officer was a short, muscular redheaded man who looked like he could eat raw lion for lunch. "We'll provide a Rigid Raider boat with a coxswain for that phase of your operation."

"What is a Rigid Raider boat?" Krauss asked.

"I'm referring to the Dell Quay Rigid Raider, sir," Major Lee said. "They are GRP-constructed—"

"What the hell is GRP?" Krauss interrupted.

"Glass reinforced plastic, sir," Major Lee answered. "The boats are a bit over five and a half yards long and close to two and a half wide. Quite good little runabouts, actually. They carry one or two Johnson outboard motors as required and can do more than thirty-five knots. I might add they're virtually unsinkable and handle quite well in high surf."

Huntington-Smythe interjected, "Your recovered operatives will be brought to this vessel on the Rigid Raiders, then transported by helicopter to the appropriate American ship." He shook his head apologetically. "I'm sorry to hear about your team that is facing a possible delay. I fear there can be no second chance for missing personnel. This must be a one-time mission for reasons I am not free to disclose."

"Of course," Krauss said. "Understood and appreciated. Our own navy's commitments precluded their participation in the water phase of the exfiltration. We are thankful to the Royal Navy for stepping in to take up the slack."

"Happy to be of service, sir," Huntington-Smythe intoned.

Krauss stood up. "I have to return and see what can be done about this mess."

"Very good, sir," Huntington-Smythe said. "I shall take you back to the landing pad."

They quickly returned to the chopper and Krauss hopped in. The aircraft lifted skyward as he buckled himself into his seat. He settled back for the ride, staring unseeing at the sights that slid by the door. His mental processes worked rapidly as a contingency plan formed in his mind. Krauss always expected the absolute worst. He was seldom wrong.

He spoke aloud to himself, the roaring aircraft engine drowning out the sound of his voice. "The first thing I have to do is put in High Priority Requisitions for six new TALON Force Battle Ensembles."

Between Saveh and Bushehr
2030 hours

Travis sat next to the window in the bus seat. It was getting dark outside and he could see his face in the reflection of the glass. His left eye was darkened and swollen almost shut, and yellowish-blue bruises marked the right side of his face. He glanced at Ramin, who sat beside him.

"How long before we reach Bushehr?"

"Another hour," Ramin answered in a soft voice. "How are you doing?"

He felt his sore jaw. "I think I'll be eating soup for a couple of weeks before tackling a steak," Travis said. He glanced back and noted that Blue T-Shirt was still in his customary seat.

Sergei, sitting across the aisle from them, slid over and joined the conversation. "If we arrested, I go first this time, hey?"

Ramin looked at him. "Maybe you won't have to. Do like Americans and cross your fingers."

"Okay," Sergei said. "My fingers I am crossing. But if we arrested again, I insist to go to interrogation first."

Travis grinned in spite of the discomfort. "Be my guest."

Ramin shrugged. "I just got hit only a few times before the police captain stopped the interrogation and told his men to take us back to the bus. I think our troubles are over."

"I'm surprised that with all that interest in us they didn't think of searching our suitcases," Travis said. "Not that I'm complaining, however."

"They were not well-trained," Ramin said. "But in Bushehr it might be different."

"If anybody finds the pistols, we'll tell them we bought them from a departing worker," Travis said. "They are just for protection."

"Okay," Sergei said. "Not much else we can say."

"Maybe it is best to throw them away," Ramin said.

Travis shook his head. "If things turn to shit—and that may well happen—we may need them. Remember, we could end up out of the loop for the pickup by the Navy."

Ramin nodded his head. "Out of the loop and into the deep shit."

"Ah, well!" Travis said. "I think I'll try to get some sleep before we reach Bushehr."

Ramin and Sergei followed his example. Within moments, all three dozed in their seats.

The door opened with a loud squeak as the driver pushed the lever. Ramin stood up and stepped back to allow Travis to proceed him off the bus. Sergei followed, and the three men glanced around as they walked into the Bushehr bus depot.

No police officers were in sight.

"Maybe they gave up on us," Travis said. He looked back at Blue T-Shirt, who had been trailing them. The agent walked through the crowd and out the front door.

Ramin was hopeful. "I am thinking they forget us now. They accept who we say we are."

"Maybe," Travis said. "But let's not try to make any contact with the Resistance right away."

Sergei nodded. "Is good idea. Maybe police set a trap, *nyet*?"

The three walked slowly across the depot and stepped outside. Immediately, uniformed men appeared from the left and right sides of the door, pinning them between both groups. Now Blue T-Shirt stepped forward. He murmured a terse order in Persian. Handcuffs were immediately slapped on the three, and they were pushed down the street toward a van.

The door of the vehicle was open and waiting for them. The arresting officers crammed the trio of prisoners inside, then slammed the door shut. The heavy snap of a large padlock could be heard as it was closed.

Ramin's voice was mute and almost mournful in the darkness of the interior. "We are not in police custody, my friends. This arrest has been made by the Military Intelligence Service."

Chapter Fifteen

Travis sat in the darkness of the dank cell with his back against the far wall. The steel chamber was completely empty except for a bucket in the corner. Not even a crude bench or stool was available for the prisoner. The only light came from a small slit that showed in the solid door's closed viewing port. Now and then the scrambling scratching of a scurrying rat broke the monotony of the silence.

Travis was dressed in a thin, oversized prison jacket and trousers. It was a tan-colored outfit with a pattern of black triangles all over it. He had no underwear, shoes, or socks.

It felt chilly in the cell and he reached down to massage his feet to keep some circulation in them. He had no idea what time of night or day it was, nor how long he had been confined. The passage of time had dissolved in the solitary gloom. Travis figured there was a good chance it might get colder. Much colder. The human body had a disagreeable habit of cutting off circulation to the hands and feet at low temperatures to keep blood flowing to vital organs. It was a situation that produced deadly gangrene infection in the extremities, which could lead to death or amputation.

The trip from the bus station had been a confusing ride in complete darkness. There were no windows or vents in the rear of the van. This hadn't surprised Travis. It was common practice to keep new prisoners disoriented prior to their introduction into an unknown environment of constraint. Even the convicts brought to the Federal Penitentiary at Alcatraz in that prison's heyday arrived at The Rock during darkness.

When the van arrived at its destination, he, Ramin, and Sergei could hear large doors opened to the front. Then the vehicle moved forward a few yards and the portals were closed to the direct rear.

They were ordered out of the vehicle, and the trio noted they were in some sort of large, bare, concrete building. No one spoke as blindfolds were silently applied to the three prisoners. Then, still handcuffed, each of their arms was grasped by persons unknown and they were led away.

Travis heard the echoing sound as his and the escort's shoes scuffed along a stone floor. Within five minutes, he sensed he was alone with the guards. He and his companions had been separated. He was led through a door and brought to a halt. Then both blindfold and handcuffs were removed.

Travis found he had been taken to a supply room. After being ordered to take off his clothes, he was strip searched and issued the ill-fitting uniform he now wore in the cell. It was ominous that he wasn't allowed to keep his shoes and socks, and that none of the blankets on the shelves were given to him. Minor but disturbing physical discomfort was going to be the order of the day.

The blindfold and handcuffs were replaced. Then he felt the chilling addition of shackles being clamped to his ankles. Now, severely hobbled, he once again was led away. The guards allowed him to proceed at his own pace with no pushing or punching. The only time they laid hands on him was to steer him in the direction they wanted him to go.

After some fifteen or so minutes of stumbling along between the guards, he arrived at the cell and was put inside. The restraints were removed, the door shut, and he was left alone. No electric lights illuminated his new quarters. Travis was acutely aware he was in a sophisticated prison instead of a police station.

Once more, Condition Black entered this thoughts. The orders had been explicit. In case of capture, the TALON Force members were to kill themselves because of the extraordinary circumstances of being in Iran. He decided to play it by ear for the time being since he didn't know if he was under observation or not.

Now, feeling the need to urinate, he crawled toward the

bucket he had seen in the corner upon his arrival. He examined it closely, noting it had no strong odors. That meant the cell had been unoccupied for some time. He relieved himself and returned to the resting spot. He knew that he was being left alone to unnerve him with the uncertainties and fear such solitude produced. That worked on most people but not Travis Barrett. He drew strength from within.

Travis took deep breaths as he began meditating to get in touch with his inner self. It helped him put his mental and spiritual processes in order to prepare for whatever ordeal lay ahead of him.

Clank!

The door opened noisily and two guards came into the cell. They said nothing as they pulled him to his feet. After turning him around they reapplied handcuffs, blindfold, and shackles. Then the two pulled him out of the cell, and he stumbled in the direction they pushed him.

As the group moved along, Travis was able to see a bit out of the bottom of the blindfold. He noted what appeared to be an ancient stone floor that was dimly lit, and he sensed he was in a corridor. Within minutes they stopped and a door to the left was opened. Travis was taken through it and placed in a cold metal chair. The door closed and he sat alone. He tried to perceive if there was another person in the room, but it seemed empty.

The handcuffs and shackles were uncomfortable, but the chair finally warmed up from his body heat. Long minutes passed, but this was something else he expected. It was another example of customary treatment to take a prisoner out of his cell and have him wait alone an inordinate amount of time in unfamiliar surroundings. It increased the natural worry and uncertainty he had already endured. He couldn't tell what he was actually waiting for. A routine interview? Bellowing abuse? A beating? A long session of agonizing torture?

Travis's stomach growled a bit, making him wonder how long it had been since he last ate. The hunger reminded him of a basic part of Special Forces doctrine: *When capture is imminent, eat and drink as much as you can.*

Travis thought about Sergei and Ramin. The Russian was as well off as he, but a fingerprint check would ID Ramin quickly and easily. Then suspicions about all of them would soar like a skyrocket on the Fourth of July. They were in the hands of the Military Intelligence Service, who had the professional expertise and training to recognize they had stumbled onto something very unusual. Once more he thought of Condition Black.

The door opened and a voice filled with annoyance spoke in Spanish. *"Que es esto?"* Some loud words in Persian followed. Someone else came into the room and removed the blindfold, handcuffs, and shackles.

Travis rubbed his wrists and looked up to see a rather decent-looking man in a khaki uniform standing at his side. The stranger seemed to be a clean-cut young guy in his early thirties, and he held a manila folder. A table was to the direct front of the prisoner with another chair. The young officer walked around and took a seat.

"I apologize for the restraints," the young officer said in fluent Spanish. "Prison people are such sticklers for routine and regulations."

"Gracias," Travis said, thanking him.

"Dios mio!" the young officer suddenly exclaimed. "What happened to your face? Did those guards beat you?"

"It happened in the town of Saveh," Travis said. "At the local police station."

"Damned bumpkins," the young officer said. He sat down and opened the manila folder he had brought in with him. Travis could see that it held the bogus documents given him by the Resistance.

The young officer looked at the first one. "Ah! An Iranian labor permit that allows you to work in this country. Mmm, seems to be in order. *Esta bien.*"

"Yes," Travis said. "It was issued by the Iranian embassy in Madrid."

The young officer smiled. "Ah, Madrid. Beautiful city."

"I am from Barcelona," Travis said.

The Spanish passport was given a thorough examination along with other documentation such as the driver's license and a Visa credit card. The final item was an airplane ticket from Bushehr to Naples. The young officer put them all back in the folder.

"Everything is in order, *señor*. I do not know why they are holding you here."

Travis shrugged. "I hope this is cleared up as soon as possible. My friends and I are on our way to Italy for two weeks vacation. I'd hate to spend most of it here before we are released."

"No se preocupa," the young officer said. "Not to worry. I'll turn in my report and you'll be out of here soon enough. And your friends as well. No doubt about it."

"I appreciate that," Travis said. *"Gracias."*

The young officer stood up and walked to the door. As he stepped out into the hall, the two guards returned. Once more Travis was blindfolded, cuffed, and shackled. He heard the young officer's voice as they led him away.

"I couldn't stop them from bundling you up that way," he said. "Prison regulations, I'm afraid. *Lo siento.* Sorry."

1200 hours

Travis pumped out fifty push-ups, then got to his feet. After performing as many deep-knee bends, he felt his way back to the wall and sat down.

He could have easily done six times that many repetitions, but he wasn't sure how his captors would feed him. Since he felt the only safe path to follow was to expect the absolute worst treatment, he only wanted to work out enough to keep limber and warm. If his caloric intake was to be greatly curtailed by the prison diet, he didn't want to weaken his physical strength by burning too much food energy.

Travis Barrett, United States Army Special Forces, was not fooled by the interview he'd had earlier with the pleasant Iranian officer. That was obviously just a get-acquainted session to feel him out. Even if they believed every word he told them and each line of printing on every document, they would give him one damned rough grilling before releasing him. The Iranian authorities had not gone to all the trouble of bringing him and his friends to a prison and issuing uniforms for just a few minutes of questioning. They were in for at least a month of unpleasantness. And that was the very best he could expect. Might as well face up to that. And the delay completely blew their portion of the exfiltration.

A sudden flash of light lit the cell. Travis glanced toward the door to see that a sliding panel in it had been opened. He got up cautiously and walked across the stone floor to the entrance. A tin plate and cup sat on a small shelf just inside the door. He reached out and took the items, pulling them inside before going back to his usual spot by the wall.

He checked the meal and found it consisted of two cold rice balls and a cup of water. He took a bite and chewed, noting the stuff was held together by some sort of date paste. It might be nourishing, he thought. He ate one, surprised at the sweetness. After consuming the second, he drained the cup of water with deep swallows. Travis had also been taught that, in addition to gorging oneself prior to capture, when nourishment and water was available, consume them all at once as soon as possible. Time limits to eat and drink were not unusual in captivity. Also it was a form of maddening harassment to put out something to eat, then withdraw it quickly before the prisoner could down it all.

Travis walked back to the door and set the plate and cup on the shelf. They were immediately withdrawn and the opening slammed shut. Now he knew he was under constant observation. He returned to the back wall and sat down.

He gave his feet a good massaging, ending the session with a few minutes of toe wiggling to keep the blood moving down below his knees. Afterward, he leaned against the wall and closed his eyes, letting his mind turn inward once again. Eventually he drifted into a nap that was filled with disjointed dreams about his Texas boyhood. He saw images of himself hunting jackrabbits, crawling under barbed-wire fences, and traipsing across prairie grass under a wide sky, and—

Clank!

The cell door opened violently and the two impersonal guards entered the cell. Travis got to his feet in a docile manner and allowed himself to be blindfolded and restrained once more. They repeated the former routine of going down the hall and entering a door to the left. Once more he was sat down in the metal chair. Travis mentally prepared himself for another period of idle waiting. But this time it wasn't for more than a minute or two.

The door opened and the blindfold came off. But the cuffs and shackles stayed. It was the young officer. He sat down with the manila folder, shaking his head.

"Excuse me," he said, continuing to speak in the Spanish language. "But I am confused."

"About what?" Travis asked.

"Certain information you have given me and a couple of these documents cannot be confirmed," Young Officer said.

"No lo comprendo," Travis said. "I don't understand. I've never had troubles with my papers before." He knew damned well they hadn't even made a serious effort to check him out. This was part of the game.

The young officer displayed a hurt expression on his face. "I trusted you, *amigo.*"

"And be assured I have been absolutely truthful with you," Travis replied.

"I must speak in a most frank and open manner," the young officer said. "This situation could turn nasty. If I don't clear this up, then I'll be taken off your case. I'll be replaced by another officer. I know him. He's a vicious man. I certainly don't want you to have to endure his cruelty."

"Ni yo tampoco," Travis said. "Me neither." He almost grinned. Here we go, his mind told him, it's time for the Good-Cop/Bad-Cop routine.

"Tell me about the discrepancies here, *por favor.* Please!"

"What discrepancies?" Travis asked.

"You know what they are," The young officer argued. "You must tell me." He shrugged. "My superiors insist."

"Hablo la verdad," Travis insisted. "I speak the truth."

"You mean you have nothing to tell me?"

"Nada. Nothing," Travis said.

The young officer sighed and stood up. "Very well. I cannot help you. But if you feel you want to fill in the blanks in your case, call for me."

The interrogator left, and the guards came in and replaced the blindfold. He was marched back to his cell. After being released and hearing the door close, Travis went back to sit down by the wall.

"Well, now, hombre," he whispered to himself, "you're about to get into some real deep shit now."

0200 hours

Travis was thirsty. He hadn't had any water since the sparse
meal of rice balls, and his lips were dry and he felt a slight
constriction in his throat. He searched around the floor of
the cell with his hands to see if he could find a pebble or
a piece of cement to put in his mouth to keep the saliva
flowing. He wasn't sure how long it had been since that
cup of water, but he reckoned it to be at least twelve hours.

Clank!

The guards came through the door again. Travis thought
it might be fun to show a bit of resistance to make sure
they weren't taking him for granted. But he knew if he put
up a fight, they would simply call for reinforcements, then
proceed to beat the shit out of him. These were unemo-
tional professionals who knew that maintaining strict and
complete control over prisoners was not only safer for
them, it made their jobs easier. He stood up slowly and
allowed them to put him under control.

This time Travis could see absolutely nothing from under
the blindfold, but he was sure they were heading back the
same old way. After a bit, however, he realized they had
come farther than before. And when a nearby door opened,
it was located to the right rather than the left. They began
going down some narrow stone steps. He counted twenty-
two before they reached the lower floor. Another walk that
took about two minutes followed, then he was pushed
through another door. This time he was left standing.

And he detected an extremely foul odor.

A long period of time passed as he stood in silence.
Travis once more sunk into himself, resting and relaxing in
spite of the physical discomfort. His breathing slowed and
deepened. His acquired self-control was to the extent that
he was no longer aware of the stench that wafted around
him.

Then the blindfold was roughly pulled off.

Travis could see an officer standing to his direct front.
The man looked familiar, and he studied the stranger's features. After a moment he recognized him as Blue T-Shirt
from the bus. He even wore a similar garment under his
uniform shirt. At that moment, Travis realized the man was

not a police agent, but a military intelligence operative. Travis turned his head and saw two large, brutal-looking men. They were dressed for athletics in tank tops, sweat pants, and jogging shoes. That meant trouble and plenty of it. They were going to have a workout and Travis Barrett would serve as the exercise apparatus.

Now he noticed a metal tank across the room. A plank with straps leaned against it. There, he knew, was the source of the horrible smell. Then Blue T-Shirt spoke. And he did so in English.

"Who are you?"

"No entiendo," Travis said. "I don't understand. I speak only Spanish."

"Let's talk about your Russian friend," Blue T-Shirt said. "His embassy knows nothing of oil workers in Iran. They cannot identify him. But other Russians from an aerospace organization said he was once a member of their group."

Travis's mind shouted the word *Frateco!* The organization had developed a working rapport with the Iranian government. He maintained a look of sincere confusion.

"Now we will consider your Turkish friend," Blue T-Shirt continued. "His embassy also knows nothing of him. Not surprising. He is not Turkish."

Travis smiled and shook his head to feign not understanding a single word being said to him.

"Then one of our guards actually recognized him," Blue T-Shirt said in a sarcastic tone. "And you know what? He is not Turkish. He is Iranian. And he was once a well-known wrestler. His name is Ramin Kahnjani. Kahnjani immigrated to Satanic America."

Travis remained silent.

"But he came back here for his father's funeral," Blue T-Shirt recited. "He was denounced by his pious neighbors as an infidel and dissident. For that he went to prison until a male relative who is a cleric got him released from confinement to serve in Iran's Grand Army. He ended up being listed as missing in action after an armored car battle. But he had actually deserted."

Travis shrugged.

"And a similarity you share with your traveling companions is that your supposed embassy also knows nothing of you," Blue T-Shirt said. "You are not Spanish. You are not Iranian. You are a foreigner. I'm thinking you are an American." He laughed. "Of course, I can't check you out at the American Embassy. We closed that down, remember?"

Travis remained impassive. Sometimes it's possible to wade through the biggest mistake ever made in an undercover mission, and other times a small, seemingly insignificant little slip can bring down hot scalding pee on even the most complex of operations.

"And strange, disturbing incidents have occurred when unknown foreigners appeared in Iran," Blue T-Shirt said. "There have been missing policemen, stolen armored cars, a Chinese rocket was destroyed along with a launch pad, and other strange events." He folded his arms and stared into Travis Barrett's face. "I ask again. Who are you?"

Travis clenched his teeth. Here it comes!

Blue T-Shirt nodded to the guards. They grabbed Travis and dragged him over to the plank by the tank of stinking liquid. He was roughly strapped down to the wide board with his head sticking above it. Now he could see the tank held feces, urine, vomit and even what appeared to be blood. It was a putrid example of all the filthy excrement the human body could produce. A couple of drowned rats, their bodies almost hairless with decay, floated on the surface.

"Who are you?" Blue T-Shirt screamed.

Travis remained silent. The board was tipped up and pushed downward. His head went into the fetid slime. He held his breath, then his head was raised after a little less than a minute.

"Who are you?"

Travis remained silent.

Once more he was thrust into the malodorous crap. This time he was kept under for so long that he felt as if his lungs would burst. Then he was again raised up.

"Who are you?"

No answer and down he went again. Then back up.

"Who are you?"

Silence.

Travis's head went down into the foul sludge again. He hadn't been able to get a complete breath before submersion, and his lungs quickly ached in their semi-inflated state.

If only he could drown himself and obey the tenets of Condition Black. But he knew his tormentors would never allow him the mercy of death.

He bore the discomfort as best he could, fighting an instinctive reflex to take a breath. His mind whirled and a strong sense of vertigo whipped through his dimming consciousness.

Then his head came up out of the crap.

"Who are you?"

Travis breathed in, feeling himself swallow bits and pieces of solid gunk.

Then he was plunged into the filth once again.

The routine began to be repeated irregularly with the time under the muck being increased. During the instances when they lifted him, he had to breathe in through his mouth since his nostrils had filled with offal. His throat burned and his temples pounded as the entire world turned into a stinking, suffocating environment. He began to ease in and out of consciousness.

Travis was barely aware he had been taken off the board until he suddenly knew he was once more blindfolded and they were frog-marching him away. A door opened and his captors roughly thrust him into what seemed a small metal box. He could neither stand nor lie down. When he sat, he could not stretch his legs out fully. His hair, ears, and nose were filled with filth. Then his mind mercifully turned off and allowed him to slip into blessed unconsciousness.

1145 hours

A dizzy confusion swirled through Travis's sense of awareness as his eyes opened. For a moment he felt completely lost, then the recent past eased into his memory. An instinctive moan escaped his lips and he became acutely aware of his physical condition.

A banging on the door caught his attention. When it opened he could see he was inside a small metal cell. A tin bowl of soup with the strong smell of fish was handed him, as was a cup of water. In his confused state, he thought of refusing sustenance and starving himself to death. But he quickly realized that would lead to the hell of forced feeding with a hose shoved down his throat. Liquid nourishment would be poured into it, to flow into his belly.

He drank the soup and the water, then set the utensils down by the door. Next, Travis removed his trousers and took the bottom of each leg to wipe off his face and hair. It didn't clean him up much, but at least he got some of the crap off him. He replaced the trousers, then went to some deep-breathing exercises to get back into some semblance of self-control.

After a half hour of concentrated meditation, he was jerked back to full consciousness by a sharp pain that went through his intestines. It was so bad, he grabbed his midsection and leaned over. Within moments the unpleasant sensations quickly evolved into watery cramps.

"The bastards!" he said to himself. "They gave me a fucking laxative."

He got the trousers off again, just in time as his bowels discharged. The physical reaction to the purge continued until he sat in his own feces. He had been infected with man-made diarrhea. This would eventually cause severe dehydration, making him acutely susceptible to mind-altering drugs.

He wondered just how much of this he could stand. Travis needed to justify his suffering and put it all into some sort of perspective that not only made sense, but also reinforced his moral and physical courage. Then he recalled a saying he had learned in a Special Warfare course on foreign military philosophies. The adage was from the Japanese warriors' Code of Bushido. It was a doctrine by which they lived and died: *Duty is heavier than a mountain; while death is lighter than a feather.*

Chapter Sixteen

Sam strolled across the thick-carpeted sitting room of the luxurious suite that he, Jack, Sarah, and Jennifer occupied in Bushehr's Iran-Metro Hotel. The high quality of the rooms, service, and food were unheard of in the typical safe house.

The hotel was just north of the downtown area and offered excellent views of the Persian Gulf to its wealthier guests who occupied the top floors. These accommodations could cost up to twenty-five hundred dollars American for a single night.

Sam paused by a table to pick an apple from the bowl of complimentary fruit placed there by the solicitous and efficient staff. He had just taken a bite when Jennifer walked into the room. She sat down on a nearby sofa and gestured to Sam. "Toss me an orange, will you, Sam?"

"Sure," Sam said, complying. "Sleep well last night?"

She caught the orange and began to remove the peel. "Not worth a damn. I hate this crap of waiting around."

"We all do," Sam said, sitting down beside her. "Especially with all the x-factors of the situation."

"When are we getting out of here?" Jennifer asked. "This unlimited luxury is beginning to wear on me."

Sam grinned. "Poor little rich girl."

They were joined by Sarah, who had just showered and changed into a sleeveless blouse, shorts, and sandals. She noticed them munching on the fruit and helped herself to some grapes. "Where's Jack?"

"Asleep," Sam replied. "He hates doing nothing. He says that sleeping makes the time go by faster." He smiled. "I had a cat that lived by that same philosophy."

"Napping's not for me," Sarah said. She pulled a grape loose and tossed it into the air, catching it in her mouth. "How'd the meeting with that Iranian guy, Hashuli, go?"

"Fine," Sam answered. "Final arrangements are being made to withdraw us from exotic Iran. As soon as everything is firmed up, we're outta here."

Jennifer asked, "Did you hear anything about any of the other teams?"

Sam shook his head. "Not much. And that really pissed me off. Of course they're not giving us full briefings for security reasons. If one bunch is compromised, they don't want them to have any information on the other guys."

"Guess we don't have a need to know," Jennifer said. "We haven't seen Hunter or Stan since we left the train. Aren't they staying at this hotel?"

"Nope," Sam said. "I did manage to find out they're at a place called the Foreign Club. It's a kind of elegant hostelry for businessmen."

Sarah laughed. "Knowing those guys, it's probably the kind of place that has hot- and cold-running call girls."

Jennifer took a slice of orange. "I suppose Travis, Sergei, and Ramin are still on some rumbling bus out in the boondocks."

"Could be," Sam said. "Or they've been stashed in a rundown fleabag hotel in the slums."

"Pity!" Jennifer joked.

"On the other hand, they may have already been exfiltrated," Sam said. "Could be they're sitting in the comfortable wardroom of an American ship enjoying plenty of delicious Navy chow and waiting patiently for our appearance." He sighed sadly. "Oh, for Cheez Doodles and a Mountain Dew."

"I'll have a burger, fries, and a chocolate milkshake," Sarah said.

"Stop it, you two!" Jennifer exclaimed.

Western District Military Prison
1430 hours

Travis's eyes opened and he closed them again, turning his head away from the fluorescent light fixture shining above him.

Fluorescent lights?

He felt around and noticed he was lying on a mattress and was covered by a blanket. He quickly sat up and a stabbing pain shot through his head. After a couple of moments he was able to slowly get to his feet. He stood a bit unsteadily as he gave his surroundings a closer scrutiny.

Travis noticed he was in a regular cell complete with toilet and sink. His small area of confinement was actually clean. He checked himself and noted he had been bathed and clothed in a fresh, clean prison uniform that included socks and cloth slippers.

The headache came back with a throbbing persistence and he sat down on the bunk to massage his temples. He felt as if he were suffering from a hangover after a three-day binge. And, like waking up after a prolonged drunk, he could remember nothing.

As his mind slowly cleared, he recognized what was behind the symptoms—he had been drugged. He let a few more minutes pass to clear the remaining cobwebs from his mind, then he got up and went to the cell door window. It was barred but open and he could see out into the steel corridor of the block. There were other doors along the wall that were close together, indicating single occupancy like his own.

Special prisoners.

That meant that he was also categorized as that sort of inmate now, and he wondered what it was all about. The sound of a door opening broke into his thoughts and he could hear footsteps approaching. He went back to his bunk and lay down, feigning sleep.

The cell door was opened and several individuals approached his bunk. Someone shook him, and Travis looked up to see three men gazing down at him. Two were in guard uniforms and the third was in a suit with a stethoscope around his neck.

One of the guards pulled Travis to a sitting position and unbuttoned his jacket. The man with the stethoscope took the instrument and listened to the prisoner's heartbeat. Then he took his pulse and examined his eyes. The doctor stepped back and nodded to the guards.

Travis was pulled to his feet and led out of the cell. With a guard on each arm, he was marched down the corridor toward an exit door. No blindfold or restraints had been put on him. The guards said nothing to him, and he made no attempt at conversation with them.

They reached a door that led from the cell block to a corridor with several doors on each side. He was taken to a small office and placed inside, then left alone.

Travis was in a twelve-by-fourteen room with two chairs on either side of a desk. He still felt a bit shaky, so he sat down to let his legs begin the process of getting back to normal. The door opened and a man wearing a well-tailored pressed-and-creased khaki uniform came in and walked around the desk. He had short-cropped hair and a trimmed moustache that matched the neatness of his clothing. He said nothing as he reached in a drawer and pulled out a tape recorder. After setting it on the desktop, he punched the play button.

The tape whirred for a few seconds, then Travis heard himself speaking English in a slurred voice. He said a few innocuous things such as hoping the Dallas Cowboys would be in the next Super Bowl and getting a tune-up for his '63 Chevy pickup.

The man hit the off-button. "That was you twelve hours ago. Let's knock off the bullshit now. It's time to smarten up and get down to the nitty-gritty."

Downtown Bushehr
1430 hours

Hunter hung up the phone in the room he shared with Stan in the Foreign Club. Stan looked at him hopefully. "I hope that was our contact instructions."

"I couldn't tell," Hunter replied. "We're supposed to go to an office building on the waterfront right now. It's called the Kaar Building. There's a room on the second floor that has a sign on it that reads Intersal Engineering. We knock and enter. Piece of cake."

"Maybe not," Stan said. "There's no way we can check this out before going to that place, is there?"

Hunter laughed. "For God's sake! We've put our asses in the hands of strangers based on information given us by a D.C. cab driver. And *now* you're getting worried? It's a little late for that, Stan." He got his jacket. "C'mon! Let's go."

They left the room and went downstairs, crossing the lobby and going outside. A doorman nodded politely to them. Hunter knew that the word "taxi" was pretty international, so he asked for one.

The doorman smiled and saluted, turning toward the street. He blew a whistle and shouted, *"Taksi!"*

Within moments the two TALON Force men were in the back of a small cab. The driver's English was poor, but he understood Kaar Building from having taken so many businessmen there in the past. He nodded enthusiastically. "I get there damn fast."

However, as it turned out, Hunter and Stan endured a stop-and-go ride that was punctuated with the driver's constant honking and yelling as the taxi inched through the heavy traffic of the narrow street. But when they reached a wide boulevard, he stomped down on the accelerator and they whipped down the street, swerving around and dodging slower vehicles and pedestrians who leaped out of the way. Then their progress slowed again when the driver had to turn off the boulevard onto another narrow thoroughfare that was choked with traffic.

When they reached the Kaar Building after fifteen minutes of honking and yelling, Hunter paid the cabby. They took careful looks at the place, also noting the surrounding neighborhood. It appeared to be an industrial park that was mostly under construction. But no workers were visible laboring at the project. Once again the Islamic Revolution had run short of funds.

The Kaar Building itself seemed to be a modern office edifice. Hunter and Stan went inside and, after walking across a marble-floored lobby, took a staircase up to the second landing. They found the offices of Intersal Engineering at the end of the hall. Following instructions, they knocked and entered.

A male secretary gave them a careful look, then wordlessly pointed to another door. They did as he indicated and stepped inside an office. The Resistance operative Hashuli was waiting for them. He was in no mood for a lot of conversation.

"You will not go back to the Foreign Club," the Iranian told them.

Hunter didn't like the sound of that. "Why not?"

"The situation has turned dangerous," Hashuli said. "You cannot return to any place where you have been before."

"You sound like we're being watched," Stan remarked.

"Perhaps you are," Hashuli said.

"Then we could have been followed here," Hunter added.

"They will see you enter," Hashuli said. "But I can assure you they will not see you leave."

Stan was edgy. "Has anybody been compromised?"

Hashuli shrugged. "The only thing I can tell you for sure is that Ramin Kahnjani has been executed by the Iranian Army."

"Aw, shit!" Hunter exclaimed. "What about the other two guys who were with him?"

"I know nothing of that team except Kahnjani's death," Hashuli said. "And that has been confirmed." He shrugged apologetically. "Please make yourselves comfortable. We'll try to get you out of here as quickly as possible."

Western District Military Prison
1835 hours

Travis sat on his bunk. He had just finished a passable, but spare, meal of rice, beans, and hot tea. A guard had sat with him the whole time, then immediately removed plate, spoon, and cup when the meal was finished. The man passed the utensils to another warder outside, then sat down on a metal stool in the corner of the cell.

Travis knew he was on suicide watch. Someone would be with him in that cell twenty-four hours a day. That would also include an additional guard at irregular times to keep him off balance. Travis would eat, answer nature's calls, shave, and sleep under their supervision. The guards' eyes would never be off him. The one with him now gazed at the prisoner dispassionately but alertly and Travis sensed the guy's tenseness and preparedness to move swiftly and effectively if he tried any self-destruction.

Travis lay down and turned his eyes toward the ceiling. He had to get his mind working now to throw off the effect of whatever drug they had injected into him hours before. He silently formed words as he tried to put the situation he was in into some sort of rationalization.

The Iranians now knew he was an American. That could not be denied. They also had undoubtedly noted that at the time of his various arrests and detentions, he possessed expertly forged documents that were graphic evidence he was no petty criminal or even a drug smuggler. The logical thing was for them to take him as a CIA operative. This made him a valuable and most unique prisoner, hence the better treatment he now received.

Travis also thought about Sergei Mongochev and Ramin Kahnjani. If they were drugged, then Ramin's mind would be literally drained of everything he knew about the Resistance. Years of work would go down the tubes, but not before the authorities managed a large, if not complete roundup of all the underground's personnel.

Sergei, on the other hand, had knowledge that was now outdated. No doubt the Frateco would have been quickly reorganized after losing the two ALAS satellites. In effect, Sergei knew nothing about them now. And his knowledge of TALON Force was nil. The Russian hadn't even known where he had been while they were out on the Mojave Desert. He could give them nothing but names of the team members, but those were matters of public record anyway. Travis grinned to himself. Right! Public records that had been carefully manipulated to throw off even the most careful investigations.

His thoughts were interrupted by voices. He looked over to see that two guards stood outside the cell door. They opened it and signaled Travis to come with them. He got up, put his feet in the cloth slippers, and walked out to join them, nodding good-bye to the guard left in the cell. The man continued to look at him without emotion or rancor.

Once more Travis was escorted down to the office where he had seen the man with the tape recorder. He was surprised to see the same individual who had played the recording during his previous visit sitting at the desk. This time there was a coffeepot and two mugs.

"Come in, sir," the man said. "May I offer you a cup of coffee?"

"No thanks," Travis replied.

"It is not drugged, sir," the man said. "Please trust me on that." He laughed. "That sounds ridiculous, I know. But I really want to have what you Americans call a heart-to-heart talk."

Travis stepped forward and waited as his host poured them each a cupful. He took one, then sat down in the chair.

"That's more like it," the man said. "By the way. My name is Naderbeti." He paused. "Would you treat me to the same courtesy?"

"John Doe. At your service."

Naderbeti laughed. "Listen to me, my friend. We are both professionals in this little game we play. We can be quite friendly and pleasant about this, don't you agree?"

"Sure."

"You did a fine job," Naderbeti said. "You resisted the vilest treatment and even under drugs, you said nothing that revealed much about yourself other than you were raised in Texas and used to hunt jackrabbits there. Although the information we garnered about that old pickup truck of yours was fascinating. It's obviously a classic. Sounds like something a Texan would take great pride in."

"Then you can call me Tex instead of John," Travis said.

"You're so amusing, my friend," Naderbeti said. "All right. I have put forward this concept of absolute honesty and openness, so I have the obligation of starting out in this manner. If I am positively candid with you, will you return the favor?"

Travis made no reply.

"Very well. Please to allow me to present a demonstration of my sincerity, Tex," the Iranian said. "Your friend Kahnjani has been executed by firing squad. Unfortunately for us, he was inadvertently and prematurely turned over to the army as a deserter. An administrative glitch on our part, no? At any rate, he was quickly court-martialed and sentenced to death. He died two hours after pronouncement of sentence. So, in truth, we have no idea of his connection with you."

Travis showed no emotional reaction to the news. If what Naderbeti said was true, however, the Iranian authorities had passed up a fantastic chance to learn all about a well-organized group of dissidents within their midst.

"Of course the man who is responsible for prematurely turning Kahnjani over to the army before he was fully investigated faces the severest penalty provided by our laws," Naderbeti added.

Travis hoped the son of a bitch was Blue T-Shirt.

"As for your Russian friend, he is useless to us," Naderbeti said. "After hours of intense interrogation, we were convinced he was an empty bucket. He talked a bit, but not much. At any rate, we turned him over to a particular organization that seemed interested in him."

Travis hoped that Sergei's death at the hands of the Frateco had been quick.

"So, you are alone now," Naderbeti said. "And all you have to do is cooperate with us and you will be well treated. Good food. Decent accommodations. Even a woman now and then." He shrugged. "Or a plump young man, if that is your preference."

Travis maintained his silence but couldn't help rolling his eyes.

Naderbeti continued, "You are being treated rather well for this prison. Yet it is still far below a decent standard of living." He waited for, but received no reaction from the prisoner. "Anyway, you will eventually be exchanged for one of our people now in your government's hands." He laughed. "And I don't mean the Texas state government."

Travis said nothing, not appreciating the humor of the poor joke.

"Look, my friend," Naderbeti said. "You and I are at a high level of sophistication in the intelligence world. We can be honest and above board when things go wrong as they have for you. Did you know I was once a member of Savat? Yes! The Shah's secret police."

Travis knew the Savat's agents had been feared and hated by the members of the Islamic Revolution.

"It's true," Naderbeti said. "And I am sure you will be amazed to find out that I was sent by the Shah's govern-

ment for an intelligence course in Israel. I do not lie! I
attended two-weeks of instruction from the Mossad in Tel
Aviv. I stayed at the Plaza Hotel there. So you can see that
I know of which I speak when I talk to you about sophistication and certain rules of etiquette between intelligence
agencies and operatives. We all bend the rules when it is
convenient, as you well know, my friend."

Travis knew he was right about that, but still declined to
agree or disagree with anything the man said.

Naderbeti continued, "But let me tell you I went through
hell when the Ayatollah Khamenei came to power. I was
down in those dungeons where you were. Eating shit like
you did. Many of my colleagues were executed but I sur-
vived. How? By cooperating of course, but actually I went
beyond that. I wrote a letter to the chief prosecutor and
confessed all my crimes. Then I asked for forgiveness and
gave advice on how to organize their own secret police.
They were so impressed with me that I was taken from the
cells and given a position in the new organization. I'm sure
you are familiar with Savama."

Travis knew this was the Islamic intelligence organization
that replaced the Savat.

"Not only myself, but several other former Savat agents
were recruited into Savama," Naderbeti said. "And here I
am. And there you are. You are in the position I was in.
It is time to apply cold clear logic in the place of any ideal-
ism you may have." He leaned forward. "Let's be professional, Tex."

Travis calmly poured himself another cup of coffee. He
offered some to Naderbeti who refused with a wave of
his hand.

The Iranian continued, "I don't wish to insult you, but
I'm sure you understand I would be remiss in my own
duties if I didn't offer you an opportunity to become a
double agent for us. The pay is good and we'll get you an
immediate release from this prison. You will stay in luxurious accommodations while we orient and train you.
Interested?"

Actually he did not have to roll over to be released by
the Iranians. All he had to do was give his real name, and
the U.S. Government would cut a deal to get him back.
But there was the Condition Black. If he gave himself up,

he would be disobeying orders. And Travis Barrett was not a spy. He was a soldier.

He shook his head to indicate a negative response to the Iranian's offer.

"I thought so," Naderbeti said. "We'll forget that and concentrate on the sensible approach. Please understand I am not going to be crude and threaten you with more physical torture if you do not cooperate. You'll not be beaten again. Or have your head dunked into vile liquids." He paused. "But we will do something, Tex. We have the drugs we need that will eventually break you down. No matter how hard you try, you cannot overcome them. You know that."

Travis was well aware of the potency of the new mind-altering drugs.

"The longer you resist our program, the worse it is for you," Naderbeti said. "If you go the limit, you will be left with terrible mental and physical disabilities from the narcotics. It will be worse than being one of those burned-out hippies left over from nineteen sixties America. You will shake like a victim of Parkinson's disease. Other times your muscles will tense up and you will be rigid and unable to move for days. Your mind will cloud up and you will be completely insane. Even when you are at your best, you will move slowly and be unable to speak plainly." He shrugged. "Unfortunately, these symptoms are permanent and irreversible."

Travis finished his coffee and sat the cup down.

"I'll have you taken back to your cell," Naderbeti said. "Think over our conversation, Tex. You are in a no-win situation. Remember that you are a professional. For the love of God, act like one." He pushed a buzzer on the desk.

The two guards came in and took Travis by the arms.

Chapter Seventeen

Drifting clouds eased across the moon's face, allowing the night to darken into a gloomy haze. Hunter and Stan gave silent thanks for the welcome murkiness around them. The two TALON Force teammates shivered slightly with the cold as they crouched in knee-deep water within the reeds of a salt-water marsh. The gentle laziness of the Persian Gulf surf could be heard some twenty yards away.

Each man held his silenced .45 automatic in his hand, ready for any contingency that bad luck might throw their way. In addition, the shirt pockets of the fatigue uniforms they wore held four extra clips. They drew comfort from the thought of the extra rounds of ammunition. In addition to the armament, they carried a couple of medium-powered Spanish antocha flashlights.

Stan spat in the water. "They're late, goddamn it!"

"I'm not surprised," Hunter said. "There was a lot of last minute, complicated arrangements that had to be made between the Iranian Resistance and the British Navy."

"I don't understand why we couldn't go straight to an American ship," complained Stan. "You'd think they'd want to follow the KISS principle—Keep It Simple, Stupid."

"There probably wasn't a U.S. vessel available," Hunter said. "Shit, you're in the Navy. You know they have other things to do besides pick up wandering operatives."

"Yeah," Stan said. "I guess we're lucky the Brits had time for us. That much coordination is enough to fuck up a train wreck." He sighed. "I was really sorry to hear about Ramin. He was a good guy."

"Tough on his family too," Hunter said. "I wonder how Travis and Sergei are doing. It worries the hell out of me that the Resistance doesn't know what's going on with them."

"Maybe that's good," Stan said. "They could be out somewhere on their own. That would mean the Iranians have no idea where they are either. Travis could get out of Hell itself if he had to. And he'd steal the devil's car for the exfiltration."

"Yeah," Hunter said. "I just hope he and Sergei have things under control."

"I never like splitting us up," Stan complained. "This mission, like all others, was rushed from the get-go and things got worse. It all started with that glider's tow hook breaking. That thing should have been made better."

"Remember, it was made by the lowest bidder," Hunter said. "It's like the old saying, 'If you can't give a guy time to do the job right, how're you going to give him time to do it over?' "

"It's always the—"

"Shhh!" Hunter cautioned him.

Stan immediately shut up. They both listened for a few moments, then picked up the growing sounds of something rustling the reeds. This was followed by voices carrying on animated conversation punctuated with laughter.

"Iranian security patrol," Hunter said.

"*Careless* Iranian security patrol," Stan added. "They sound more like a Boy Scout troop out on a weekend hike."

"Except these Boy Scouts carry AK-47s," Hunter said.

They squatted deeper in the water and lowered their heads when it became obvious the patrol was moving in their direction. The clouds over the moon drifted under the influence of the winds, allowing an intermittent light to brighten the area a bit. The sounds of splashing as the security men moved through the water were easily discerned. The two TALON Force men looked upward and could see dull silhouettes of the patrol against the grayish-black sky. The apparitions were moving directly toward them.

Suddenly the winds aloft washed the moon free of the clouds and a near-daylight brilliance flooded the scene. Stan looked into the startled countenance of an Iranian sailor armed with a Russian assault rifle.

Stan instinctively raised his .45 and fired.

Western District Military Prison
0255 hours

Travis walked down an alley that shimmered in shades from complete black through various grays to stark white. No color was visible in his troubled vision. It was like one of those old 1940s B movies that crop up on cable TV now and then.

The urban lane undulated and swayed like a pitching ocean in slow motion. He fought to keep his balance as he made his way along. The buildings on either side closed in on him until they touched his shoulders, barely giving him enough room to move along. Then suddenly they parted, going out half a football field's length before once again surging back to pin him in.

He felt nauseous and a little drunk as he struggled to get through the area. A small white dot appeared in the distance, dancing crazily up and down. Then it moved toward him, gaining speed with each passing moment. The orb grew in size until it evolved into the large face of a fat, bald man with black lips and pointed teeth. There were no pupils in the eyes, yet they seemed to gaze piercingly through Travis's body and into his soul to rip away any secrets he possessed.

The mouth opened in a silent scream as the face jiggled up and down directly in front of him. Travis could not control his feelings no matter how hard he tried. He was frightened witless with alarming sensations of helplessness. He turned to run but could make no headway against the swaying alley and buildings that hemmed him in.

Finally he stumbled free of the obstacles out into an open field. He looked back to see that the face was gone. He had to get his bearings to decide in which direction to go. A loud continuous buzz began close by that increased until it was a pulsating roar.

Travis looked down to see that he was surrounded by thousands of rattlesnakes that stretched from horizon to horizon. He whirled desperately as he tried to find a way out. But the rattlers were everywhere, looking at him as they coiled to strike.

Now Travis began to run desperately through the serpents. He could feel hundreds of stinging bites as the snakes struck at his legs. He moved in slow motion as if his shoes were made of lead. But the snakes whipped around lightning fast.

Travis fled like a man possessed while fangs sunk time and again into his flesh. The rattlers he stepped on exploded, covering him with the same vile liquid he had been dumped into during his interrogation in the prison's dungeon.

Then Travis's eyes opened.

He was in his cell lying faceup on his bunk. His clothing was soaked in sweat, and his throat was dry while his tongue felt as if it were made of sandpaper. He turned his head and saw the guard on the stool in the corner, calmly observing him.

As his mind cleared a bit, Travis realized his nightmare was the result of drugs. An adhesive bandage in the crook of his arm covered the needle punctures through which the narcotics had been injected into him. It had been one hell of a dose.

Travis sat up unsteadily, then forced himself to stand. He staggered over to the sink and drew a cupful of water from the tap. His hands trembled with such violence that he spilled most of the water. After managing to get a few drops swallowed, he lurched back to his bunk and collapsed on it.

He lay still, breathing heavily. His left hand shook with a slight irregularity. He tried to make it stop, but the palsied movement continued. He put it under his leg and could feel the involuntary movement. It was as if his hand had a mind all its own.

Travis clenched his teeth in the knowledge that neurological and protoplasmic damage to his body and nervous system from the potent drugs had already begun.

On the beach
0300 hours

The lead man in the Iranian patrol took Stan's bullet in the forehead. The unlucky guy's left eyeball popped out as the back of his skull blossomed outward from the pressure of the exiting slug.

Hunter, who had not been spotted by the patrol, fired at almost the same instant that Stan did. He capped three shots at the two men directly behind Stan's victim. The trio of rounds all hit flesh, knocking the sailors kicking and yelling into the water. At that moment the clouds once again darkened the moon and the scene turned as black as ink, effectively blinding everyone involved in the impromptu firefight.

Stan and Hunter, well aware of each other's positions, instinctively moved in closer together until their shoulders were touching. They were now down on their knees in the marsh water and mud, soaked to the waist. Suddenly the Iranians began firing blindly and madly, forcing the two to duck even lower to avoid being seen in the brief instances of brilliance made by the muzzle flashes.

Hunter whispered in Stan's ear, "I counted seven of them. Three of the bastards are dead, so we've still got four to deal with."

"Gotcha," Stan replied softly. "Stick close or we could end up shooting each other."

The patrol leader yelled some orders in a hoarse voice and the Iranians stopped their useless shooting. There were some distinct metallic clicks as a couple of the sailors changed magazines. After that, the area went silent. Only the breeze moving through the reeds disturbed the night as six men, nerves primed and adrenaline pumping, knelt in the wetness while they waited for something—anything— to happen that would break the Mexican standoff in that isolated salt marsh.

A strained quarter of an hour passed as the tension mounted. Then there was the slight sound of rippling water off to the right. Three AK-47s blasted out in that direction. A man screamed, then splashes followed as he thrashed about in his death throes. Both Stan and Hunter shook their heads in silent contempt. The Iranians had killed one of their own.

The scene began to brighten slowly as the clouds once more eased past the moon. After a few more moments it was almost like daylight again. The three surviving Iranians, now panicked beyond reason, fired rapidly and blindly all around their position in the wild hope of hitting their adversaries.

Stan and Hunter ducked as 7.62-millimeter rounds cracked through the air above them. But they had now made the Iranians' exact location. Acting with the instinctive coordination and rapport built up in months of training and operation on the TALON Force, the two fired in the direction of the incoming rounds. Shrieks and wildly churning water followed.

Then silence.

Stan and Hunter reloaded fresh magazines into their .45s and waited. No noise came from the Iranians other than some bubbling sounds in the water. These ceased after a few moments.

The teammates rose to crouching positions and cautiously moved forward. When they reached the spot where the Iranians had been lurking, there was nothing but bodies in the reddening water around blood-splattered reeds. Then the clouds eased through the sky again, once more bringing darkness into the area.

Stan smiled. "Well! That little problem is solved."

"There may be more to it than that," Hunter said glancing at the landscape opposite the coast. "If somebody heard those shots, there'll be another patrol here PDQ."

"Good point," Stan said. "Let's move the hell away from here and get closer to the surf. That's where we're supposed to be now, anyway."

They pushed their way through the water until they reached a strip of sand. At that point the marsh ended and the two walked across the beach to a place where the shallow waves off the Persian Gulf washed up. The foam was slightly fluorescent in the fading moonlight.

"Hunter!" Stan exclaimed, pointing.

Hunter glanced in the indicated direction and could see a blinking light. The illumination showed long—long—

short—long—long. He raised his flashlight, flashing back short—short—long—short—short.

Within moments, the sound of an outboard motor could be heard growing louder. The Eagle Team men splashed out into the surf in time to see the outline of a Rigid Raider boat ease toward them in the waves. When it drew up to them, both hopped over the gunwale.

A lean, hard-as-iron Royal Marine corporal grinned at them. "I 'eard all the shootin' over there. I thought you blokes might be goners."

"Piece of cake," Stan said. "Thanks for waiting around for us."

"Right," the corporal said.

The coxswain in the aft end of the boat at his console added, " 'ang on then."

It took an hour for the small craft to get back to the frigate that awaited them. The coxswain skillfully maneuvered the small craft up to the accommodation ladder, reversing the engine. The corporal grabbed the ladder and held it to give their passengers a steady footing. Hunter and Stan hopped onto the lower rungs, and turned to give the pair of Royal Marines a salute as they sped off into the darkness to return to their own ship.

As the men headed up the ladder to the British crewmen waiting above, Stan turned to Hunter.

"Know what? We've been exfiltrated."

Downtown Bushehr
0530 hours

The pink had faded from the dawn and the city of Bushehr's downtown area began to stir with life. Pushcart vendors, merchants, and others with businesses to set up for the new day had begun to appear on the street.

Inside the Iran-Metro Hotel, one of the elevators reached the lobby after completing a descent from the lavish suites on the top floor. When the door opened, a slightly built Asian man rushed out.

"Isma minni!" he called out loudly in Arabic to get people out of his way. *"El amir!"*

The Arabian prince, the nobleman's two wives, and a bevy of bellboys struggling with their luggage closely followed him. The group, moving *en masse,* hurried across the lobby toward the door leading to the street.

A large van, almost a bus, awaited their pleasure. The windows were tinted dark and it was impossible to see inside. The attentive driver had all the doors open in readiness to accept his passengers and their baggage. The prince and the women immediately stepped inside to settle down in the ample seating provided for them. The Asian man, nervous and gesturing excitedly, supervised the loading of the suitcases and trunks into the back.

When the bellboys had stowed the load, they stepped back with looks of resignation. They had learned days earlier that the prince's entourage did not tip generously. But this time they were most happily surprised. The Asian not only gave them all abundant gratuities, but the money was in American dollars. They waved happily as the small man joined the others inside the vehicle.

Sam settled down across from Jack, and caught sight of the Iranian Hashuli in the passenger seat. He nodded to the Resistance operative. "How goes it?"

"We're trying to put things together," Hashuli replied as the driver put the van in gear and merged into the growing traffic.

Everyone settled back, looking out at what they hoped would be the final sights of Iran as they made their way through the city. Jack, Jen, and Sarah peeled off their Arabian clothing to reveal the sporty attire they wore underneath. They were grateful for the thermos bottles of hot coffee that Hashuli passed back to them.

"We have now received word that the team of desalination engineers is aboard the British frigate awaiting helicopter transport to the American vessel." Then he added, "That is your destination as well."

The driver turned from the urban area and eased onto a highway heading south. Jack took a heavy swig of the hot brew, knowing the caffeine would help dissolve the drowsiness of a rare long night's sleep.

"What about the others?" he asked.

"I'm afraid I've bad news in that area," Hashuli said. "Ramin Kahnjani has been executed."

"What happened?" Sarah asked.

"They were captured," Hashuli said. "The entire team. That unhappy intelligence has been confirmed now. The Russian fellow is missing. Nobody seems to know what has happened to him."

"Goddamn it!" Jack said angrily. "What about the American?"

"The American?" Hashuli asked, puzzled. Then he nodded. "Ah! You mean the fellow playing the Spaniard. He is in the hands of Savama. The Islamic Republic's Secret Police."

Jack leaned forward toward the Iranian. "Then that's something that's got to be taken care of right away."

Hashuli shrugged. "Sorry. It is a situation the Resistance is not prepared to handle at the moment."

Jack reached out and grabbed his jacket, shaking him violently. "Then you damned well better *get* prepared."

Hashuli shook himself loose. "If we could do something without endangering our own organization and missions we most certainly would. You must believe that."

"So the Resistance can't do anything?" Sarah asked.

"I am so sorry, miss," Hashuli said. "We were fortunate that Kahnjani was shot before they had taken time to give him a thorough examination. The brave man might have saved his life if he had volunteered to betray us. But he remained silent and was martyred by the fanatics."

"Good man. He knew the score," Jennifer said.

"As do we," Hashuli said. "If there was anything we could do about your friend, rest assured steps would be taken right now. But the Resistance will not take further chances."

Jack felt helpless rage. Condition Black would doom Travis eventually. It was just a matter of time. He remembered what Sun Tzu said about the five types of secret operatives: indigenous, double, traitors, scouts, and expendable.

"I guess we're expendable," Jack said to himself.

Sarah turned to him. "Hmmm?"

"Just thinking out loud," Jack said. He looked at Hashuli. "We appreciate the risks you're taking in getting us out of Iran."

"Listen, my friend," Hashuli said. "We have information

that your people will find useful if they wish to attempt a rescue."

"You can bet we aren't going to be sitting on our asses," Jack said.

The van left the main highway and spent the next half hour on a narrow country road. Hashuli gave Jack all the details regarding Travis's captivity. Eventually the watery horizon of the gulf could be seen to the west, then a small fishing village came into view. They turned off the road to enter the hamlet's one street. They went out to a small dock and came to a halt.

"We are here, my friends," Hashuli said, opening the door and getting out.

TALON Force joined him on the dock. The Iranian led them down to a small fishing boat. He nodded to them. "Here is your transportation to the U.S. Navy. Good-bye, my friends. And good luck always."

Jack offered him his hand. "Sorry about blowing up. You folks have done a super job."

"No apology is necessary," Hashuli said. "I understand your feelings. And if anyone can get your friend free of the Savama, it will be your organization." He smiled. "I have met General Krauss."

"He won't sit still," Sarah said.

"I am of the opinion that he, indeed, plans on rectifying this situation that is so distressing," Hashuli said.

The four Eagle Team members stepped from the dock to the boat's after-deck. The captain nodded to the mate in the pilot house. The engine quickly kicked into life as a crewman forward cast off the line.

Jack, Sam, Sarah, and Jennifer turned for what they thought would be a last look at Iran as the small boat chugged out into the waters of the Persian Gulf.

Chapter Eighteen

Travis had been left in peace for four complete days. The prison authorities had even increased the amount of food given him, and on two occasions he received extra helpings of bread. It was far less food than he was used to, but he appreciated what little extra strength he garnered from it.

The twenty-four-hour suicide watch was still in effect, but aside from that he was unmolested. The interrogator Naderbeti had surprised him with a recent copy of the *Houston Post,* and Travis brought himself up to date on the latest news.

He knew why he was being left in relative peace and given a few minor perks without any real pressure being put on him. It wasn't out of kindness on Naderbeti's part. The prisoner was being allowed a complete recovery from the latest injection of drugs.

The reason?

So his mind would be clear enough to converse calmly and logically about the Iranian's offer for him to roll over and then be exchanged. There was a great deal of seriousness behind the offer.

But Travis was sure as hell not going to roll over for anybody, and that meant he would eventually be pumped up with drugs until his brain exploded and his asshole puckered. His captors could well turn him into a slobbering, stuttering idiot barely able to walk, talk, or even feed himself.

Travis was a Texan. And he was a proud and stubborn Texan. He had decided he would, at least in spirit, follow the advice given by Rudyard Kipling in his poem "The Young British Soldier":

When you're wounded and left on Afghanistan's plains,
And the women come out to cut up what remains,
Just roll to your rifle and blow out your brains
And go to your God like a soldier.

Travis couldn't blow out his brains, but he could go out
in a flash of glory and report in at St. Peter's Gate like a
soldier. The next time the bastards came for him, Travis
was going to fight. He would kick ass, bust jaws, break
teeth, and flatten noses. They would whip him, sure, even
if it took a dozen of them to do it. But after he had been
beaten to a pulp, those sons of bitches would know they'd
been in a fight.

It didn't make obvious sense to put himself through that
much additional punishment. It appeared to be a useless,
losing fight, and he was nearing the end of an ordeal he
couldn't possibly win. But it was the closest he could come
to obeying the Condition Black order. If the SOBs wouldn't
let him kill himself, he'd allow them to destroy his mind.
The big test would be having the inner strength not to
reveal any real information to them until they had messed
up his mental processes so badly that he wouldn't be able
to remember anything anyway.

In the meantime, he would treat himself to the pleasure
of kicking some towel-headed butt. Travis glanced over at
the guard on the stool and grinned viciously at him.

The guard gazed back at him impassively.

The Persian Gulf
1800 hours

The United States guided missile cruiser *San Ysidro* moved
through the waters at one-third speed ahead. The vessel's
Cruise and Tomahawk Missiles were ready for action but
were on a stand-down status like the crew. Only those on
watch were active while the others relaxed and enjoyed a
respite from their usual hectic activities.

The vessel had been pulled from its normal routine for
a special operation. The seven people involved in that mission were deep in the iron bowels of the powerful warship.

Brigadier General Krauss and TALON Force Eagle Team were situated in a compartment just large enough to accommodate them.

Krauss stood to the front of the others who occupied chairs in two uneven rows on the steel deck. Directly behind the general were a bulletin board and a map of the Iranian coastline just south of the city of Bushehr. The exact position of the Western District Military Prison was highlighted on the chart.

"Listen up," Krauss commanded. "I know you are all unaware of the fact that the Condition Black status was lifted the moment all TALON Force gear was destroyed back there in that Iranian forest."

Jack leaned forward in his chair. "How come we weren't told?"

"I tried to tell Travis during that last commo session with him," Krauss explained, "but the stubborn mule was so pissed off that he took off his helmet and broke off transmission before I could let him know. I tried to contact the rest of you, but couldn't raise anybody on the TALON net."

Sam nodded. "Travis was the only one wearing his helmet at that time. And he told us our gear had to be destroyed then and there."

"Damn!" Sarah exclaimed. "He may have killed himself by now."

"We know that as of yesterday afternoon he was still alive," Krauss said grimly. "Normally, in a case like this, the government would get into some supersecret negotiations to get him—or any of you—brought back in from the cold."

"But if Travis hasn't done himself in by now, he still might at any moment," Stan said.

"That is why we have to move fast," Krauss said. "Time is working against us." He took a pointer and turned to the map of the Bushehr region showing the location of the prison. "If Travis is still alive, this is where he is right now. You are now charged with getting him the hell out of there."

Hunter stared at the map. "I'll assume there's some useful information you'll be giving us about the place?"

"Give the man a cigar," Krauss said with a bit of a smile.

"Actually, I can give you a whole lot of poop on that lockup. There is an asset from the Resistance inside. We can't communicate with him because it's a one-way street. He gets information out to the Resistance, but can't be contacted himself. Security is as tight as a gymnast's pussy in this situation—uh, sorry, ladies."

Jen and Sarah shrugged.

"Shit!" Hunter exclaimed. "Then we can't have the asset tell Travis that the Condition Black is lifted." He shrugged. "He probably wouldn't believe the guy anyhow."

"Now you see the reason we have to move fast," Krauss said. "That's the bad news. The good news is that we've managed to gather the most critical of intelligence that we require to get in and out of the place with Travis."

"So?" Stan said. "Spill it."

"Okay," Krauss said. He pulled a large piece of paper from his briefcase. After unfolding it, he tacked it to the bulletin board. "This is the layout of the target area. As you can see, the prison is on top of a hill not far from the beach. You'll be going in there by Rigid Raider boat."

Stan asked, "Are the Royal Marines going to give us a hand?"

"Negative," Krauss answered. "The Brits don't want to get involved in this and the feeling is mutual. A stray operative that needs rescuing is our business alone. So we've purchased the boat. All identifying markings on it and the engine have been removed or filed away. The damn thing has even been painted a different color."

Stan liked the idea of using the watercraft. "I take it I'll be the captain of the Rigid Raider?"

"I think the title 'coxswain' would be more appropriate," Krauss said.

"That's okay, Stan," Hunter said. "We'll call you 'Skipper' or 'Gilligan' or whatever you want."

"Back to the issue at hand," Krauss said. "A narrow road leads from the beach up to the hill where the prison is located. The target is a three-story affair with a subterranean area not so creatively dubbed the Dungeon. Right now Travis is on the third floor in cell eight. That is the elite prisoner section. He's getting pretty decent treatment, but we don't know what's happened to him prior to this. He could be a battered, drugged-out mess."

Sarah spoke up. "Will the asset give us physical help once we're inside?"

"I'm afraid not," Krauss responded. "He'll be unattainable as far as we're concerned. That's at the specific request of the Resistance. I've been informed he will not be physically present during the rescue. You'll be on your own. The place is surrounded by a fence with one sentry post at the main gate. You will go to that point and wait. A semitruck carrying weekly supplies for the prison will go past there. When it's inside, you'll take out the guard in order to get past him."

"He'll have the key to the gate, right?" Hunter asked.

"Negative," Krauss replied. "It's a new setup and is opened by a switch from inside the prison. You'll have to go through the fence. Fortunately it's nonelectric since it's just about impossible to escape the main building. There is also no alarm attached to it. Actually, the barrier is well-designed to keep prisoners *in* rather than other people *out*. That, of course, will work in your favor."

"Sounds like plain ol' wirecutters will do the job there," Jack said.

"Right," Krauss said. "Now when you're within the fence perimeter, move to the north side where there is good cover available. Find a place where you can observe the loading dock. The warehouse there will be opened up for the delivery. That'll provide you an entry into the prison itself. The truck will be there, and you'll see some trustees unloading it under the supervision of three or four guards."

"How are we supposed to deal with the trustees?" Hunter asked.

"Consider them hostile," Krauss said. "In other words: Use extreme prejudice."

"Shoot down unarmed men?" Sam asked.

"This isn't a play-nice situation," Krauss said. "There're reasons why they've become trusted prisoners." He turned back to the map. "After taking care of the personnel on the loading dock and at the entrance to the supply warehouse, you will launch the attack through there into the prison itself."

"Silent kills in that location?" Hunter asked.

"Forget it," Krauss said. "Don't even worry about it. From that point on it's going to be a pitched, noisy, no-holds-barred battle. Can't be avoided. You'll have surprise on your side and that's worth a lot. Your fighting skills will get you through. These are prison guards, not infantry troops."

"What route do we take when we breach the warehouse area?" Sarah asked.

"Go directly forward to the central rotunda," Krauss instructed. "It's a big, high-ceiling mosquelike area with a dome. Go through the east door, take the stairs to the left, and head up to the third floor. It's a winding staircase that leads to just one exit. Bust in."

"And we'll find . . . what?" Jennifer wanted to know.

"A long narrow cell block," Krauss answered. "It's an old-fashion setup and the cell doors are opened mechanically rather than electronically. A large lever in the wall by the guard sergeant's desk can open them all at once."

Stan rubbed his hands together. "Then we'll let everybody out."

"That's fine," Krauss said. "But once the doors are open, go directly and quickly to cell eight. That's where Travis is." He nodded to Sarah. "You check him out. I want you to take care of him if he's in a drugged stupor. Or injured."

"There're some things I'm going to need," Sarah said.

"I've already anticipated that, Doctor," Krauss said. He reached over to his briefcase and pulled out a small box of vials and hypodermics. "Catch!"

She caught the box and opened it. It contained secobarbital, a drug that induces a deep, but short nap; morphine for pain; norepinephrine for mood elevation and physical stimulation; and a bottle of Bayer Aspirin.

Krauss grinned. "The last item was my idea."

"Probably the most useful," Sarah replied with a smile. "By the way, a fold-up stretcher might come in handy."

"I'll see that you get one," Krauss said. He turned his attention back to the group. "When you have Travis in hand, head back to the loading dock and out the prison compound to the beach and the Rigid Raider boat. Return here to the *San Ysidro* as quickly as you can."

Hunter had a question. "General Krauss, you've told us what to do, where to do it, and how to get there and back. But you haven't mentioned *when*."

Krauss checked his watch. "You'll jump off in two hours."

"What about combat gear and weapons?" Jack asked.

Krauss grinned. "Surprise! There's a crate of brand-new TALON Force Battle Ensembles in the next compartment, made to your personal specifications. Complete with XM-29 rifles and grenade launchers. By the way, everybody will pack grenade launchers along with bounding fragmentation as well as high-explosive projectiles. The former will come in handy for clearing corridors."

"What about CS gas?" Jack asked.

"Negative," Krauss said. "That could affect Travis as much as it does the unfriendlies. You better take it easy with those grenades too unless you know his exact location." Once more he turned to Sarah. "That reminds me. Also bring a helmet and automatic trauma med pack for Travis."

"Yes, sir," Sarah replied.

"All right then," Krauss said. "You've got your orders, and a design of the objective up here on the wall. Powczuk, you're in command. DuBois will second you." He walked toward the door, then paused and turned. "I know how much Major Barrett means to all of you. I share your deepest emotions right now. So go get him the hell out of there!" He stood and gave Eagle Team an emotional salute, his prosthetic hand rigid at his forehead. Eagle Team returned the salute.

After General Krauss left the compartment, Stan went up to the front. He faced the team, folding his arms across his barrel chest.

"Okay, boys and girls, here's the way we're gonna get it on! Jen and I will be on the point as storm troopers. Sarah and Hunter stay in the center while Jack and Sam bring up the rear."

The team listened as Stan launched into his operational plan.

Western District Military Prison
1830 hours

The cell door opened and the current guard's relief stepped inside. Both men remained silent, their eyes drilled on

Travis, lying on his bunk. The new guy took the stool while the other went out the door, locking it after he stepped into the hall.

Travis yawned and stretched, giving every indication he was in a tranquil mood. He even hummed a few bars of "The Jailhouse Blues." After a few moments he sat up and nodded to the new guard. The Iranian, a muscular young man with an intelligent face, gazed back without acknowledging the greeting.

Travis got up and walked over to the sink, filling his tin cup with water. He took a swallow, then another mouthful that he gargled and spit out. Humming once more, he returned to his bunk and sat down, pushing himself back to lean against the wall. He nodded and smiled to the unresponsive guard one more time.

Travis picked up the copy of the *Houston Post,* mentally doing the crossword puzzle. Prisoners on suicide watch were not allowed pens or pencils. The mind game went on for ten minutes until interrupted by the sounds of guards coming down the hall. They stopped outside the door and Travis knew they'd soon be escorting him down for another interview and discussion period with Naderbeti.

Travis stood up the moment the guards came into the cell. One motioned for him to approach them. He took three slow steps, then exploded into a spinning *takai* head-kick that sent the man crashing against the wall. After whirling completely around, Travis delivered a lightning fast *massuguna yubi kansetsu* punch into the other's face. The Iranian's nose exploded blood and he stumbled backward out of the cell into the hall.

The guard on the stool was athletic and launched himself into an instinctive attack. Travis caught sight of him out of the corner of his eye and turned to deliver a *hiraita te* jab. The guard deftly ducked the punch and slammed Travis in the midsection with three rapid punches. The American gasped and violently jabbed his knee into his opponent's groin. The kid screamed in pain and Travis finished him off with an old-fashion bolo punch that lifted his feet off the floor. The unconscious kid crashed back to the floor and rolled under the sink.

Now three fresh guards joined the fray as they charged through the door in a single formation. Travis went on the defensive with an *uwamuki no* kick. It hit the middle guy, but it didn't slow him down as he and his buddies overwhelmed the prisoner. Travis went down with the three of them on top of him.

The young cell guard regained consciousness and writhed in agony on the floor as the other escort guards jumped back into the fight. The five Iranians began to play a violent and concentrated game called Beat The Shit Out Of The American.

After ten minutes of hard physical abuse, a semiconscious and bleeding Travis was dragged out into the hall. The escort guards hauled him to his feet. Travis was able to open one eye, but he was smiling. He found himself looking straight into the face of Naderbeti.

The Iranian interrogator shook his head disapprovingly. "I am very disappointed in you, Tex. What you have just done was not only unprofessional; it was crude and barbaric. Tsk! Tsk! Such bad manners!"

Travis grinned through battered lips. "Fuck you very much."

Naderbeti, switching from English to Persian, spoke to the guards. "Take him down to the dungeon!"

Chapter Nineteen

The Rigid Raider rocked gently on the ocean's swells as Stan stood at the coxswain's console. He was in his element and worked the wheel with a smooth expertise, steering the craft toward the high hill that showed on the shore to the direct front. The ominous outline of the Western District Military Prison was a mournful silhouette against the night sky.

Stan could hear the rumbling splashing of surf as it spilled over the beach to roll back into itself. As the sound grew louder, he cut the engine to silently ride the natural flow of the ocean into the shore. At his signal, Jen tipped the motor to get the propeller out of the water, and Stan turned back to his piloting duties.

Although the movement toward land was slow and almost gentle, he had to keep the boat's bow directly aligned with the rolling surge to avoid broaching. Stan was an experienced sailor, and the movement of his craft showed no hesitation as it became one with the ocean's movement.

The Rigid Raider slid up on the beach, then came to an abrupt stop as the bottom of the boat made contact with the sand. Stan quickly left the console and joined Jennifer as she rushed forward to set up security. The rest of the team pulled the boat into the brush and made sure it was out of sight.

Stan and Jen used their battle sensor devices to quickly but thoroughly check out the area. She spoke into her commo system. "All clear."

"Same here," Stan said. "Let's move out, babe."

Stan took up a forward position on point with Jen a few yards behind him. They moved silently across the marsh through the reeds in the shallow water until reaching solid ground. Stan, speaking softly through his battle sensor helmet, ordered everyone to halt. He moved forward with Jen until reaching the road. They settled in the brush and once more flipped down their battle sensor devices for a period of observation.

The road came in from the north, then curved in front of their position before running past a guard shack. From that point on, it continued up to the prison through the electronic gate.

After five minutes, Jen and Stan heard what they were waiting for. The supply truck rolled toward them, then eased up to the sentry post. It pulled up to a stop.

The guard on duty phoned up to the prison to have the gate opened. As soon as its electronic lock popped, the barrier swung back. The driver put his truck in gear and headed for the loading dock. The gate closed automatically.

Stan handed his XM-29 rifle to Jen. After pulling his knife from its sheath, he moved forward toward the sentry shack. The guard manning the post strolled in a circle in front of the place, obviously bored with the monotony of the job. Stan reached a place where the brush ended, then moved swiftly to the shadows of the shack.

As the man walked past, he stepped out behind him. In one movement, the Navy SEAL clapped his hand over the Iranian's mouth and drove the knife into his lower back under the ribs. The blade went upward into vital organs and was twisted. The Iranian struggled for a brief moment, before collapsing from heavy internal bleeding. Stan lowered him quietly to the ground, then sliced the knife across his jugular vein.

"Move up!" he said over his helmet.

He pulled the corpse out of sight so that no casual passersby would see the dead man. Anybody noting his absence would think he had stepped off into the brush to take a piss or he was sneaking a catnap somewhere.

Jen hurried forward and handed Stan back his rifle as the others came up to follow. The first to show up were Hunter and Sarah, each on opposite sides of the road. Jack and his little buddy Sammy brought up the rear. Sarah, in addition to her own equipment, also carried a helmet, automatic trauma medical pack, and extra medical gear for Travis. Jack toted bolt cutters and the folding stretcher, both strapped to his wide back.

When Jen and Stan reached the fence, he again ordered a halt. At that point Jen headed north for a short reconnaissance while Stan went south. As the naval intelligence officer moved along the fence, she glanced up at the prison. The large stone building was bleak and foreboding. There was a dome in the center with narrow slits in the walls for cell windows. Large sections of the wall had no such openings, showing where the more unfortunate prisoners were locked into the hell of solitary confinement.

Jen considered the fact that there were many people inside suffering. Not only torture and hunger, but that worst of agonies to humans or animals—the loss of freedom. Even if they were being treated relatively well, they endured that psychological agony. Her thoughts turned to her comrade-in-arms.

"Hang tough, Trav, we're coming for you," she swore under her breath.

She reached the end of the fence and turned, retracing her steps back to the area near the road. Stan was already there. He moved close to her. "Everything's fine down that way."

"Right," Jennifer said.

Stan spoke into his commo. "All clear, everyone. C'mon up!"

The team moved to the fence. Jack approached it with the bolt cutters and examined the barrier. It was made up of ten-millimeter wire mesh. He went to work on it with Sarah watching over his shoulder.

"Be sure and make the opening big enough to accommodate Travis on a stretcher if we need it," she said.

"Right," Jack said as he worked the handles of the tool.

In spite of his great strength, he was fatigued after only a couple of minutes of laboring. But he gritted his teeth and forced himself on as shoulders and upper arms ached from the tremendous effort. Within ten minutes he was able to quietly pull the cut section free. Wordlessly, he led the way into the prison area as the others followed.

They moved across a grassy expanse to a stand of trees

that looked down at the loading dock. The team observed for several moments as a crew trundled out boxes and bales on handcarts from the truck's trailer to the open doors of the prison's supply warehouse. Stan led the team into the shadows cast by the prison building.

They moved up to the dock and silently hopped up on it. After Stan made sure everyone was ready, they charged the door. The crew inside turned in surprise at the intrusion. One guard raised his AK-47.

Bad mistake.

A half-dozen XM-29 rifles barked, their powerful 4.55-millimeter slugs ripping and punching into the flesh of his body. Before the guard even hit the floor, the remainder of the firepower hit the supply crew, other guards and trustees alike, twisting and toppling them down amidst the crates and boxes.

Stan ran forward toward the door leading the way into the rotunda. Jen was on his heels, sticking close. The others were right behind the pair as they burst into the large open chamber. A half dozen guards were responding to the sound of the gunfire as Stan and Jen came into view. The guards beat the two TALON Force troopers to the draw, and it was Jen who took three hits on the bullet-resistant fabric of her camo suit. She gasped aloud and staggered under the triple impacts, violently bumping into Stan. Both went down to the stone floor.

Hunter and Sarah leaped over them and pumped bursts of full automatic fire into the group of guards. The front three buckled under the blows of the slugs, but the rear three returned fire while moving backward toward the safety of a far door.

Sarah responded with a bounding fragmentation grenade that flew toward the bottom of the wall they were approaching. The projectile hit, bounced five feet into the air, then exploded. Three hundred pieces of notched steel wire shredded the three Iranians into hunks of raw meat.

Stan carefully helped Jen to her feet as the others rushed past them. "Are you okay?" he asked.

"Ooh—uh—wind knocked out—wait," she said. She managed a breath and checked her vital signs—courtesy of the micro-biochips embedded under her skin—via the readout in her BSH. "I'm—all right. Let's follow the others."

The team had rushed across the rotunda to the door in the east wall. Jack pulled the portal open and fired in a high-explosive grenade. It exploded on impact and he charged in with Sarah, Hunter, and Sam on his heels. The ripped carcass of a dead guard slumped against the wall. The entire team pounded up the spiral staircase to the top. A frightened middle-age guard stood there with his hands raised in surrender. Jack rushed to the lever by the wall and pushed it, opening all the cell doors.

"Everybody stay here," Jack ordered. "Sarah! Let's go!"

Dazed and confused prisoners stepped out into the corridor as the two ran down to cell eight. It was empty. They hurried back to the entrance to the cell block. Jack glared at the terrified old guard and spoke to him in his broken Persian.

"Where prisoner cell eight?"

"Th-th-they took h-h-him down to the d-d-dungeon," the man stammered.

"Lead us dungeon!" Jack growled, shoving the muzzle of his rifle up under the man's chin. "Or you dead."

"I shall take you," the guard said. "Don't kill me, by the mercy of Allah."

"Hurry!"

Jack turned to the released prisoners. "Stay! Big fight! Run later. *Khodahafez!* Good-bye!"

"Mersi!" some yelled back at him in gratitude.

The old guard took them back down the stairs to the exit door. When they entered the rotunda, incoming shots splattered around the door, kicking up stone dust from the walls. The team withdrew inside.

Jack rapidly reloaded his launcher with four bouncing fragmentation grenades. Then he opened the door a crack and fired rapidly, not bothering to aim. A series of detonations, flying shrapnel, and screams immediately followed.

Jack charged through the door with a wild yell. There was no one to resist him or his teammates. Mangled men, pieces of arms and legs lying next to them, were scattered across the rotunda. Pools of blood oozed across the floor, running together and seeping into the cracks between the stones.

One of the guards was still alive, even though he was disemboweled and both legs were blown off. He had a dazed look on his face and showed a half smile. Hunter started to put a mercy shot into the man's head, but Sarah stopped him.

"Don't waste the bullet," she said. "He's in shock. He can't feel a thing. He'll be dead in a minute or so."

The horrified hostage stumbled through the gore as he took his captors to a door on the south side of the chamber. Jack signaled a halt.

"We can't use grenades when we break in there," he said. "Travis could be too close."

Sam, fired up emotionally from the fighting, leaped forward and opened the door. He rushed down the stairs on the other side with his XM-29 ready for action. The others followed him down to the bottom of the stairs. There were no guards around.

"Travis! Travis!" Jack bellowed. "Hey! Boss!"

A familiar voice not faraway answered a bit weakly, "Yeah? What do you want?"

"What the hell do you think we want?" Jack yelled back. "You, man!" He grabbed their captive guard. "Keys!"

The man stumbled over to a metal box mounted on the wall. He opened it and produced a set of keys on a ring. Jack grabbed them, and ran down a row of cells.

"Travis! Travis!"

"Here I am, damn it!" came the reply. "I'm not going anywhere."

Jack found the cell and fumbled with the keys trying to open it. The third one did the trick and Travis stumbled out. He was in his prison uniform and barefooted. "I kind of thought it might be you guys. What's going on?"

Jack grinned and tousled his friend's hair. "We were wondering if you wanted to go out for a beer."

"Sure," Travis said, smiling back. "I reckon I have an opening on my schedule."

They went back to the others. Happy greetings and embraces were exchanged. Sarah hugged Travis. "You look great!"

"Liar," Travis replied with a grin.

Stan and Jen now joined the rest of the team. She had recovered enough from the bullets' impacts to throw her arms around him and give him a deep kiss.

"Hey! Watch it, Olsen," he said. "I've been locked away from women for a while."

She gave him a special look that made any further remarks unnecessary.

"C'mon!" Stan said. "Let's boogie."

"Wait!" Sam cautioned them. He moved toward a desk and walked around it, pointing his rifle beneath it. "Out!"

An Iranian scrambled into sight. He got to his feet, holding his hands high.

It was Blue T-Shirt.

Travis's eyes lit up. He went over and grabbed the man, dragging him across the hall to another room. The others followed to see what was going on.

"Man!" Sarah exclaimed as she walked into the torture chamber. "It smells like shit in here!"

Travis pushed Blue T-Shirt up to the vat of filthy liquid. "Care to go for a swim?"

Blue T-Shirt, knowing there would be no mercy shown him, remained silent, begging only with his eyes.

Travis threw him bodily into the muck. The Iranian went under, then came to the surface coughing and hacking. The putrid liquid dripped off him in streams.

"Jesus Christ, Boss!" Jack yelled. "Why'd you throw that poor bastard into the shit?"

"I have my reasons, believe me," Travis replied. He turned back to Blue T-Shirt. "Go under!"

Blue T-Shirt hesitated, then knelt down in the muck.

"All the way under, goddamn you!" Travis roared.

Blue T-Shirt started to obey, but he hesitated. Then he stood back up. He had decided to die on his feet. Travis was only too glad to accommodate him. He reached over and took Sarah's rifle, firing one round into Blue T-Shirt's belly.

The agent doubled over and fell face down, slipping under the surface. His head came up and he gasped. He grabbed the edge of the vat and tried to pull himself out, but he quickly weakened. Slowly he lost strength and then slipped under the liquid offal. Some rippling and a few bubbles followed, then the pool of crap moved no more.

Travis handed the rifle back. "Thanks. Now I feel like my old self."

"You must have really had it in for that guy," Sarah said, as she began examining him.

"Yeah," Travis said. "He sent me into that shit a couple of dozen times. Head first. And there were a hell of a lot of other poor bastards before me."

"Then the world is better off without him," Sarah said. She cut off his prison uniform shirt and took a close look at Travis. "You've had some good beatings, Trav. I'll patch you up some here, then we'll be ready to get the hell out of this place." She pulled the medical pack off her shoulder. "I've got some stuff that'll relieve any pain PDQ."

"Just gimme a couple of aspirin," Travis said.

Sarah laughed loudly, remembering General Krauss's remarks.

"What's so god damned funny?" Travis asked.

"I'll explain later," Sarah said.

"These cuts and bruises aren't from interrogation," Travis said. "I picked a fight with the sons of bitches and got my ass kicked pretty good."

Sarah grinned as she pulled the Bayer from the pack. "You can take the man out of Texas—"

The elderly guard trembled with fear. Jack took pity on the old fellow. "Not hurt you."

"*Mersi!*" he blubbered and fell to his knees, weeping and praying in thanks.

Travis put his new battle sensor helmet on and followed along with Sarah at his side as the team moved upstairs. They crossed the butchery in the rotunda and went back through the warehouse to the dock. Travis's bare feet didn't bother him much as they traveled across the grass of the yard.

Jen and Stan, back on point duty, ran a quick recon up to the fence, then commoed the others to join them. After crawling through the opening Jack had made, they were all back on the road and headed for the beach.

The point team stepped out to get a ways ahead of the rest of the column. They had gone some fifty yards when their automatic battlefield motion sensors picked up a disturbance. Jennifer flipped down the battle sensor device on her helmet for a look to the north. She picked up the disturbing image of armored cars heading rapidly in their direction.

"Everybody down!" she ordered through her commo gear. "It's *déjà vu*, folks! Four BRDM-2 armored cars approaching. The Iranian Paramilitary is on the march."

"Shit!" Stan swore. "Somebody in the prison must have got the word out about our raid."

"Too bad we didn't have time to knock out radios or telephone lines," Jennifer said.

While Jack halted the team, Jen and Stan moved into position to observe the arrival of the armored cars. Within five minutes the quartet came into sight on the road. The commander in the first vehicle was surveying his surroundings through his binoculars, making sweeping gazes over the nearby terrain. When he spotted the smoke coming out of some of the prison windows, he turned his observation toward the fence. It didn't take him long to catch sight of the opening that had been cut in the barrier.

The Iranians came to a halt and the gun turrets turned toward the area where the team had taken cover. Eight machine guns—four 14.5-milimeter and four 7.62-milimeter—immediately opened fire with sweeping, forward-stepping fusillades that progressed from the road up toward the fence.

"Keep down!" Stan ordered his charges. "They can't see us, but they know we're out here someplace. This is reconnaissance by fire." From his vantage point he could see where the rounds were striking as ricochets of tracers bounced off the ground and streaked into the air. "They'll be on 'em in a minute. Fire at the last car to block any escape."

He and Jennifer opened up. She sent a high-explosive grenade into the rear tire that blew it and the entire axle off. Stan raked the hull with his XM-29 rifle, pocking the armor with dozens of penetrating rounds.

The two center vehicles quickly established the source of attack. They turned their machine guns on Jennifer and Stan. The two team members crawled backward under the hail of incoming fire that raked the ground around them. Stan took a hard hit in the shoulder by one of the large 14.5-millimeters. He was rolled through the grass just as Jennifer's calf was hit by a smaller 7.62. The bullet passed completely through.

She moved painfully over to join a very dazed and confused Stan as her trauma pack activated. Her imbedded biochip sensors transmitted quick but accurate diagnostic data to the ensemble. Bladders in the suit inflated at the source of the wound to apply pressure and prevent loss of blood. Then a combination of anesthesia and antibiotics was injected to enhance the treatment. Her primary shock and confusion rapidly dissipated and she was again clear-headed. Jen turned her thoughts to Stan.

"You okay?" she asked.

"I feel like I've been kicked by a mule," Stan said. "How about you?"

"I, uh, think I may need a hand," Jennifer said reluctantly.

Hunter and Sam immediately sized up the situation. Both jumped up and charged across the road in full view of the Iranians. They dove into the brush and scrambled on their bellies deeper into the cover as bullets snapped the air around them, cut vegetation, and kicked up dirt in their faces.

They both emptied their magazines of fifty armor-piercing bullets into the first vehicle. Its machine guns went silent. Next, Sam loaded a high-explosive grenade into his launcher and aimed, using the XM-29's millimeter wave sensor, at the open driver's viewing slit in the second armored car. The projectile went straight into the vehicle. Ammunition and gasoline exploded inside, sending sheets of flame out of the crevice between turret and hull. The turret cover blew off and flew fifty feet straight up in the air. When it came hurtling back to the ground, a 200-pound piece of steel plate narrowly missed Sam and Hunter, hitting the ground between them without a single bounce. Hunter frowned at his companion.

"Whose side are you on anyway?"

"As Confucius say, 'Oops!,'" Sam said, grinning.

They moved forward another ten yards, then both opened full automatic fire on the third vehicle. Within seconds it was as punctured as a piece of Swiss cheese.

And just as silent.

Sam spoke into his helmet mike. "All clear!"

The team assembled down by the last car where Stan and Jennifer waited. She had her arm around his shoulder, holding her injured leg up off the ground.

"I'm all right," she said. "Let's get the hell out of here."

"Come on," Stan said to Jen. "I'll carry you."

"Sure," she snarled. "You just want to grab my ass."

"Olsen, this isn't the time for this."

"Okay. You're right," she said. "Kneel down." She climbed up on Stan's back.

He grinned and jiggled her a bit. "All right, I'll admit it. I just wanted to try it with you on top."

Jen seethed. "Powczuk, after you finish saving my life, I'm going to kill you!"

Meanwhile Jack offered Travis the same personal service. When the ex-prisoner hopped up, Jack grinned. "Hey, Travis. You're light as a feather. You on a diet?"

"Yeah," Travis answered. "The most effective weight-loss program known to man. It's called Iranian prison food. I don't recommend it." He turned his head for a last look at the prison. "The other prisoners are making their breaks now."

The team glanced back to see dozens of inmates from the third floor streaming out, rushing for the road and freedom.

"Right now we've got to worry about ourselves," Jack said. "Let's go!"

They reached the marsh and splashed through the water and reeds to the edge of the beach. Sarah and Hunter dragged the Rigid Raider out of the brush and down to the beach.

Jen and Travis got in as the craft was maneuvered into the surf. Stan hopped up into the coxswain's station while the others pushed the boat into deeper water. As he dropped the motor down and started it up, everyone else jumped in.

Sarah checked Jennifer and noted she was holding up fine. Travis was tired but in good spirits. Sam took up a watch position in the bow, using his battle sensor device to scan the watery horizon that surrounded them. Within five minutes he sounded an alarm.

"Small, fast vessel approaching. Two thousand meters." Moments later, he added, "Iranian naval patrol boat."

Stan grumbled, "Goddamn it! Ain't this shit ever gonna end?"

Sarah stood up with her XM-29 and fully loaded it with four high-explosive grenades. As she flipped her own battle sensor device down, she said, "Stan! I'll take them out—just follow my lead."

"Aye, aye," he replied.

A minute later, Sarah said, "Target one thousand meters. Turn three degrees left."

"Port," Stan said testily. "We're at sea. Port is left. Starboard is right."

"Whatever," Sarah said. A few moments passed. "One degree *starboard*, okay? Target five hundred meters." Then a full minute eased by as she checked the angle of the approaching Iranians. "Steady as she goes, Blackbeard."

"Wiseass," Stan muttered.

"Target in range!" Sarah exclaimed. She flipped up the battle sensor device and took aim, counting, "One! Two! Three!" Then she fired.

The projectile flew in a lazy arc and fell dead onto the approaching enemy boat. The explosion rocked the vessel. Sarah aimed and fired again. Another hit. The patrol boat suddenly went dead in the water. Sarah announced, "And now for the *coup de grâce*."

The third grenade launched beautifully into a graceful curve. It landed directly on the boat like its predecessors and detonated. The Iranian vessel began to rapidly settle in the water as the Persian Gulf seemed to move up to swallow it.

"I think that pretty much wraps things up," Sarah said. "I won't need the fourth grenade." She looked at Stan. "Set a course for the *U.S.S. San Ysidro*."

Stan took his right hand off the wheel and saluted. "Aye, aye, sir—aw, fuck—you know what I mean!"

The Rigid Raider boat danced over the waves toward its destination.

Jen parked her new Lincoln LS in the parking lot. She had bought the car a few days after her return to the States as a personal consolation gift for getting shot in the line of duty.

The young woman had to struggle to get out of the vehicle because of the bandages on her leg. After balancing on her good leg while retrieving her crutches, she closed the door and locked it, then headed for the front door.

As she approached the entrance, Jen caught sight of Travis's '63 Chevy pickup. The battered old vehicle looked out of place among the chic vehicles of other patrons, such as Hunter's Dodge Viper and Stan's new Corvette. Sarah's bright yellow new Volkswagen Beetle was down a few spaces.

When Jen reached the door, an elderly couple came out. The lady noted Jennifer's condition. "Oh, dear!" she exclaimed. "How in the world did you injure your leg?"

Jennifer, leaning on her crutches, gave her a grin. "Rollerblading accident."

"You really should stick to more ladylike activities, young woman," the lady counseled her.

"Yes, ma'am," Jennifer replied. "But then I wouldn't have near as much fun as I do."

As the couple walked out toward their car, the husband said, "This younger generation!"

Jennifer thought, You don't know the half of it, Pops.

She went through the door, making her way up to the host's station. Elmo Gleason, the proprietor of the place, was acting as the *maitre d'* that evening. He had done his own share of clandestine intelligence service for twenty-five years before retiring and opening up his establishment. In spite of its simple name, Elmo's Bar and Grill was a four-star restaurant, its popularity growing rapidly among the area's wealthy and elite residents.

The place was not only a fancy gourmet eatery, but was an official U.S. government safe house. This was something the greater majority of its plush clientele did not know. Special rooms were sound- and bug-proofed. A number of the serving staff were government people who played their roles while providing security for special gatherings.

Heads of state had dined incognito and conducted important meetings within the confines of Elmo's. The back entrance was designed as a secure and private access into the interior of the building, so the visits of the VIPs could remain unobserved and unknown.

"Hey, Olsen!" Elmo said when she swung up to him on the crutches. He had thick gray hair and lined craggy features. His left elbow didn't bend properly because of a bullet wound incurred during a black op in Peru. A chance encounter with some Red guerrillas.

"Hello, Elmo," Jennifer said.

"How're you doing?" Elmo asked.

"Not bad," she answered.

Elmo lowered his voice, "Caught one, hey?"

"Yeah," Jen said. "It was the old story of zagging when I should have zigged." She shifted the crutches. "Where's the party?"

"Number two," Elmo said. "You're the last to arrive, but I guess you have a good excuse."

"I'm going to milk this injury to the max," she replied with a wink.

Jennifer made her way down the hall to the proper door. She shifted her crutches to one hand and twisted the knob, stepping inside. The entire team, along with Brigadier General Krauss, was scattered around the room enjoying cocktails and the gourmet snacks set up for them.

"At last!" Krauss said, catching sight of Jennifer's entrance.

"Hey, Toots," Stan said. "C'mon and grab a seat. I'll get you a drink. Scotch, neat, right?"

"Thanks," Jennifer replied.

As Stan fetched her drink, General Krauss called them all together. "Now that Lieutenant Olsen is here"—he looked at her—"*finally* here, we can get our debriefing out of the way, then we'll be able to go back to socializing."

They all filled their plates and freshened their drinks, then took some chairs around Krauss. The general waited as they settled down before he began speaking.

"Nice to see you again under more pleasant circumstances," Krauss said. "I hope you fully realize what you accomplished during those long weeks you spent in Asia and the Middle East. The world could well have been at the permanent mercy of the Frateco except for you. If those Aimed Laser Attack Satellites had become fully operational, and those bastards had been able to construct a few more, there would have been no defeating them. I particularly wish to commend your finding that second, unknown launch site. Believe me, there are some important international circles that are breathing easier because of how things turned out."

"That was a real fluke," Travis said. "If we hadn't stumbled across it, they would have been able to launch it that very day."

"True," Krauss agreed. "And Tel Aviv, along with a large area of Israel, would not exist at this very moment."

Jack asked, "You ever find out what happened to Sergei Mongochev?"

"I'm afraid so," Krauss said.

"That doesn't sound good," Sarah said.

"A headless, footless, and handless body was found floating in the Moscow River two weeks ago near the Kempinski Hotel," Krauss reported. "DNA testing identified it as Sergei's."

"Bummer," Sarah said. "Good man. What about his family?"

"That's a real sensitive area," Krauss said. "We can't do a hell of a lot without compromising ourselves. Some contacts have seen to getting his wife good employment. She's an educated woman with a degree in economics. Once her English improves, she'll be offered a good government job by some folks that can really help her. It'll be up to her to take care of the kids. But the lady will be earning a good civil service salary, so she shouldn't have any trouble."

"Does she know her husband is dead?" Sam Wong asked.

"No," Krauss said. "And she never will. His fate cannot be revealed to her under any circumstances. Can't be helped. It would cause too much natural curiosity."

"Same for Ramin Kahnjani's family?" Sam asked, taking a slug of a vile green liquid that could only be Mountain Dew. "I believe he lived with a sister who took care of his kids."

"The Iranian Resistance will handle that end of the affair," Krauss said. "If they pull off their counterrevolution, he'll become a national hero. But at least the sister knows he died for the cause. She can take pride in that, as can his sons when they're old enough to appreciate what their dad did."

Jack was more interested in tactical and strategic matters. "What about the Frateco?"

"Alive and kicking," Krauss said. "They may be out of the satellite-launching business at the moment, but they're still well connected and financed. We'll hear from them again. There's plenty of mischief they can get into. Drugs. Smuggling. Money laundering. Extortion. And any other rotten business that springs into their twisted minds. They've relocated their headquarters to parts unknown in Eastern Europe. I'm sure they're controlling organized crime from Warsaw down to Sofia."

"Anything on the horizon for us?" Hunter asked.

"Not today," Krauss said. "By the way, sorry about that glider."

Travis shrugged. "Fuck us all if we can't take a joke."

"Good attitude," Krauss said. He raised his glass with his prosthetic hand. "Ladies and gentlemen! Here's to you. May you all be put out of business by a sudden outbreak of peace. But if there is another mission, may it be a success, may casualties be nonexistent, and may it result in less evil in the world."

TALON Force Eagle Team joined in the toast, calling out together:

"To peace!"

After the toast they got up and went back to their cocktail hour. Sarah went up to Travis. "How're you doing?"

"Great," Travis said. His face still showed some fading

marks from his brawl with the guards. "I had a complete physical down at Fort Bragg. Turns out I got very lucky. My body has evidently thrown off the effects of the drugs they gave me."

"That's what I was worried about," Sarah said.

Jack Krauss interrupted them. "I have a note for you," he said to Travis. He handed him a folded piece of paper with typed words on it.

Travis opened it and read:

Dear Tex,
Glad to hear you got out okay. We'll meet again.
Naderbeti

Travis frowned. "The son of a bitch!" He looked at Krauss. "What's the status on that guy?"

"Double agent," Krauss replied. "He works for us. He did the same thing when he was on the Shah's payroll with Savat."

"It's a good thing I didn't take him up on becoming a double for the Iranians," Travis said. "He'd have sent me over."

"Yeah," Krauss said. "They'd be fishing *your* headless torso out of some river." He walked away.

Author's Notes

Aerospatiale SA-341 Fighter Helicopter French-manufactured aircraft with armament available for specific missions, e.g., antitank, antipersonnel, bunkers, buildings, etc. This helicopter has a cruising speed of 161 mph. In use in several nations, including Iran.

APC Armored Personnel Carrier.

BRDM-2 Armored Car Russian-manufactured wheeled vehicle with a one-man turret armed with a 14.5-millimeter and 7.62-millimeter machine guns. Powered by a GAZ-41 V8 water-cooled engine with a maximum road speed of 62 mph. Currently in use by thirty-five nations and considered an excellent vehicle.

HE High Explosive.

Hind Mi-24, 25, and 35 Helicopters Russian-manufactured attack helicopters. Armament varies, but can include various types of heat- and radar-seeking rockets for numerous types of targets, FAB-250 bombs, and a 30-millimeter twin-barreled cannon in the nose. Maximum speed 199 mph.

MT-LB Armored Personnel Carrier USSR-manufactured tracked amphibious vehicle armed with one 7.62-millimeter machine gun in a single forward turret. Powered by YaMZ 238 V8 diesel engine with a maximum road speed of 38 mph. Currently in use by Bulgaria, the Czech Republic, Finland, Hungary, Poland, Russia and others.